JUDGE

BLACKWINGS MC - DEVIL SPRINGS

BOOK TWO

BY

TEAGAN BROOKS

Cathy

♡ - Teagan Brooks

ACKNOWLEDGMENTS

Cover Design: C.T. Cover Creations

Cover Model: Andrew England

Cover Photographer: James Critchley

Proofreading/Editing: Kathleen Martin

Special thanks to Melissa Rivera, Tina Workman, Jennifer Ritch, and Katherine Smith.

Dedication
To those who've struggled
with addiction.
To those who've been affected
by addiction.
To those who've loved someone
with an addiction.
To those who've lost someone to
an addiction.

CONTENTS

PROLOGUE

The day I gave birth to my daughter was the happiest day of my life.

I sat at the breakfast table waiting for my twenty-year-old daughter to come downstairs, and I sat there until after one o'clock in the afternoon.

"Morning, Mother," she grumbled as she stumbled past me to the refrigerator.

"Afternoon," I said calmly. It was a struggle, but I forced myself to keep my voice even and soft despite how much I wanted to scream at her. "Please, sit; I want to talk to you about something."

With a great display of her disdain, she dropped into a chair across from me and glared. "What?"

I wanted to ease into the conversation. I thought I would have a better chance of getting her to agree with me if I worked my way up to my point; but, after one look at her tangled hair and the day-old makeup smeared across her sallow face, I jumped in head first.

"How long have you been using heroin?"

For a brief moment, her eyes widened in fear, maybe shock, before she masked her expression and lied. "I don't know what you're talking about, Mother."

"You know exactly what I'm talking about. And forget about trying to lie your way out of this. I've seen the track marks on your arms, and I found used syringes in the trash. But, I think this is more than enough proof," I said firmly and held up a little bag of whitish-brown powder. "Now, answer my question. How long have you been using heroin?"

She swallowed thickly and stared at me in silence for long moments. Finally, she said, "A few months, I think."

A few months. I thought she had been using much longer than that.

"And what were you doing before? No one just decides to start shooting up one day."

She shook her head and looked down at her clasped hands. "I just tried a few different things with friends. Smoked some weed, took some pills, snorted a little coke. Stuff like that."

"Tell me about the first time you tried this!" I screamed and shook the bag fisted in my hand. "Tell me!!"

Tears began to slip down her cheeks, turning black as they slid through the mascara and eyeliner crusted beneath her once bright eyes. "I spent the night at a friend's house. We'd been drinking, and she was passed out in her bed. When I got up to use the bathroom, her brother was in the living room with his best friend, his best friend's brother, and his best friend's dad. They had some heroin and asked me if I wanted to try it. I don't know why I said yes," she sobbed. "But I did, and I liked it! I loved it, Mother! I loved it!!"

I fought to contain my rage. She didn't say it, but I knew exactly who she was with—her cousins and her uncle were the ones at her best friend's house. I silently fumed as I wrapped my arms around my baby and held her against my chest while she went on and on about how much she loved heroin. How it made her feel. How she only lived and breathed so she could poison herself with it. She spoke of it as though it was the key to eternal happiness.

"Sweetheart, do you want to stop?"

She nodded her head against me. "Yes, please."

"I'll get you the help you need," I said and continued to try to soothe her. "It'll be okay. Everything will be okay."

Everything was not okay.

Twelve hours before my baby girl was supposed to check in at the rehab center, she went to tell her best friend goodbye.

Six hours later, her best friend called to tell me she had been taken to the hospital for a suspected overdose.

She was pronounced dead at the hospital, though I later learned she had been dead for hours before anyone found her.

The day my daughter died was the worst day of my life.

The day I buried her was the last day of my life.

CHAPTER ONE

RIVER

Out of all the places in the United States, I had to be sent to the one place I never wanted to return to—my hometown of Devil Springs. Years ago, when I finally got away from that dreadful place, I promised myself I would never return. Unfortunately for me, I signed a contract as a traveling nurse and agreed to go wherever the agency sent me. Never in a million years did I think they would send me to Devil Springs. But they did. And I had to go unless I wanted to pay the price for breaking the contract, which was equivalent to an arm and a leg and possibly my firstborn child. Not to mention, I would likely never be able to work as a traveling nurse again.

With no other options, I sucked it up and headed to Devil Springs. The contract was only for three months—which happened to be the same amount of time I had left on my general contract with the agency. Three months wasn't that long. If I only went to work and did my shopping in a neighboring town, I had a good chance of making it out of Devil Springs without running into my mother or my brother. Right?

Despite my disdain for the place, I sagged with relief when I finally pulled into the driveway of the rental house after spending two days driving from my previous assignment. At least I had a few days to get settled before I started working in the Emergency Department at the local hospital.

I grabbed my purse, my book bag, and my small suitcase from the car. Everything else would have to wait until after I showered and placed an order for delivery.

I unlocked the door and pushed it open to find a quaint, but cozy, living room, with the lights and television on. I glanced from the paper in my hand to the gold number on the front door. I was in the right place. Maybe the cleaners forgot to turn everything off before leaving.

I locked the door behind me and made a beeline for the bedrooms. I was told the place had two bedrooms with a Jack and Jill style bathroom. I entered the first door I came to, dropped my bags on the bed, and ran to the bathroom.

I let out a contented sigh as I began what had to be the longest pee of my life. It had been hours since I stopped for a bathroom break, because I hated public restrooms with a passion and would risk permanent damage to my bladder to avoid them.

After placing an order for delivery, I showered, dressed, and started unloading my car. I didn't have a lot of stuff with me, so by the time my food arrived, my car was unloaded, and I was halfway through unpacking.

I plopped down on the sofa and made a total pig of myself as I devoured every single bite of my meal. I didn't allow myself to indulge in takeout or fast food often, so I ended up looking like someone fresh out of prison whenever I did have it.

And then I would feel awful, consumed by

feelings of guilt and shame. My rational mind knew one extra-large, grease-laden combo meal wouldn't cause me to be overweight. But at one time, I had been overweight because I took comfort in food. I was an emotional eater, which is why I felt so guilty. I had been back in Devil Springs for all of an hour, and there I was stuffing my face like I did as a teenager.

I shook my head and tried to clear my thoughts. I was hungry, and there wasn't any food in the house. On that note, I cleaned up my trash and grabbed my car keys. I needed groceries and some other necessities, and I was going to drive to a store at least two towns away to avoid running into anyone I might know.

After finding a super Walmart almost an hour away, I loaded up on as much as I could fit into my little car. I truly did not want to see anyone from my past, and the less I went out, the less chance there was of that happening.

I pulled into the driveway of the little rental house and sat for a few minutes, trying to find the energy to deal with the groceries. I hated grocery shopping. Take it off the shelf, put it in the cart, out of the cart, into a bag, bag into the cart, bag into the car, bag out of the car and into the house, food out of the bag and into the cabinets or refrigerator. It was just monotonous and exhausting. If I ever had an excessive amount of money, I was going to pay someone to take care of the grocery shopping for me.

Taking a deep breath, I heaved myself out of my car and started carrying load after load into the house. By the time everything was put away, it was late, and I was exhausted.

I quickly fell into a deep sleep. So deep, that I was completely disoriented when I suddenly woke in the early morning hours. I rubbed the sleep from my eyes and glanced around the room, confused as to what woke me.

VROOOM!

VROOOM!

VRRRROOOOOOOOM!

I flopped back onto my pillow and covered my eyes with my arm. Just great. It sounded like one of my new neighbors had an obnoxiously loud motorcycle. Or maybe it was just someone passing by. Hopefully, it wouldn't matter in the future. I was going to be working the night shift at the hospital, so I normally wouldn't be home or asleep at this time. With that thought, I rolled to my side and went back to sleep.

CHAPTER TWO

RIVER

I was on my fourth day at the hospital, and things had been going well. I was surprised to find that I liked the people I was working with. Most of the time, agency nurses were brought in as a last resort, and the environments weren't always pleasant to work in, which is part of why they paid us so much. However, Devil Springs truly had a minor nursing shortage and only needed a few bodies to fill positions temporarily until reliable permanent staff could be hired and trained.

"River, can you see what's going on with the patient that just came in? Karen said he has a blood-soaked rag held to his hand," the charge nurse asked.

I knocked on the door twice before entering the room. "Hello. I'm River, and I'll be your nurse this evening," I said as I hit the hand sanitizer and reached for a pair of gloves. "We're still working on getting your chart created, but the receptionist said your hand was bleeding significantly. Can you tell me what happened?"

"Yeah, I cut it," a deep male voice rumbled.

My head shot up, and I blinked in surprise. Holy shit! I was pretty sure Jonah Jackson was sitting in front of me, and damn, he looked good. Too good. The cute boy who was once friends with my brother—that I may or may not have had a tiny crush on years ago—had been replaced by one hell of a man with broad shoulders, messy, dark hair, and a chiseled jaw covered with just the slightest bit of scruff. His eyes were the same though—sparkling blue with a hint of mischief.

Fuck me. The tattoos covering his arms, as well as the nose ring he was sporting, completed the I-will-need-to-buy-new-batteries-before-morning look.

I snapped out of my daze when he cleared

his throat. Shit. Had I been staring? I needed to focus on the task at hand and pretend like I didn't know him so I could get out of there before he recognized me. I was not going to get sucked back into the pit of Devil Springs because of a hot guy, no matter how fuckable he was.

I grabbed some gauze and stepped closer. "Can I take a look at it, Mr...?"

"Jackson," he said, confirming my suspicions, "but most people call me Judge."

"Well, I'll be calling you Mr. Jackson," I informed him.

He grinned, and a dimple popped up along his jawline. "That works, too."

I picked up a stack of gauze pads and reached for his hand. "What happened?"

"Box cutter slipped and stabbed my hand. I'd just put a new blade in, and it sank into the skin like a hot knife through butter," he explained. I started to remove whatever he had wrapped around it, but he pulled his hand back. "Fair warning, when you take this off, it's going to spray you."

I highly doubted that. He would have had to hit something significant for it to be spraying blood and, judging by his calm demeanor, that wasn't the case. "Noted," I acknowledged and reached for his makeshift bandage.

"Oh! You weren't lying!" I shrieked when blood started to shoot up from his skin. I quickly pressed his bandage back down and held pressure to it. With my foot outstretched, I kicked the door open wider and shouted, "Dr. Daniels! I need you in room seven, stat!"

Jonah laughed. "Told ya."

I smiled. "Yeah, you did."

Dr. Daniels entered the room moments later. "What's going on in here, River?"

"Mr. Jackson has a small, but deep, laceration on his palm. I believe he may have nicked an artery."

Dr. Daniels chuckled. "What'd you do this time, Judge?"

"Box cutter slipped while I was opening some new equipment for an install."

"All right, let's have a look," Dr. Daniels said and moved her body to the side. She carefully lifted the bandage and just as quickly pressed it back down. "I do believe you're correct, River. Will you draw up some lidocaine for me and then get a laceration kit?"

"Yes, ma'am," I said and left the room as she started explaining what was going to happen to Jonah.

When I returned to the room, the two were

chatting and laughing like old friends. I drew up the lidocaine and handed the syringe to Dr. Daniels.

"River, could you go over and hold Judge's hand?" Dr. Daniels asked. I found the request odd, but didn't argue and reached to steady my patient's injured hand.

Dr. Daniels laughed and said, "I meant the other one. This big galoot doesn't like needles, and I don't want him to punch me again."

"That only happened one time, Doc, and I was five years old," Jonah retorted.

Dr. Daniels continued to guffaw. "Yeah, but you sure threw one hell of a punch. I couldn't believe it. Just an average sized five-year-old, and he blacked my eye and damn near broke my cheekbone."

Judge laughed. "I bet my ass hurt worse than your face after my daddy spanked the daylights out of me."

Dr. Daniels patted Jonah's thigh. "I'm sure it did, sweetie." I wasn't sure what, but something in the atmosphere changed at the mention of Jonah's father. "All right, this is going to sting," Dr. Daniels announced and proceeded to numb Jonah's hand before cleaning the wound and closing it with sutures.

"All finished. Same aftercare as usual, except I want to leave those sutures in for fourteen days since it's so deep."

"Thanks, Doc."

"Give me just a few minutes, and I'll be right back with your discharge papers," I told him.

When I returned with his discharge instructions, he was standing by the door, clearly ready to go. I went over the necessities, had him sign on the dotted line, and then he was gone, leaving me to wonder when Jonah started going by Judge and why I was disappointed that he didn't recognize me.

That was my last twelve-hour shift for the week, and I was ready to crash. As I was walking out, the charge nurse, Kennedy, sidled up next to me and asked if I had any plans for the weekend.

"I wasn't planning on doing anything other than laundry, binging some shows on Netflix, and sleeping. Why? Do you need me to cover a shift?" I asked.

"No," she said and shifted her weight, suddenly seeming nervous. "Uh, okay, this is kind of embarrassing, so I'm just going to say it. Um, I have a blind date this weekend, and I'm supposed to meet him at a bar in town. I was wondering if you would go with me in case he stands me up or turns out to be a creep. I know we just met, but you seem like a fun girl, and if I end up being humiliated, well, you're only here for a few weeks…" she trailed off and slapped her hand over her mouth. "Sorry! I didn't mean for it to come out like that. Oh, hell, you probably think I'm a loony bird."

"Kennedy, it's fine. You don't have to explain. Where are you meeting this guy?"

"Precious Metals. It's a bar off Old Devil Springs Road. Kind of a hole-in-the-wall place, but it's never overly crowded, and I've always had a good time when I've been there."

I sighed. I really didn't want to, but she was a nice girl, and it seemed like she needed someone to go with her. "Yeah, I'll tag along, as long as you don't mind me leaving if you two hit it off."

"No problem. Can you meet me there at seven?"

"Tonight?" I asked in surprise.

"Oh, yes, tonight. Is that okay?"

I gave her a fake smile and hoped it looked real. "Sure, tonight's fine. I better get going so I can get some sleep."

Well, crap. I guess it really didn't matter when we went out. I just thought I would have more time to mentally prepare myself to step out into the general public of Devil Springs.

CHAPTER THREE

JUDGE

I walked into Precious Metals behind Batta. Apparently, Layla joined a dating website on his behalf, unbeknownst to him, and had been searching for a woman for him. Last week, she found one and somehow managed to get him to agree to meet the woman. So, there I was, by his side, to play wingman or run interference if she turned out to be one of the crazies.

"Do you see her, man?" I asked.

He didn't answer until we reached the bar. "How the hell should I know? Layla said she would be wearing a black shirt. Look around, brother. Almost everyone in here is wearing a black shirt."

The bartender handed us each a beer without us having to order, and I took a sip while I glanced around the bar. I smiled with my lips still on the bottle when my eyes landed on a familiar face sitting a few stools down from where I was standing.

"Well, if it isn't Nurse River. We meet again," I said jovially.

She turned, and her eyes widened at the sight of me. "Mr. Jackson. How are you?"

I stepped closer to her, almost too close, and I heard her suck in a sharp breath. "Call me Judge."

"Uh, okay, Judge. How are you?" she stammered.

I stepped back and gave her my panty-dropping smile. "I'm good. What brings you to Precious Metals tonight?"

"My friend is meeting someone here. I'm just keeping her company until he arrives."

"Your friend meeting a guy named Trey by chance?" I asked.

Before River could answer, her friend leaned around her and looked me up and down. She grinned. "Yes, I am. Are you Trey?"

I shook my head. "I'm not, but he is," I said and pointed behind me to Batta with my thumb.

The girl's eyes widened and her mouth slightly parted. River reached over and pushed her mouth closed, bringing the girl out of her trance. "Oh, hell yes," she breathed. "I'm giving that dating site a five-star review as soon as I get home."

"Batta," I called. "Found your girl." Batta picked up his bottle and joined us.

"This is River," I introduced her first since I didn't know the other girl's name.

"And I'm Kennedy," the other girl said and held out her hand.

Batta reached for her hand and grinned, "Kitty?"

"No, Kennedy," the girl said loudly as her cheeks flushed.

Batta smiled and took her hand. "Hi, Kennedy. I'm Trey, and this is my friend Judge. Would you ladies like to get a table?"

"Sounds good," Kennedy beamed while River grimaced.

I moved to stand beside River, allowing Batta to move in closer to Kennedy. "Judging by the look on your face, I'm guessing you got roped into tagging along, too."

She picked at the label on her beer bottle. "Yeah, this isn't really my kind of place."

"Mmm...and what is your kind of place?"

"Honestly? The couch or bed wherever I'm staying at the time."

"You move around a lot?"

She bobbed her head. "I'm a traveling nurse."

"So, you're a traveling nurse that likes to stay at home?" I asked, even though it was obvious she had no interest in carrying on a conversation with me.

She shrugged. "I guess you could say that. There's no point in going out and getting to know people when I'm only going to be in one place for a short amount of time."

"Yeah, but it's good for the soul to go out and have fun every once in a while."

"And why are you concerned about my soul?" she asked snarkily.

I raised my hands in surrender and took a step back. "I was just trying to make conversation while our friends are getting to know one another. I'll leave you to enjoy the rest of your evening."

I turned and headed for my previous spot at the bar, passing Batta and Kennedy along the way. "You guys feel free to grab a table if you want. I'm going to hang out at the bar," I said and pointed to my intended destination. Batta gave me a strange look while Kennedy's eyes shot to River.

"Sorry," Kennedy said softly. "I knew she didn't want to come, but I hoped she would change her mind once we got here."

"No worries, darlin'. There's a game on I want to watch. You two enjoy your evening," I said with a chin lift to Batta and made my way to the bar.

I shook my head and glanced over at River. She had her pretty blue eyes focused on the bottle in front of her while her long, dark hair hid most of her face. She was hot as hell on the outside, but she was a block of ice on the inside, and I didn't have the time or energy to waste on trying to warm her up.

I ordered another beer and tried to focus on the game, but my team was crushing their opponents, and it wasn't holding my interest. After finishing my beer, I signaled to Batta and headed to the bathroom to take a piss before I left.

I was almost to the hallway that led to the bathrooms when a noise off to the side caught my attention. It was a feminine yelp followed by a male shouting, "You fucking bitch!"

Batta stood as I turned to find some jackass holding River by her upper arms while his buddy closed in behind her. I was across the room and had my arm wrapped around the guy's neck in a flash. "Let her go and apologize!" I ordered.

"Fuck you, cunt!" he spat as he released one of River's arms and hit her across the face.

And that was it. I yanked the piece of shit away from River and let my fist fly. If there was one thing I couldn't stand, it was a man putting his hands on a woman in anger. Unfortunately, I only got to hit him three, maybe four times before he was out cold. I glanced to the side to see the other guy already on the ground. Batta was standing a few feet behind him with his arms wrapped protectively around Kennedy and River.

A bag of ice was pressed against my chest, drawing my attention to the man standing in front of me. "Here. Take this to her. We'll take out the trash," Sam, the bartender, said.

"Thanks, man. Get a pic of their IDs. They'll be permanently banned once I let Copper know about this," I told him and took the ice to River.

When I reached them, Batta removed his arm from her shoulders, and she turned to look at me. Her cheek was red and already starting to swell. I gingerly held the bag to her face, and she covered my hand with hers. "Are you okay?"

"Yes," she croaked and cleared her throat. "Thank you."

I shook my head. "Don't thank me. If I hadn't given him the chance, you wouldn't be standing here with a busted-up face."

"If you hadn't been here, it would have been a lot worse. So, yes, thank you." She turned to look at Batta. "And thank you, too."

"Any time, sweetheart," he replied with a nod. "Let's have a seat," he said and gestured to the table he and Kennedy had been sitting at.

"Is Sam gonna let Prez know?" Batta asked when the girls were in front of us.

"Nah, I told him I'd tell him. Just waiting on Sam to send me the pics of their IDs." As if on cue, my phone chimed letting me know I had a new text message.

Sam and his newest employee reappeared behind the bar a few minutes later. "They give you any trouble?" I asked.

"Started to," Sam said with a sly grin. "But they changed their tune real quick when they found out just who they were fucking with."

I turned back to the table to find Kennedy

gawking at Batta with her mouth agape, and River staring at the table with furrowed brows. "The bar was recently sold, and the new owner is a well-known businessman in the area with a lot of powerful connections," I explained. I didn't particularly care what River thought, but Batta seemed interested in Kennedy, so he could tell her about the club when he was ready.

When he'd asked me to tag along, he'd also asked me not to wear my cut. Normally, I would have told anyone else to fuck off for asking, but I understood why he made that particular request. Batta was a big guy—an extremely big guy. His size alone was intimidating to most people, but when he added his club cut, he scared off most women before he even had a chance to show them he was a good man. While I understood his point of view, I had a completely different opinion in regard to myself. If a woman was scared of my cut, she wasn't the woman for me.

River suddenly gasped and pushed away from the table. "Judge! Your hand! Let me see," she blurted and reached for my injured hand.

"It's fine, sweet cheeks," I said and held out my hand for her to inspect. "I only hit him with my good hand."

"The fuck did you do this time?" Batta asked

with a chuckle.

I held up my hand to show him my latest set of stitches. "Box cutter slipped while I was making a cut getting stuff ready for the install I have scheduled for tomorrow."

"What's the total count now?"

I smiled proudly. "Two hundred and forty-seven."

"What?" Kennedy asked.

"Judge is a bit accident-prone. To date, his injuries have resulted in two hundred and forty-seven stitches," Batta explained.

"And seventeen staples," I added.

"You should be more careful," River chastised.

"You sound like my mother," I snapped back. It wasn't like I enjoyed having to stop whatever I was doing and go get sewn up, and I wasn't purposefully careless. Shit just happened.

"Well, thank you again for your help this evening, but I think I've had all the fun I can handle for one night. So, I'm going to head out," River said.

"Yeah, me, too," I said. "I'll walk you out."

"Oh, that's not necessary. I'll be fine."

"I wasn't asking," I said pointedly and stood. "Let's go."

CHAPTER FOUR

RIVER

I bit back the snarky reply trying to burst from my mouth and said goodbye to Kennedy and her date before allowing Jonah "Judge" Jackson to escort me to my car.

I just wanted to go home and pretend like the night never happened. Arguing with him would only delay my ultimate goal. My headache was getting worse by the minute, and my cheek was starting to throb.

He followed me out to my car and even held the door open while I slid into the driver's seat.

"Well, thanks again. Take care," I said awkwardly.

"No problem. See ya around," he said with a wink and walked across the parking lot to a shiny black motorcycle. He swung his leg over the seat and slid on a helmet before the engine roared to life. When he revved the engine twice, I realized I was staring at him with my lips parted.

I shook my head to clear it and backed out of my parking space. Yes, the man was sexy as sin and then some, but I was in town for a job, nothing more. Feelings were not included in my five-year plan, especially feelings that had anything to do with Devil Springs.

At the first red light, I noticed Jonah was in front of me. When he was still in front of me fifteen minutes later, an uneasy feeling started to form in my gut and continued to grow as he took every turn I needed to take. When he turned on to my street, I still didn't know what he was doing until he pulled into the driveway of the house next to mine. Without a single glance in my direction, he pulled his motorcycle into the garage and closed the door. What the hell? He was my next-door neighbor?

I couldn't stop myself, even though I knew I should have. I stomped across the lawn and pounded on his front door.

The porch light came on, and the front door opened to reveal a smiling Jonah. "It's a little late for visiting, don't you think?"

"Oh, shut it. You live here?" I asked incredulously.

"For now, yes."

"Why?" I asked, even though it was none of my business.

"Well," he drawled, "I sold my old house, and they're not finished building my new one yet. Since I'm a little too old to be living with my mother, I'm renting this house until mine is ready."

"Why didn't you tell me you were my neighbor?" I asked, clearly unable to shut my big mouth.

"I didn't know until just now. Might've figured it out over drinks, but you had no interest in talking to me."

"I never said that."

"You didn't have to, sweetheart. It was written all over your pretty face," he pointed out.

I sighed and studied my feet. "You're right, and I'm sorry." I cleared my throat and nervously twisted the toe of my boot against the ground. "I, uh, I'm not very happy with my assignment, but I shouldn't have held that against you."

He stepped back and opened the door wider. "Want to come in and put some ice on your face?"

I hesitated for a few seconds before I decided that it might not be a bad idea to have a friend close by. "Okay," I said and followed him into his living room.

"Have a seat, and I'll grab some ice for you. Want something to drink?"

"No thanks. I'm good."

He returned with a vacuum-sealed frozen steak and handed it to me. "I was planning to cook that tomorrow night. Two birds, one stone."

"Glad I could be of service," I said with a smile.

His lips pressed into a thin line. "I'm not."

"Sorry, I didn't mean it like that."

"What happened with that guy?" he asked.

I really didn't want to tell him and thought I had gotten off lucky when no one asked at the bar. "The same thing that happens at bars all across the country. Guy approaches girl. Girl isn't interested. Guy doesn't want to take no for an answer. Girl tells him to suck his own dick. Guy gets pissed. Girl underestimates his anger." For the most part, that was what happened. He didn't need to know that I knew the guy from high school or that I'd had problems with him back then, too.

He nodded in understanding. "So, why aren't you happy with your assignment?"

I laughed nervously. "Straight to the point, huh?"

"You brought it up. For most people, that means they want to talk about it, even if they think they don't."

His insightfulness was spot on and really starting to piss me off. "So, I work as a traveling nurse for an agency and have been assigned to work in Devil Springs for three months. My assignment itself isn't the problem. The people I work with are great, and the hospital has the equipment and supplies necessary to provide adequate care for the patients. My issue is of a personal nature. I, um, I have family that used to live in this area and maybe still do, and I have no desire to see or speak to them."

"When's the last time you spoke to any of them?" he asked.

I shrugged. "I don't know, maybe six or seven years ago."

"Can I ask why?"

"My mother is the very definition of a junkie whore. My brother took off when he turned eighteen," I said flatly, doing everything in my power to hide my emotions. "I know my brother came back at some point, but I don't know if he's still here, and I have no idea what became of my mother."

"Hold up," he said, leaning forward and bracing his hands on his knees. "You're from Devil Springs?"

Well, fuck me sideways. I hadn't realized I was inadvertently sharing that information with him. "Yep," I said.

"How old are you?"

"It's not good manners to ask a lady her age," I said playfully.

"Oh, please. I'm just trying to figure out how I don't know you. This isn't a huge town, and there's only one high school in Devil Springs."

I studied him for a few moments. His eyes never left mine as he waited for my answer. "You're not going to let this go, are you?"

He shook his head. "I'll find out one way or another. You can tell me, or I'll find out on my own."

I figured it would be better to tell him than to have him calling attention to my presence in town by asking questions about me. I inhaled deeply and squared my shoulders. "Well, Jonah, you knew me as Rain Lawson."

CHAPTER FIVE

JUDGE

I blinked stupidly at the woman sitting on my sofa with a huge steak held to her face. "You're little Rain Lawson?"

She scoffed and rolled her eyes. "I was never little, Jonah."

"Do not even try to start that shit with me. So, you've known who I was this whole time?" I asked, a little pissed at her for deceiving me.

"If by 'the whole time,' you mean at the hospital and the bar, then yes," she answered with a hint of attitude in her voice.

"Why didn't you tell me who you were?"

"I just told you. Because I don't know where my mother and brother are, and I have no interest in seeing either one of them."

"And why'd you start going by River?"

She sighed. "Because I wanted to distance myself as far away from this place as possible, physically and figuratively. Rain was the poor little fat girl with no future. River is the healthy, college graduate with a solid career and a promising future."

"I see," I said. I wanted to argue with her about her description of her younger self, but I knew it was pointless. "Well, I don't know shit about your mother, but Da—Reed doesn't live here. He hasn't lived here for a long time," I told her.

"Oh, well that's good to know. With any luck, my mother is dead, and I have nothing to worry about for the rest of my contract," she chirped.

"Your brother isn't a bad man, Rain," I said.

"River. My name is River," she corrected.

I held my hands up in surrender. "Sorry. Your brother isn't a bad man, River."

"Never said he was a bad man. I said I didn't want to see or talk to him. And I don't," she stated.

I sighed, knowing what I was about to tell her would not make her happy in the slightest. "You remember the Blackwings MC?"

"Yeah, why?"

"The club moved to Croftridge a while back. A few years ago, a new chapter of Blackwings was started in Devil Springs. Anyway, your brother is a member of the Croftridge chapter," I told her.

"Okay. Why are you telling me this?"

"Because, I'm a member of the Devil Springs chapter, and I have to tell him you're in town," I said.

The steak landed hard against my chest seconds before she walked out and slammed my front door in her wake.

***

I hoped River would knock on my door after she'd had some time to cool down, but three days passed, and I hadn't even caught a glimpse of her in passing. So, I sucked it up and knocked on her door, but, if she was home, she didn't answer.

I went back to my place and picked up the phone. I'd already waited too long to call, and I couldn't put it off any longer.

"Judge, what's up, man?" Dash answered.

"Hey, brother, uh, I ran into your sister a few days ago," I said.

"No shit. Where?"

Dropping down on my sofa, I filled him in on my encounters with River.

Dash blew out a slow breath. "I hate to say it, but I'm not going to bother her. I know she doesn't want to see me. She made that clear the one time I was able to track her down a few years ago. If she's in trouble or she needs my help, I'll do anything I can for her, but otherwise, I'm going to leave her be."

"Can I ask what happened between you two?"

He let out a humorless laugh. "Honestly, Judge, I don't fucking know myself. When I was discharged from the Marines and came home, she was gone. Took me a few years to find her, and she flat out told me she would press charges if I came anywhere near her again."

"What about your mom? Do you know anything about her?" I asked.

"Last I heard, she was still using and was whoring herself to pay for her drugs, but that was also a few years ago. Bitch is probably dead by now," he said, his voice full of disgust.

"Gotcha. So, do you want me to tell her I

talked to you?" I asked.

"No, probably better if you don't. But I do want you to keep an eye on her. Regardless of what she thinks, I do love her and care about her. Now, my mother? I don't give two flying fucks what happens to her," he said.

"Will do, man. How's Ember doing?" I asked.

The tone of his voice noticeably changed. "She's doing great. Only a few weeks left before we get to meet our baby girl."

"Awesome, man. Keep me posted."

After getting off the phone with Dash, I sat back and wondered what could have happened that made River hate her brother so much. I could understand her dislike for her mother, but her brother was a good guy.

Before I could talk myself out of it, my phone was in my hand making another phone call.

"Brother Judge," Harper answered cheerfully.

"Hey, little sister cousin. You busy?"

"Not at all. What's up?"

"I think she may have been a grade or two ahead of you in school, but do you remember Rain Lawson?" I asked.

Harper inhaled sharply. "How could I not remember her?"

"What do you mean?"

"You seriously don't know? The whole thing that happened at prom the first year I went? I didn't think people would ever stop talking about it."

"Well, they did, because I have no idea what you're talking about," I grumbled.

"From what I remember, she went to prom with that douchebag, Brett Owens. They had been dating for a few months. Anyway, she went to talk to some friends and then went to the restroom. She came out of the bathroom to find her mother sucking Brett's dick in the girls' locker room. She started screaming at Brett and kicked the shit out of her mother. Some teachers came in to see what was going on, and it turned into a huge ordeal. Her mom started having a seizure and foaming at the mouth while her wrinkled, saggy tits flopped around for all to see. Brett's junk was hanging out on full display, and they were threatening to arrest her for aggravated assault. If that wasn't bad enough, Brett told everyone Rain's brother paid him and her mother to do it."

I was on my feet and pacing from one side of my living room to the other. "What happened next?" I asked through clenched teeth.

"Nothing really. I don't think she came back

to school after that. It was near the end of the year anyway, but I don't remember seeing her again after prom. Why are you asking about her?"

"I ran into her a few days ago. So, I'm guessing you don't know who her brother is?" I asked.

"No, should I?"

I snorted. "Yes, Harpy. Her brother is Dash."

Harper's shriek damn near busted my eardrum. "He would never do something like that!"

"Yeah, I know, but listen, this isn't our business. He knows she's back in Devil Springs, but she's asked him to leave her alone, and he's respecting her wishes. So, can you not mention this conversation we just had? It just seemed like there was something I was missing, and obviously, I was."

"Yeah, I can keep it to myself. I mean, my big scary biker is right here listening to everything we're saying, but he knows how to mind his own business. Right, pumpkin?"

"Call me pumpkin in front of a brother again, and I'll put you over my knee," Carbon rumbled in the background.

"And that's my cue to go. Talk to you later, Harper. Love you," I said and disconnected the call before I heard anything that would mentally scar me. Even though Harper was technically my first cousin, she came to live with my mother and me when she was ten years old and has always been more like a sister than a cousin to me.

I sat back and wondered if what Harper had said was the reason River hated Dash. But then I reminded myself that we were all adults, and it really wasn't any of my business.

CHAPTER SIX

RIVER

You can ask any nurse who's ever worked in a hospital what happens when it's a full moon, and they will all give you the same answer. The crazies come out to play. It didn't matter if it was a big city or a tiny town. So, I wasn't surprised when I dealt with difficult patient after difficult patient, followed by a "you waited until two o'clock in the morning to have someone look at the golf-ball sized cyst on your leg" and a few "you really didn't need to come to the ER for that."

Kennedy sped past me with a wad of papers in her hand. "I've got discharge orders for two of mine. Can you check in on the abdominal pain that they just brought back to room four?"

"On it," I said and went to see our newest patient. I should've looked at the board. Should've at least checked the name. But we were crazy busy and doing everything we could to stay on top of the madness.

I knocked and pushed the door open. "Hi. I'm River, and I'll be one of your nurses tonight. What seems to be—?"

"Is that any way to greet your mother, Rain?" the toothless, wrinkled woman asked before dramatically clutching her stomach.

Okay, I just needed to make sure she wasn't actively dying, remain professional, and get the hell out of her room as fast as possible. Most hospitals wouldn't make you take care of a family member if you didn't want to; some wouldn't allow it even if you did want to.

I cleared my throat, "What are we seeing you for tonight, ma'am?" No way in hell was I calling her any form of mother, and I didn't have a clue what last name she might be using.

She scrunched her face and moaned. "My stomach. It hurts. Please make it stop. Oh, the pain. It's killing me," she wailed.

"I see. And where does it hurt?" I asked.

"My stomach, you stupid bitch. Just told you that," she spat, no longer clutching her stomach.

"And on a scale of zero to ten, what would you rate this pain?" I asked.

"A twelve," she yelled and fell back onto the bed dramatically.

"Have you had this pain before?" I continued.

"Yesss!!!" she screamed.

"And what helped it?"

She sat up quickly and said, "Dilaudid. Only Dilaudid. They gave me some through a needle in my arm and sent me home with pills. Made it all better."

"Okay, the doctor will be in to see you in a few minutes," I said and got out of there as fast as I could without actually running for the door.

I looked around but didn't see Kennedy or Dr. Daniels anywhere. The two other nurses working were with Dr. Alvarez getting a patient ready to take to surgery. I waited at the nurse's station, hoping one of them would return soon. And then room four's call bell went off.

Shit. Shit. Shit.

With no other choice, I walked back through the portal to hell with a fake smile on my face.

"Did you need something?"

"Pain medicine! I need something for pain before I die!" she cried.

"Okay, let me see if I can find the doctor," I said and turned to leave the room only to be shoulder checked by a greasy, dirty, stinky man who was clearly on some kind of drugs.

"Why the fuck are you just standing there? Get my woman something for pain," he shouted.

I left the room again and blessedly found Dr. Daniels at the nurse's station. "Everything okay, River?"

"No, ma'am. Uh, the patient in room four is complaining of severe abdominal pain, and, um," I sighed and covered my face with my hands. "And she's my mother, so I would like to trade patients with another nurse, please."

Dr. Daniels frowned. "Um, that's fine, as soon as Kennedy comes back. She got puked on and went to shower and change," she said as she clicked through the computer. "So, Spring Lawson is your mother?"

"She gave birth to me, yes," I answered. She didn't deserve the title of mother.

"I see," she said kindly and patted my hand. "I'm familiar with Ms. Lawson. Let me go see if I can get her out of here so you don't have to deal with her."

"Thank you, Dr. Daniels," I said and breathed a sigh of relief.

True to her word, Dr. Daniels called my mother on her bullshit and sent her packing with nothing stronger than acetaminophen. "She comes in and tries that abdominal pain bit every couple of months, hoping a new doctor will be working. What she doesn't realize is that her history is listed right there in the chart for all to see," she said. "So, hopefully you won't have to see her again."

Unfortunately, she was wrong. My mother and her male friend were waiting for me in the parking lot. How they knew which car was mine, I have no idea, but there they were with their disgusting asses resting on my bumper.

My plan was to completely ignore them, get into my car, and drive away with or without them still sitting on my car. They had a different plan. One that involved the male party wrapping his hands around my throat and choking me while my mother spewed spittle all over the side of my face as she flapped her toothless gums at me.

"I'll be back tonight, and you will make sure I get some pain pills or I will fuck you up, you hear me, whore. Fuck. You. Up. You owe me, and now that you're back, you're gonna pay."

With that, I was released and shoved away as they scurried off and disappeared between the cars. And at that moment, all I could think was, I hope they didn't give me lice.

I went home, showered, and slept. Or tried to. Despite my best efforts, my mother and her friend had gotten to me. I wasn't scared of them, but I didn't want to have to deal with them. And I knew I would, because addicts were relentless, and she saw me as a means to an end.

After staying in bed for hours and not falling asleep, I got up and moved to the couch hoping I would fall asleep while watching my beloved *Golden Girls* DVDs. Finally, somewhere between the fifth and sixth episode, I did fall asleep only to be woken up some time later by someone knocking on my front door.

I got up and peeked through the window, groaning when I saw Jonah standing on my front porch, staring at me. Growling to myself, I opened the door and didn't bother to hide my annoyance. "What do you want?"

He stepped forward and tried to crowd me into my own home, but I refused to move, and he ended up with his body pressed almost flush to mine. "The fuck happened to your neck?"

"None of your business. Why are you here?" I asked.

"I wanted to talk to you about the other day, but now I want to know who did that to you," he demanded.

"I like rough sex, and I don't want to talk about the other day. Now, if you'll excuse me, I need to get ready for work," I huffed and closed the door in his face.

"River! Damn it. We're going to talk about this!" he yelled through the door.

"No, we're not. Go away, Jonah."

Things only deteriorated from there. When I got to work, it was still a madhouse. On top of that, Kennedy was off and so was the doctor I usually worked with, but I couldn't complain too much, at least not about the staffing. I had yet to meet anyone who wasn't confident and friendly, which had never happened to me in my few years as a nurse, even as a student nurse.

As promised, my mother showed up about halfway through my shift claiming she broke her finger. Once she was triaged, the charge nurse assigned Virginia to be her nurse, and I breathed a sigh of relief until Virginia returned and said the patient was asking for me to be her nurse.

Instead of putting up an argument about it,

I sucked it up and accepted the assignment. I knew she wouldn't go away until I made it clear that I would not help her in her quest to acquire prescription narcotics. And that's exactly what I was going to do.

"What brings you in tonight, Ms. Lawson?" I asked in an overly cheerful tone.

She held up her hand and pointed to an extremely swollen and misshapen finger. "I broke my finger."

Yeah, I had to agree with her. Yuck. "Okay, let me get the doctor for you," I said and quickly left the room.

"Dr. Alvarez, the patient in room three appears to have a broken finger. Would you like for me to go ahead and get an x-ray?" I asked.

"Yes, please. And thank you," she said with a smile as she continued typing and clicking on the computer in front of her.

It didn't take long for the x-ray to confirm the break, causing my mother to smile with glee. Dr. Alvarez placed her in a splint, went over her discharge instructions, and gave her a prescription for ibuprofen.

"I want something stronger," she demanded.

"I'm sorry, Ms. Lawson, but your injury doesn't warrant something stronger," Dr. Alvarez said and left me standing there while my mother fumed at me.

"You go after her and get me something else!" she screamed.

"It doesn't work like that. It's people like you who've made it damn near impossible for people who actually do need pain medication to get it. Now, you have your paperwork, and it's time for you to leave."

"I'm not going anywhere until I have something for pain!" she screeched.

"You have a prescription for pain medicine. If you don't leave on your own, I will call security and have you escorted out," I told her.

"I'd like to see you try," she spat.

I didn't have the time or patience to deal with her shit. I wasn't kidding, and I proved it ten minutes later when two security guards entered her room and told her to leave. She made a huge scene and threw herself onto the floor kicking and screaming with a tantrum that any three-year-old would have been envious of.

Dr. Alvarez stepped into the doorway and took in the scene. "River, call the police while I order a psych consult," she said loudly.

Silence suddenly fell over the room. My mother got to her feet, glared at Dr. Alvarez, and stomped out the door.

My mouth dropped open in shock, and Dr. Alvarez grinned. "Works every time."

I was so relieved to have my mother out of the hospital that the rest of the night's craziness didn't bother me. And when I got home, I fell asleep the second my head hit my pillow.

CHAPTER SEVEN

JUDGE

The one thing I didn't like about living in the rental house was the distance it was from my office. My mom's house, the clubhouse, and my new house were all on the other side of town where my office was located. Since I tended to do a good bit of work at home, I set up a makeshift office in one of the guest bedrooms of the rental house.

It didn't happen very often, but occasionally I would get an alert that needed immediate attention. So, when one of those alerts came to my phone Saturday morning, I stopped what I was doing and went back to my home office to see what was going on.

When my eyes landed on not one, not two, but four sensors picking up smoke or fire in River's house, my heart skipped a few beats before my body sprang into action. I knew the system was wired to call 9-1-1, but I called from my cell phone anyway as I ran over to her house and started pounding on the front door.

River didn't open the door, but I knew she was home. I saw her pull into her driveway when she came home from work, and her car was still sitting in the same spot. And I knew she was probably asleep.

I gave the dispatcher the address and told her what was going on before I ended the call and moved around to the back of the house. Luckily, I had just done the security install on the house right before River moved in, so the layout was still fresh in my mind.

After I checked the back door knob and found it cool to the touch, I gave it a turn, but it was locked. Taking a step back, I raised my booted foot and planted it squarely in the center of the door. The wood creaked, but the door didn't open. It took two more solid kicks before it finally flew open, and thick, white smoke poured out at an alarming rate.

I covered my face with my shirt and ducked down low, following along the wall to what I hoped was the bedroom River was using. Flinging the door open, I rushed inside and closed it behind me. The room was filled with smoke, not as bad as the hallway, but bad enough that I couldn't see clearly.

"River!" I yelled, followed by a fit of coughing. "River! Are you in here?"

"Jonah?" she croaked and coughed.

"Keep talking," I ordered.

"Can't. It hurts."

I went for the window I could barely make out through the smoke and tripped over something.

"Ow! Fuck, Jonah!" River groaned from below me. I reached down and grabbed for anything I could get my hands on while keeping my eyes focused on the window. When my fingers made contact with cloth, I grabbed and pulled, dragging her along with me as I tried to get us to the window.

My eyes were burning, and it was becoming more and more painful to breathe. I was struggling, and I wasn't sure we were going to make it out of the house. I knew smoke inhalation was usually the cause of death for victims of fires, and I now fully understood why.

My steps faltered, and I fell against the window as I gasped for breath and tried not to acknowledge the absence of River's coughing. With the last bit of strength I could muster, I flipped the locks and raised the window. Pressing my face against the screen, I sucked in a huge lungful of air while I pushed it out of the frame.

I squatted down and scooped River's limp body into my arms. I hated to do it, but there wasn't time to be gentle. I dangled her as far as I could out the window before I let her fall to the ground below. At least it was a one-story house, so the fall wasn't too far.

I attempted to land on my feet, but fell on my ass the second my boots touched the ground. I scrambled to grab her and pull her to me, so I could press my lips to hers and breathe what little breath I had into her smoke-filled lungs. And that's how the fire department found us. Passed out on the ground with my arms around her and my lips pressed to hers.

***

"Judge! Knock this shit off!" Copper ordered

from beside me.

I shoved my President as hard as I could and jumped up from the stretcher they were trying to keep me on. "Where is she?" I roared and then damn near collapsed as I gasped for air through a fit of coughing.

I steadied myself, caught my breath, and pushed past the men surrounding me. Or I meant to. I was captured from behind by the big bastard I thought was my best friend. "Let me fucking go, Batta."

Kennedy suddenly appeared in front of me and placed her hand on my cheek. "Judge, please get back in the bed. River's in the next room, and we're trying to help her, but you're pulling resources from her by not cooperating with us. Sit down, put that oxygen mask back on, and breathe so I can go back in there."

I nodded and did everything she said without a word. The moment I was settled, Kennedy disappeared and Batta gently squeezed my shoulder. I tilted my head to the sky, closed my eyes, and prayed that I didn't get to her too late.

The room remained unbearably silent until it was broken long minutes later by a cry I'd only heard a handful of times in my life. The familiar comfort of my mother's soft hand landed on my cheek as she dropped her head to my chest and sobbed. "Oh, my baby boy. Thank God you're okay."

I hugged her with my arm that wasn't holding the oxygen mask to my face. "Sorry I scared you, Mom. Just a little smoke inhalation," I rasped and started coughing again.

"You're not supposed to be talking," Copper grumbled.

"Right," I agreed and fell silent, but I couldn't release the tension from my body, and Mom picked up on it immediately. I wasn't one to sit back and watch while others handled things, even when I could barely move without hacking up a lung.

Mom pointed an accusatory finger at Copper and Batta. "You two aren't helping him by sitting there like bumps on a log. What's happening right now? Did they get the fire under control? Any idea what caused it? Have the police been called? Did somebody let Tiny know so he can start getting the security reports together?"

Copper grinned and shook his head. "Leigh, he's only been awake for a few minutes, and he was fighting with the staff for half of 'em."

Mom whirled around and glared at me. "Jonah, why on earth would you try to fight the staff? Wait, don't answer that."

Batta sat forward and answered for me. "He was a little disoriented when he regained consciousness and was demanding to know about the girl he saved."

"You saved a girl?" Mom asked.

I nodded slowly and waited for one of the guys to fill her in on what they knew. None of them knew how close we came to not making it out of that house, and I hoped none of them ever would.

"Yeah, as soon as he got the alert on his phone, he ran next door and found the girl on her bedroom floor. They were on the ground outside of the house when the trucks got there," Copper explained.

"I thought you said it was the rental house," Mom said, her forehead scrunched in confusion.

Understanding washed over Copper's face and he clarified, "Sorry, Leigh. We recently bought the property next door to the one Judge is renting. It was that house that caught on fire, not his."

Mom turned back to me with a mix of anger and pride on her face. "Jonah," she sighed. "I love you, Son, but I think this is the closest you've ever come to giving me a heart attack."

I squeezed her hand in apology. She knew good and well there was no way I wouldn't help someone in need, even if it meant risking my own life.

After that, the room fell silent as we waited for news about River. And we waited for a long time. I tried my best to keep my eyes from straying to the clock so I wouldn't know exactly how much time had passed, because the longer we waited, the more worried I became.

Finally, Kennedy came back, looking like she was ready to fall over herself. "They're keeping her overnight for observation, but she's awake, and it looks like she's going to be okay."

"Can I see her?" I asked.

Kennedy nodded. "They're discharging you now. As soon as she's moved to her room, I'll take you to see her."

CHAPTER EIGHT

RIVER

I was only granted a few minutes of peace once I was transferred to my hospital room before the door opened and a host of people filed in one right after the other. Some I knew, others I'd never seen before, but one I owed my life to.

"Jonah," I said and my voice cracked with emotion. "Thank you."

He stepped forward and took my hand. "You doing okay?"

I nodded and swallowed over the lump in my throat. "Yeah, all things considered. How about you?"

"I'm okay," he said hoarsely, and I automatically kicked into nurse mode.

"Did someone look at your throat?"

His brows furrowed, and he turned to Kennedy.

"Yes, they did. He had the same workup as you," she assured me.

"So, uh, who are all these people?" I asked, eyeing the strangers gathered in my room.

"You know Kennedy and Trey. This is my mom, Leigh, and these are my friends, Copper, Bronze, and Tiny," Jonah said.

"Hello," I said awkwardly.

"Not sure if you knew, but the club owns the rental property, and we wanted to stop by and make sure you were okay," Copper said, stepping forward and extending his hand to me.

"Oh, I had no idea," I said and shook his hand. "Thanks for stopping by."

"Also, when you're released from the hospital, we'll put you up in a hotel until the property is in livable condition again or another property becomes available," Copper continued.

I hadn't expected that. To be perfectly honest, where I would live hadn't even crossed my mind at that point. At least most of my personal belongings were in a storage unit in Baltimore. I never took much with me on assignments because more times than not, the contract would end early, and I would find myself packing up within a week or two of finally getting unpacked and settled.

A throat clearing pulled me out of my thoughts. "We'll get out of your hair and let you get some rest. Here's my contact info," he said, holding up a business card before placing it on the bedside table. "Call me if you need anything."

"Thank you. I appreciate the offer, but I'm sure I'll be fine," I said, even though I wasn't completely sure about that.

With that, he nodded and left the room. His friends following behind him like dutiful soldiers and left Kennedy and I alone in the room.

She plopped down in the oversized chair in the corner and made herself comfortable. "What are you doing?" I asked curiously.

"Getting comfortable. I'm not letting you stay here by yourself," she informed me.

Normally, I would have argued and insisted I didn't need a babysitter, but truthfully, the near-death experience had shaken me, and I was grateful to have the company.

***

After an uneventful night in the hospital, Kennedy drove me to the hotel where Copper had booked a room for me. Correction, he booked a deluxe suite for me. Kennedy squealed in delight, "Oh, I think I need to stay with you for a few more nights."

"Kennedy, this is too much. I can't stay here. Really, I just need a place to sleep and shower," I said as I stared wide-eyed at the lavish room.

Before she could reply, someone knocked on the door. She peeked through the peephole and yanked the door open to reveal Jonah and Trey.

"What are you guys doing here?" I blurted.

Trey chuckled, and Jonah held up a set of keys. "Dropping your car off for you. The house hasn't been cleared yet, but Splint got one of the firefighters to grab your keys when they were wrapping things up last night."

"Oh, uh, thanks," I said and took the keys from him.

An awkward silence fell over the room for several uncomfortable minutes. Finally, Jonah clapped his hands together and said, "Well, I've got to get to work. Your car's downstairs in the front lot. Take care."

Trey kissed Kennedy on the cheek, "See you later, Kitty."

Once they were gone, I sat down on the bed and started perusing the room service lunch menu. "So, things are going well with you and Trey, Kitty?"

"Oh, shut it. When I first told him my name, he thought I said Kitty, not Kennedy. But, yeah, things are going okay. We're taking it slow and getting to know each other. What about you and Jonah?"

I blinked in surprise. "Say what now?"

"Don't play dumb with me, missy. The way he looks at you. Damn girl, even I got a little wet from the fire in his eyes."

"Kennedy!" I gasped. "He does not look at me *like that.*"

"Yes, he does. He also beat the brakes off a guy for bothering you, escorted you home, saved you from a fiery death, and had to be forcefully restrained when he didn't know where you were at the hospital," she said, holding up a finger for each point she made.

"That proves nothing other than he's a nice

guy who looks out for other people," I retorted.

She grinned mischievously. "If that's so, then why is he staying in the room next door?"

He was what? "Uh, his house was probably damaged by the fire, too. You know how newer neighborhoods are; the houses are built so close together they're practically touching. Are you hungry? I'm going to order some room service," I said, hoping she would drop it.

"Yeah, I could eat," she smiled. "Want me to go next door and see if Jonah wants to have lunch with us?"

"No!" I shrieked causing Kennedy to burst into a fit of giggles. His presence meant nothing. Absolutely nothing.

CHAPTER NINE

JUDGE

I dropped into a chair in Copper's office at the clubhouse. "What's up, Prez?"

"Fire Marshal called with the preliminary results from the fire. He said it was clearly arson. Whoever did it, didn't try to make it look like an accident. They went with the classic can of gas and some matches," Copper told me.

"They got any leads?" I asked.

"Not yet. I know we didn't have any external cameras at that house, but I need you to check the feeds for the ones at yours. See if they picked up anything."

"Got it. Anything else?" I asked.

He sighed and rubbed his chin. "I don't like this. River is a traveling nurse and only in town for a three-month contract, so no one would be targeting her, which means this was likely aimed at the club. I can't have innocent people being hurt or killed because of the club."

And that's when I realized he didn't know who she was. "Uh, Prez, I forgot to mention something, that at the time didn't seem important, but now—"

"Spit it out, Judge."

"River Rain Lawson is Dash's little sister."

Silence.

"He knows she's here, but I guess there's some bad blood between them. He asked that I keep an eye on her, but to also be respectful of her wishes, which include having nothing to do with him," I explained.

"What caused the bad blood?" Copper asked.

I shrugged. "I don't know for sure. He doesn't know, and she won't talk about it."

"But you do know something," he observed.

"Harper told me what she could remember from high school, and really, it isn't my business," I said.

"You're right, it isn't your business. But it is mine if it's affecting my actual business. I'll stop by the hotel and have a word with her."

"Give me a chance to go through the security footage first. Might not need to bother her with all this if the cameras caught something useful," I suggested. I didn't know why, but I didn't like the idea of him, or anyone, prying into a part of River's life she clearly wanted to forget about.

Copper studied me for a few long moments before nodding in agreement. "Yeah, okay, but I need you to go through the recordings today."

I left the clubhouse and went back to my office to start sifting through the footage. It didn't take long since I knew roughly what time the fire started. Within fifteen minutes, I had clear shots of the vehicle, the tag number, and the two occupants. The only thing I didn't have was a video of them actually pouring the gas and lighting the fire, but I had the next best thing. My cameras had audio recordings.

I downloaded the recordings to three different flash drives and took them over to the clubhouse. "Here's one for the Fire Marshal, one for the police, and one for the club," I said and placed the drives on Copper's desk.

Copper grinned and inserted the flash drive

into his computer. We watched as the rusted-out sedan rolled past my house at a snail's pace, giving us a clear shot of the license plate, which I already had Spazz running. The car passed again headed in the opposite direction. Moments later, you could hear doors opening and closing followed my muffled voices.

The video cut to the camera mounted on the side of my house that faced the side of River's house. A man and a woman were each carrying a red jug presumably filled with gasoline. They were only on the screen for a few seconds before they disappeared.

The third part of the video was from the camera mounted at the back of my house. This one didn't show anything, but it picked up parts of their conversation that were crisp and clear.

"That little bitch always thought she was better'an everybody else....knock her off her high horse....refusin' to help her momma," the woman grumbled.

"Will you shut the fuck up and just pour the damn gas? I swear, Spring, if you still had teeth, I'd knock them the fuck outta your mouth right now," the male said.

"Roy! You're pouring that shit on my feet!"

"Yeah, 'cause I might just set your ass on fire

*too if you don't get busy," he spat followed by
the sound of a slap and a female yelp of pain.
"Gimme those matches and take these jugs to the
car."*

Several minutes later, the video became
noticeably brighter before smoke started wafting
across the screen. Then, you could hear me
screaming River's name before kicking her door
three times.

Right on cue, Spazz entered Copper's office
with a paper in his hand. "Here's the info on
the plates you wanted me to run. Plates are
registered to a 1992 Toyota Corolla belonging to
a Roy Mayfield."

"I'll be damned. I would've thought for sure
the plates were stolen," I blurted.

Copper laughed. "What a fucking dumbass.
Before I call this in, do we know who the woman
is?"

I nodded slowly, "Yeah, that's Spring Lawson,
Dash's and River's mother."

Copper's hand slammed down on his desk,
knocking a few pens and papers to the floor.
"You've got to be fucking kidding me."

"I've never met her personally, but Dash
said her name was Spring and described her as
a junkie whore. Harper's description was much

the same," I told him.

"Fuck," he breathed. "That makes this club business."

"Not necessarily. When I talked to Dash, he said he didn't give a shit about his mother."

Copper arched a brow. "Well, guess it wouldn't hurt to give him a call first."

I was right; Dash didn't care what happened to his mother, but he was very concerned about his sister. He offered to send one of the guys from Croftridge to tail River until their mother was arrested, but Copper assured him we could handle the job.

"I'm going to put the new prospect, Grant, on River. It'll be a good test to see if he's cut out for the club. Plus, I figure you won't be far from her, anyway."

"Sounds good, Prez," I agreed.

When I finally left the clubhouse, the evidence had been turned in and arrest warrants were issued for Roy Mayfield and Spring Lawson.

CHAPTER TEN

RIVER

After spending the entire day with me, Kennedy finally left, and that was only because she had to go to work. I, on the other hand, was being forced to take a week off. Well, technically, it was just the next three days because I was already scheduled to be off the following four. Still, I didn't need a week off to recover.

I wandered around the hotel room, wondering what I could do to entertain myself. I wasn't tired, and I only liked to watch certain shows on television, none of which were on. The existence of my e-reader and my laptop were still unknown. I really hoped they survived the fire. I had rental insurance to cover them, but it would likely be weeks of back and forth with the insurance company before I would be reimbursed to replace them.

I was studying the dinner menu, reminding myself that I couldn't order any of the delicious, unbelievably fattening meals when someone knocked on the door. Don't ask me how I knew it was Jonah at the door; I just did.

I quickly straightened my clothes and smoothed my hair. Then, I wanted to smack Kennedy for putting any kind of thoughts about Jonah in my head. I refused to allow myself to feel self-conscious around him, or anyone for that matter.

I opened the door and smiled. "Jonah, I wasn't expecting to see you."

"I need to talk to you about something. Can I come in?" he asked.

"I don't know. Can you?"

"Cute. May I come in?"

"Of course," I said and gestured with my hand for him to enter. "What do you need to talk to me about?"

He took a seat on the small sofa and patted the spot beside him. "You should probably sit for this," he suggested.

For reasons unbeknownst to me, I didn't argue with him. I sat quietly beside him and waited for him to continue.

"My rental house has security cameras mounted on each side of the house. After the Fire Marshal told us the preliminary findings indicated the fire was arson, I went through the footage to see if the cameras caught anything useful. The people who set fire to the house were Roy Mayfield and Spring Lawson," he said slowly while watching my every move.

I tried to swallow, but my mouth was suddenly dry. My mother set my house on fire, with me inside. I thought her threats were just that, threats. "I can't believe she actually did it," I breathed.

"The fuck did you just say?" he shouted.

"Huh?" I asked, confused by his outburst.

"You knew she was going to burn your house down?"

"No, I didn't. Well, not exactly. Shit," I stammered and pinched the bridge of my nose. "She came to the hospital trying to get a prescription for pain pills. She threatened me in the parking lot and told me she would be back. She came back the night before the fire and didn't get what she wanted. She was escorted out by hospital security, and she was pissed. I didn't think she would try to burn my house down, though. I'm not even sure how she knew where I was staying," I told him.

Before I could register what was happening, he had his cell phone pressed to his ear and walked away from me as he quietly spoke to someone. When he ended the call, he turned back to face me, "An officer will be coming by to take your statement in a little bit."

"What? I don't want to make a statement," I shouted.

"You have to. Your mother and her whatever tried to kill you. They've already issued warrants for their arrests, but this new information proves it was premeditated."

"I fucking knew this would happen if I came back here! For the last eight years, I've managed to live my life without that woman infecting any part of it, and now, after two weeks of living in the same town with her, she has affected my job and destroyed my home!" I screamed as tears of frustration ran down my cheeks.

And then something happened I didn't see

coming and wasn't prepared for. He pulled me against his chest and wrapped his arms around me. "It's going to be okay, River. Everything's going to be okay." As he gently rubbed my back and whispered reassuring words, I was almost tempted to believe him.

I allowed myself to be comforted by him, to enjoy the safety of his arms around me, to let his masculine scent wash over me and relax me before I pushed against his chest—his undeniably rock-hard chest—and took a few steps back to put some much-needed distance between us.

Jonah stepped forward with his hand extended, but three sharp knocks on the door halted his movement. After checking the peephole, I opened the door and let the two female officers into my hotel room.

While I was silently scolding myself for my stereotypical thoughts as I was one hundred percent expecting the officers to be male, I apparently missed something.

"River? You okay?" Jonah asked, appearing directly in front of me.

"Yeah, I'm fine. Sorry, what did I miss?" I asked and felt my cheeks redden.

"Just the introductions," the first woman

said. "I'm Officer Dunk, and this is Officer Underwood. Are you ready to give us your statement?"

"Yes?" I said, though it came out like a question. "Sorry, I've never done anything like this before, so you'll have to talk me through it."

Officer Dunk smiled kindly. "No problem, sweetie. You tell us what happened. We'll ask any questions we have, then we'll put it all into a formal report, have you read it, and sign it if you agree with everything on the report," she explained.

So, I spent the next thirty minutes telling them what happened with my mother in the hospital parking lot. "I'm sorry, but I'm not comfortable discussing what happened while she was a patient without the presence of a representative from the hospital," I said and shrugged. "HIPAA."

They both nodded in understanding. "Honestly, the threats and the physical contact happened outside when I was off duty and she was no longer a patient."

After a few more questions, they said someone would call me when the official report was ready for me to review and sign. "Ms. Lawson, we've issued warrants for their arrest, but as of right now, neither are in custody. It would be wise to be alert and cautious until they have been apprehended." Then, she pointedly looked at Jonah and lifted her chin before letting the door close behind her.

"What the hell was that about?" I asked.

He grinned. "She's a family friend. Well, they both are, but that was her way of telling me to look out for you without actually saying it."

I rolled my eyes. "I don't need a babysitter."

"No one said you did. But would it hurt to have someone watching your back? At least until they've been arrested?" he asked.

Sighing in exasperation, I admitted, "I guess not."

Jonah tried to convince me to have dinner with him, but I was exhausted and wanted to go to bed. Before leaving, he finally told me, rather awkwardly, that he was staying in the room next door until his home was cleared and to let him know if I needed anything. I agreed and then fell face down onto the softest mattress in the world and drifted into a deep sleep.

Brrrrnnnngggg!

Brrrrnnnngggg!

Brrrrnnnngggg!

The loud and obnoxious noise startled me

awake. My eyes flew open but immediately slammed shut when the bright white flashing light assaulted them. It took two seconds for me to realize the fire alarm in the hotel was going off.

"You've got to be fucking kidding me!" I screamed to the ceiling as I slid my feet into the slip-on sneakers I borrowed from Kennedy.

I startled again when someone pounded furiously on the door. "River!" Jonah screamed. "Rivvveeerrr!"

"I'm coming!" I yelled and grabbed my car keys from the small desk as I made my way to the door.

I yanked the door open and stepped out into the hallway. Jonah tossed me over his shoulder in a fireman's carry and sprinted for the stairs.

"I can fucking walk!" I yelled and punctuated it with a slap to his back.

"Not as fast as I can run," he retorted and moved down the stairs faster than a gazelle running from a cheetah.

When we made it to the ground floor, he set me on my feet while we followed the crowd of hotel guests outside. The flashing lights of rapidly approaching fire trucks could be seen in the distance, and the hotel staff were strategically stationed to guide us along to the designated safe location. But what no one planned for was the spray of bullets that tore through the crowd from the two cars that flew by at top speeds.

"Down!" Jonah roared as he threw, yes threw, me to the ground and landed on top of me. "Everybody, get down!"

It lasted all of five seconds, maybe seven, and then a deafening silence filled the night air before complete and total chaos erupted.

CHAPTER ELEVEN

Judge

"What're you thinking?" Copper asked.

"That it's a fucking miracle no one was hurt," I said honestly. At least fifty people were standing outside the hotel when two cars raced by and opened fire.

"You think it was intentional?" he asked, and I couldn't help but look at my President like he had lost his damn mind. He rolled his eyes, "Not the shooting. I meant do you think they intentionally didn't hit anyone?"

"Why in the hell would anyone do a drive-by shooting if their intention wasn't to shoot someone?" I asked.

"To scare someone. To cause a distraction. As part of a gang initiation. Because people are fucking crazy. There could be a number of reasons. I just think the whole thing seems weird and wondered if you were getting the same vibe?"

He had some good points, but I hadn't considered any of them. "Honestly, Prez, I haven't had the time to do much more than be thankful I didn't shit myself while covering River."

"How is she?" he asked and jerked his chin toward the ambulance River was standing beside.

"Physically, she probably sprained her wrist when we went down, but otherwise she's fine. Mentally, I'm guessing she's freaked the fuck out. Back-to-back near-death experiences is a bit much for anyone to handle."

"Yeah, I have to agree with you on that one. I'm going to see if I can find out what triggered the fire alarm. You staying at the clubhouse tonight?"

"Not sure yet. I'm going to go check on River. I'll catch you before you leave," I told him and clapped him on the shoulder.

I did know one thing for sure; River would not be spending the night by herself. She could bitch about it all she wanted, but that's how it was going to be.

She looked up when I was a few steps away. "Jonah, any news?"

I frowned and shook my head. "Not yet. How's your wrist?" She instinctively put her arms out to catch herself when I tossed her to the ground. With my much larger frame coming down on top of her, she was damn lucky her arm didn't break.

She shrugged. "It's fine. A little sore, but nothing a few days rest and some ibuprofen won't fix."

I nodded to Splint. "Is she good to go, brother?"

"She is. Now, it's your turn," he said and pointed to my hand.

I opened my mouth to protest, but he didn't even let me get started. "It probably just needs to be cleaned and closed up with some glue. Quit being such a pussy and sit down."

River burst into laughter, and Splint actually looked embarrassed. "Sorry, please forgive my language," he said softly.

"Oh, no apologies necessary," River said and snorted comically. "I had to hold his hand while he got a shot once."

"Both of you can fuck right off. Splint, make it quick. I've got shit to do," I snapped.

Splint made quick work of cleaning and gluing my hand. Two stitches had torn through the skin, but the majority of the wound stayed closed. Once he was finished, River asked, "Are they going to let us go back to our rooms any time soon?"

I scratched the back of my neck. "Uh, about that...I don't think it's a good idea to stay here. It's still early, but as of right now, they don't know if the fire alarm and the shooting were related or completely separate incidents."

"Okay, so where am I supposed to stay?" she asked.

"My place—"

"Oh, hell no," she answered immediately.

"Hear me out. Your mother and her boyfriend or whatever haven't been picked up yet. My place is the last place they'll look. You can park your car in the garage, and no one will know you're there. I have an alarm system and cameras that have already saved your life once, and it's close to the hospital," I explained.

While she was thinking it over, I added, "You'll have your own bedroom and bathroom. Plus, I work days, and you work nights; we'll hardly see each other."

She blew out an exasperated breath. "Fine. I guess I'll stay with you until I can move back into my place."

I grinned and pulled her along behind me by her uninjured wrist. "Wait! Where're you going?"

"Home," I said over my shoulder and continued toward my bike.

"But my stuff," she protested.

"I'll have someone bring it over. I don't want to be here any longer than I have to be," I confessed. Copper could speculate all he wanted, but regardless of intent, any time a gun was fired in the direction of people, it should always be assumed that someone would be hit. Since we weren't, I didn't want to push our luck any further.

When we reached my bike, River held up her car keys and jingled them in front of my face. "I'll follow you," she announced smugly.

Her jaw dropped when I snatched the keys from her and tossed them over her head. "No, you won't. One of the boys will drop it off when they bring your stuff. Now, quit stalling and put your fine ass on my bike," I growled. She had about two seconds to move before I placed her on it myself.

She stiffened and shot me a scathing look, but silently climbed onto my bike. I didn't have a spare helmet with me, so I pushed mine onto her head and climbed on in front of her. Grabbing her thighs, I pulled her forward until her thighs were snug against mine and her hot little pussy was pressed against my lower back. "Put your arms around me and hold on," I ordered but didn't wait for her to comply, because I knew she would the moment I pulled onto the road and the bike lurched forward.

Fuck. I was hard as a rock by the time I pulled into my garage, and there was a large part of me that didn't care if she saw it. But, the part of me that did care tapped her thigh and let her get off first while I discreetly readjusted myself.

She stayed silent as I escorted her into my temporary home and showed her to her room. "Bathroom's through that door. There should be plenty of towels and toilet paper in there. Help yourself to anything that's in the kitchen. Good night," I said and went to my bedroom, closing the door behind me and my hard dick. Fuck, maybe having her stay with me wasn't such a good idea after all.

CHAPTER TWELVE

RIVER

Surprisingly, Jonah was right; we didn't see much of each other. However, it wasn't because of our work schedules, or at least not mine. I hadn't been scheduled to work since I'd been staying at his house. And it looked like I would be there for a few more weeks before I could move back into the rental house next door.

Spending the better part of a week pretty much alone with little to no interaction with any humans whatsoever had just about sent me over the edge. So, I was more than happy to be returning to work.

I tried to take a nap in the afternoon, but never fell asleep. After growing more and more frustrated, I finally got up and started getting ready for work. After my shower, I put on a pair of panties and a camisole and spent the next fifteen minutes drying my hair and doing my makeup. By that time, I was starving and went to the kitchen to make myself something to eat. Since I knew Jonah wouldn't be home before I left for work, I didn't bother putting on any other clothes.

So, when I walked into the open part of the house to find a woman wearing what could only be described as material masquerading as a dress sprawled on the sofa, I was shocked to say the least. Before I could ask her what in the hell she was doing, my eyes shot to the fifty-inch flat screen mounted on the wall and all words left the building. Why? Because this barely dressed woman was watching porn. Hardcore, fetish porn. In Jonah's house.

While I stood gaping at her trying to formulate words, she got to her feet and had no problem speaking. "Who in the fuck are you?" she asked in an annoying nasally voice.

"The woman who is supposed to be here. Who the fuck are you?" I shot back, happy that my brain and mouth were finally in sync.

"I don't think so, honey. I'm Judge's girlfriend, and I can assure you, I'm the only one who's supposed to be here. Now get your skank ass out of here before I bash your snot-nosed face in," she screamed, slowly advancing toward me.

I snorted and rolled my eyes at her ridiculousness. "Okie dokie, Imposter Barbie," I said and crossed my arms. I was in no way, shape, or form intimidated by her in the slightest. She was wearing five or six-inch heels, and she was unnaturally top heavy; with one good push, she'd hit the floor like a sack of bouncy balls.

Moments later, she proved to be dumber than I originally thought when she tottered closer and slowly cocked her arm back giving me full warning of what she was about to do. She swung her arm in a wide arc aiming for my face. My left hand shot out and wrapped around her wrist stopping her momentum while I bashed her snot-nosed face in with my right fist. Her arm was ripped from my grasp when she flew backward off her spiked heels and landed with a plop on her ass.

"Ahhhh! You broke my nose, you crazy

bitch!" she shrieked.

I shook my hand out and momentarily regretted hitting her so hard. But then she got to her feet and came at me again. What happened next wasn't my fault. Not entirely.

Jonah came through the front door as she was charging me and I was gearing up to knock some teeth out. He grabbed me by my waist and swung me around with the intent to move me out of her path, I assumed. I used it for the opportunity it was and kicked my foot out, making contact with her jaw. She hit the ground with a muffled scream.

"What in the motherfuck is going on?" Jonah roared.

"Your girlfriend attacked me!" I roared back.

"What?" he asked with a confused look on his face.

I pointed to the heap of whore on the floor. "Your girlfriend attacked me."

His confusion quickly morphed to anger. He spun around and lifted the girl to her feet. "Get the fuck out of my house, and don't you dare come back. Got me?"

She whimpered, but nodded her head and moved to the door. "And Didi, you're officially banned from the club, too. Now, get gone." I almost felt bad for her when she started to sob as she fled, but my throbbing hand made me realize the error of my ways.

"Are you okay?"

"Yeah, I'm fine," I chuckled humorlessly and held up my hand. "My hand's a little sore. I'm just gonna grab some ice for it."

"What happened?" Jonah asked in a much softer tone.

"I found her on the couch when I came to make something to eat. She said—"

"Oh, fuck. Mmmm, you like it when I fuck your ass, you dirty little whore?"

Jonah whirled around and his eyes widened comically. "Oh yeah, she was watching that when I came out."

I almost laughed as I watched him scramble to turn it off. The screen turned black, but the sound was still going. *"Such a tight ass,"* was moaned followed by the sounds of skin meeting skin. Jonah yanked all the cords from the wall, and suddenly we were surrounded by silence.

"So, yeah, she said she was your girlfriend and demanded to know who I was. Then, she said she was going to bash my face in, some words were exchanged, and I was the one to do the bashing," I explained.

I didn't realize Jonah had come up behind me while I was filling a bag with ice for my hand, so I jumped when his arms came around from behind and took the bag from me. He turned me around and cradled my hand in his, gently placing the bag on top of it. "Are you sure you're okay?"

"I'm good," I assured him, feeling very uncomfortable with the way he was looking at me. "What?" I asked.

"I'm sorry," he said simply.

"For what?"

"Didi. I promised you would be safe here, and you weren't. It won't happen again."

"It's fine, Jonah. I don't have a problem with you having your girlfriends or whatever come over. I mean, it's your house, and I don't expect you to change your lifestyle just because I'm staying with you for a little while."

"She's not my girlfriend."

"Fuck buddy or whatever," I said dismissively and glanced away.

He slid his hand under my jaw and tipped my face up to his. "Don't know what she was up to. Never laid a hand on her. Never wanted to," he said softly, and I was all too aware of how close his lips were to mine.

I gently pushed against his chest. "It's really none of my business."

"Maybe it should be," he breathed and captured my lips with his. And he kissed me. Oh, holy hell, did he kiss me.

There was nothing hesitant or unsure about the way he devoured my mouth. He took from me, and for a few minutes, I forgot about everything except the way he made me feel.

Then, his phone rang, and I was thrust back into reality. I broke the kiss and shoved him back. "You should get that. I need to get to work," I said and bolted from the room.

CHAPTER THIRTEEN

JUDGE

"What?" I barked into the phone while I watched River run from the room.

"Got some info about the shooting. Is now a bad time?" Copper asked.

"Sorry, Prez. Now's good."

"The shooting was a distraction. The new gun store in town had just been robbed. They just happened to be flying by the hotel at the same time some kids that were staying there pulled the fire alarm. The whole thing was a total coincidence, but they were hoping to keep the cars from being identified by letting off a few rounds. Didn't work out like they thought," he explained.

"I see. Any word on River's mom and her boyfriend?"

"Nope. The detective I spoke with said they'd sent some officers out to check their local haunts and listed addresses, but hadn't had any luck finding them."

"Figures," I grumbled. "Let me know if you hear anything. Oh, one more thing. I came home this afternoon to find Didi and River going at it in my living room. Didi thought it would be okay to let herself into my home and start a fight with my houseguest. Kicked her out and told her she was banned from the club."

"Good. That bitch had trouble written all over her. I'll let the other brothers know. If she was ballsy enough to show up at your place, I don't doubt she'll try showing up at the club to test your word."

I laughed, "Yeah, she probably will, but it might be a minute. River broke her nose, and I'm pretty sure she fractured her jaw, too."

"No, shit. River okay?"

"She's fine. Girl didn't even split her

knuckles," I said proudly.

We talked for a few more minutes before ending the call. As soon as I hung up, I went in search of River, but the sneaky little shit had already left for work.

***

I had been in my home office for hours trying to get caught up on billing and filing invoices, which I hated doing, when my phone rang. Figuring it was one of the guys, I ignored it and kept working. I ignored it the second time it rang, but when Copper's designated ring sounded next, I answered.

"Get your ass to the hospital right now!" he yelled and disconnected before I had a chance to say anything.

I grabbed my keys and hauled ass to the hospital, hoping and praying the whole way that whatever happened to River wasn't that bad, but knowing full well that it would be. Copper wouldn't have called like that if it wasn't an emergency.

Copper and Bronze were waiting for me right inside the doors of the Emergency Room entrance. "What's going on? Did something happen to River?"

As I stepped farther into the waiting room, I noticed Tiny standing next to Batta who had his arm around Copper's Old Lady, Layla. She was visibly upset and that scared the shit out of me. Layla didn't know River, but she was very close to the other woman in my life.

Copper grimaced and shook his head. "No, brother, she's okay. Sit down, Jonah."

Jonah. He hadn't called me Jonah in years, not since long before he started the Devil Springs chapter of Blackwings. My instinct was to argue; I didn't take orders from just anyone, but I knew he only had my best interest in mind and that scared the shit out of me. So, I sat my ass down and waited for him to speak.

"Splint's working tonight, and he was on the call. Leigh was out with some of the Old Ladies and collapsed. They think it's a heart attack. I don't know anything other than that right now."

I nodded in acknowledgment and dropped my face into my hands. I couldn't lose my mom. I lost my dad way too early in life; I wouldn't make it through losing my mom, too. What had I done to deserve this? What had she done? We were good fucking people.

"Fuck!" I yelled as uncontrollable emotions exploded within me. I got to my feet and launched the chair I was sitting in across the room.

I heard a female scream in the background as I unceremoniously hit the hard tile floor, and a crushing weight landed on top of me.

"Rein it in, brother. Your momma is going to whoop your ass if you aren't there when she's allowed visitors because you're in jail. And I'm telling you right now, ain't none of us leaving here to bail your ass out until we've seen her. Breathe it out, man, and I'll let you up," Batta said as he held me down.

"We've got it under control. He just got some bad news, but I'll have him removed myself before he does anything like that again. And let me know who I need to speak to about covering the damages," Copper said to who I assumed to be hospital security.

"I'm good," I said quietly.

"You sure about that?" Batta asked.

"Yeah, man. You're right; Mom would have my ass. Probably will anyway when she finds out about this."

"Prez?" Batta asked.

"Let him up." I got to my feet, and Copper got in my face. "But damn it, Judge, don't make me have you hauled out of here because I will fucking do it. We all love that woman. She's been a mother to all of us and then some—"

I interrupted him when something suddenly occurred to me, "Harper," I croaked. "Somebody needs to call her."

"I called Carbon and Duke as soon as we heard," Bronze said. "They're on their way."

"I don't know what to do," I confessed and didn't give the first fuck how broken I sounded.

"Nothing you can do right now but wait," Copper said. "And we'll all be right here with you."

The waiting was excruciating. Knowing my mom was back there, possibly dying, while I sat helplessly on the other side of the doors.

I don't know how much time passed, but finally a familiar face stepped out. "Jonah, come with me," Dr. Daniels called from the doorway and led me to a small room off to the side.

"We believe your mom has a blockage in one or possibly more of the large vessels that supply blood to the heart. They're taking her to do a heart cath right now. Usually, they can place a stent to open up the blocked vessel and restore blood flow to the heart," Dr. Daniels explained.

"What happens if they can't place a stent?

Or what if it's not her heart?"

"It is her heart, Jonah. That I can assure you. If they can't place a stent, she'll need to have heart surgery."

"You mean open heart surgery? Like a bypass or whatever it's called?"

"Yes, that's exactly what I mean. But let's not get ahead of ourselves. In your mother's case, it's highly likely that a stent will take care of the problem," he said confidently.

"Yeah, okay," I agreed. I trusted Dr. Daniels. She'd been friends with my parents since before I was born. Her reassurance alleviated a tiny bit of my worry.

"Do you want to stay back here or go back out there with your friends?"

"I should get back out there. My cousins will be here soon, and Harper's going to be a mess."

"I would imagine so. I'll let you know the moment I hear something."

"Uh, one more thing. Is River Lawson around? I'd like to talk to her if she has a minute," I said nervously.

The corners of Dr. Daniels's mouth tipped up in a small grin before she spoke. "She's in the cath lab with your mom. She volunteered to assist the cardiologist on call so they wouldn't have to wait for the on-call nurse to get here."

I nodded and swallowed thickly. No matter how things turned out, I would be forever grateful to River for going out of her way to help my mother. "Thanks, Doc," I managed to say and went back to the waiting room to update everyone else.

During another agonizingly long period of waiting for any news, Harper came through the doors like a woman on a mission. She spotted me immediately and threw herself against my chest where she dissolved into a fit of gasping sobs. Carbon was right behind her with Duke by his side. "How is she?" Duke asked.

"Haven't heard anything in a while. They're doing a heart cath now," I shared as Harper continued to break my heart while she cried all over me. "Come on, sister cousin, let's go sit down."

Sometime later, Dr. Daniels called me, Harper, and Duke back to the same little room where a woman dressed in hospital scrubs was waiting inside.

"I'm Dr. Kenny, the cardiologist taking care of Mrs. Jackson. We did find a significant blockage in the left anterior descending artery and were able to place a stent. Blood flow was immediately restored to the heart, but she did not show any signs of regaining consciousness. Because of that and her heart stopping en route, we've initiated a protocol called therapeutic hypothermia to reduce the risk of damage to her brain from the decrease in oxygenated blood flow. That's a fancy way of saying we're going to keep her sedated while we lower her temperature and give her body a chance to recover," she explained. "I know this is a lot to take in. Do you have any questions?"

"When can we see her?" Harper asked.

"Is she going to make it?" I asked.

"Will she have brain damage?" Duke asked.

All at the same time.

Dr. Kenny sat patiently and answered all of our questions. Unfortunately, her answers, though honest, did little to comfort us. It would be a few more hours before we could see her. As for the rest, only time would tell.

As we waited for her to be moved to a room, I was lost in my own thoughts. I knew she wouldn't want me to keep her alive if she didn't have any brain activity, but could I do it? Could I give the okay to pull the plug on my mother? And what if she did live, but was massively impaired. Would she want that?

"Brother Judge," Harper said as she nudged me. "You ready?"

I shook my head. "I'm sorry. What?"

"She's in her room. We can go see her. You ready?"

I nodded sharply. Was I ready? Hell, no. But that wasn't going to stop me from being by my mom's side.

CHAPTER FOURTEEN

JUDGE

I stayed by Mom's bedside for two days straight before Harper insisted that I go home.

"You need to get some sleep, and please, take a shower. I love you, but you stink."

I started to protest, but she was ready for it. "I won't leave her side. You heard what the doctor said this morning. Today is going to be a slow day. So, go home and come back rested and refreshed for when they start warming her up tomorrow."

Reluctantly, I agreed. As much as I didn't

want to leave, Harper was right, on two counts. I did want to be well-rested before they started the warming process, and I smelled like two-day-old ass.

I pulled my bike into my empty garage and wondered why River's car wasn't there. Then, I glanced at my watch and realized it was barely seven o'clock in the morning, and she usually didn't get home from work until around eight.

Once inside, I went straight for the shower, kicking off my boots and shedding my clothes along the way. I sighed when the hot water hit my body and soothed my sore muscles. Hospital furniture was not fit to be slept on for more than a few hours at a time.

When the water started to run cold, I put on my usual black boxer briefs followed by a pair of black drawstring pants and went out to the kitchen to make myself something to eat.

I was putting my dishes in the dishwasher when River came through the garage door. She kicked her shoes off and dropped her purse on the kitchen table before she saw me and yelped.

"Shit!" she cursed and placed a hand on her chest. "I didn't know you were here."

I arched an eyebrow. "You didn't see my bike?"

"Obviously not. How's your mom?" she asked and reached into the refrigerator for a bottle of water.

I waited for her to finish drinking and took the bottle from her hands. Then, I pulled her into a hug and held her against me while I spoke. "Thank you for being there. For helping her and stepping in so she could get the help she needed faster."

She looked up and met my eyes. "You're welcome. It was—"

And I couldn't hold back any longer. I lowered my head and kissed her while she was still talking. And she didn't resist. No, she melted into me and kissed me back with just as much fervor.

"Jonah," she moaned and thrust her fingers into my hair.

I reached down and hoisted her up by her ass. She wrapped her legs around my waist and held on while I moved down the hall. Kicking my bedroom door shut, I moved to my bed, dropping her on it and following her down.

She wiggled underneath me while I devoured her mouth. I broke the kiss and studied her face. "You want this?"

Her cheeks flushed, but she nodded. When I

just stared at her, she whispered, "Yes."

With that, I ripped her top over her head and yanked her pants from her legs. She was fucking gorgeous laying there almost naked with her dark hair fanned around her, her flushed cheeks, and her swollen lips. "Fuck, River," I breathed and reached for her bra, but she beat me to it.

She unclasped her bra and tossed it to the side, slowly lowering her arms and revealing a perfect set of tits. When she kept her eyes cast down, I realized she needed some reassurance. She was a beautiful, confident woman, but I knew she hadn't always felt that way about herself, and I wasn't going to let those old feelings resurface for her.

"You're fucking gorgeous," I told her as I leaned down and captured her nipple with my lips while my fingers teased and toyed with the other. I alternated between her breasts, and soon, she was moaning and grinding her cunt on my thigh.

Releasing her nipple with a pop, I slowly moved my hands down her stomach to slip between her skin and the band of her panties. With a firm grip, I tore the flimsy material from her body like a greedy kid ripping open presents.

And what a present she was.

I was like a ravenous beast ready to devour every inch of her, but I wanted her to be as hungry as I was. Grabbing her by her waist, I lifted her as I rolled to my back and placed her perfect pussy right over my waiting mouth.

"Jonah," she gasped in a weak protest.

"Ride my face, River," I ordered. When she didn't move, I placed my hands on her hips and started to guide her. As I licked, flicked, and sucked, she began moving on her own and soon the room was filled with her moans and gasps.

Despite her obvious enjoyment, I knew she was holding back, and I wasn't having it. "I'm not stopping until you come on my face," I said and punctuated my words with a light slap to her ass.

"I-I can't," she groaned.

The fuck she couldn't. The next time her hips rose, I latched on to her clit and slipped two fingers inside of her. With a firm grip on her thigh, I held her against me as I picked up the pace.

The sound of her hands slapping against the wall echoed through the room followed by her moans while her body spasmed. She rested her forehead against the cool wall and heaved in breath after breath. "Holy fuck," she panted.

I quickly slid out from underneath her and grabbed a condom from the nightstand. Once I was covered, I moved behind her, wrapped my arm around her waist, positioned myself at her entrance, and thrust inside.

"Oh, fuck, Jonah," she groaned and pushed back against me.

"Fucking hell, woman," I gritted out and held her in place while I tried to keep from embarrassing myself. I slapped her ass when she pressed back again. "Don't move."

"But I—" she started, but I silenced her with my mouth. When I finally had a handle on things, I broke the kiss and started to move.

My hands slid up her torso and cupped her breasts while I watched my dick disappear every time the round globes of her ass met my hips over and over.

My eyes focused on a drop of sweat that fell from my nose and slid down the track of her spine highlighting the sheer perfection of her body. Suddenly, I wanted to see her face. I needed to take in her every reaction and see if she was feeling the same intense connection I was.

Within seconds, my eyes were locked to hers

while I moved inside of her. She placed her hand on my cheek for a moment before sliding her fingers into my hair and pulling my lips down to hers.

I slowed my pace so I could savor every second of our sweat slicked bodies sliding against each other.

The hand in my hair tightened at the same time I felt her nails dig into my back. "Please, Jonah," she whispered against my lips.

I slid my arms underneath her to grip her shoulders and buried my face in her neck so I could give her everything I had. I didn't want to stop until she could feel my soul the way I felt hers. Because I'd never felt anything like what I was feeling with her and I knew it was an intensity I would chase forever. With her.

Her body tensed and her nails dug deeper into my skin. "Jonah," she exhaled followed by a gasp. My lips covered hers and our bodies melded together as she reached her climax and pulled me along with her.

I broke the kiss, breathing heavily, our bodies still connected, and rested my forehead against hers for long minutes.

"Jonah?"

"If I move, you'll leave. And I want you to

stay," I whispered.

"I'll stay," she said softly and placed a gentle kiss on my lips.

"Okay," I said but didn't move. For several minutes, I stayed right where I was, enjoying the feeling of her body surrounding mine. For those few moments, I was at peace.

All too soon, it became apparent that I had to get up or things were going to get extremely messy. With a groan of discontent, I went to the bathroom to take care of the condom and returned to the bed with a warm washcloth for her.

She squirmed and wiggled uncomfortably when I ran the cloth between her legs, but I was finished before she could find the words to protest. Tossing the rag to the floor, I slid into the bed beside her and pulled the covers over both of us. Within minutes, we were wrapped in each other's arms sound asleep.

CHAPTER FIFTEEN

RIVER

When I woke, Jonah was still asleep. I quietly slipped out of bed and went back to my room to take a shower and get ready for work.

Tilting my head back into the stream of water, I raised my arms to start rinsing the conditioner from my hair. I heard the shower curtain rustle followed by, "It's just me."

"What're you doing?"

"Same thing you are. Taking a shower," he said and pulled me against him as he pressed his lips to my neck.

To my surprise, he grabbed the bar of soap and lathered us both in suds. Once we were rinsed, he quickly washed his hair and turned off the water.

He caught the look of disbelief on my face and smirked. "Expecting something else?"

"I guess," I shrugged. "I've never had a guy get in the shower with me. It's a natural assumption that more would be involved." Reaching for a towel, I stepped out of the shower and wrapped my hair up before I started drying my body with a second towel.

I shrieked when Jonah scooped me up and carried me into my room. He dropped me onto my bed on my stomach and crawled up behind me grabbing each cheek of my ass and gently squeezing. "This wasn't my original intention, but, fuck, it is now," he growled.

Moments later, he'd divested me of both towels and was lavishing my breasts with his tongue and teeth. My hands were everywhere—pulling at his hair, clawing at his back, desperately trying to pull him impossibly closer to me.

His hand trailed down my torso to the apex of my thighs. He slowly moved his fingers through my wetness before teasing my clit with light circles.

"Jonah, please," I begged.

I could feel him grin against my skin. "Please, what?"

I wiggled and lifted my hips trying to get his fingers to go where I needed them. "Say it, River. Tell me what your wet pussy wants."

Any other time, I would have rolled my eyes and said something sarcastic, but I wanted him so damn bad all I could say was the truth. "Fuck me."

"With what?" he asked as he teased my entrance with the tips of his fingers and flicked my nipple with his tongue.

"Your fingers. Your cock. I don't care! Just fuck me!" I shouted.

He reached between us and I wanted to scream out in victory. But then he suddenly dropped his head to my shoulder. "Shit," he swore and started to pull away.

"No," I snapped and grabbed for his shoulders so my body followed his when he sat back on his heels.

"Just need to grab a condom. I'll be right back."

"Wait!" I said more forcefully than I intended and proceeded to imitate a contortionist in order to reach the tote bag on the floor beside the bed. I quickly found the foil square and held it up for Jonah to see. "I have one," I announced proudly.

He immediately reached for it, but I pulled my hand back and shook my head. With a little smirk, I brought the package to my mouth and carefully tore it open with my teeth. He watched me like a hawk while I slowly rolled it down his length.

With his attention focused on his cock, I was able to catch him off guard and push him to his back. I climbed on top of him and grinned. "My turn," I declared before I slid down his shaft.

I wanted to tease him, to drag it out until he was begging me to move faster, but I was too worked up. The moment he was fully inside me, I started moving. My hips rose and fell maybe a half a dozen times before Jonah took over. He curled up into a sitting position with one hand going around my back and the other threading through my hair.

The hand in my hair tightened and he pulled my head back exposing the column of my neck. His lips and teeth scraped along my skin from my collarbone to my earlobe where he gently bit down. "You," he breathed, "will not fuck anyone else while you're fucking me."

I gripped his hair in return and pulled his head back until he was looking me in the eyes. I didn't even have to say it. "Only you, baby. I only want you," he promised.

"Okay," I whispered and lowered my mouth to his.

And that was it for Jonah's control. He flipped us over and proceeded to do things to my body I'd only known to exist on the pages of a dirty romance book.

Once again, we reached our climaxes together, which was something I'd never experienced with anyone other than him.

As much as I wanted to stay in his arms and enjoy being fully sated, I rolled to my side and sighed. "I need to take a quick shower and get moving. I've got less than an hour before I need to be at work." And for the first time since I'd arrived in Devil Springs, I didn't want to go to work.

"Yeah, I need to get back up there, too. Can I catch a ride with you?" he asked.

My forehead scrunched. "Uh, sure, but you know I have to work all night, right?"

He chuckled. "I know. I'm planning on spending the night in Mom's room. They're supposed to start warming her in the morning, so I won't be going anywhere for a few days. If I need to leave, one of the guys can give me a ride."

When I was ready to leave, Jonah held his hands out for my keys. "Mind if I drive?" he asked. And because he asked, I didn't mind.

Working in the ER in a somewhat small town was hit or miss. Some nights were nonstop craziness while other nights were so slow a twelve-hour shift felt like twelve days. I didn't have a problem with the crazy shifts, but the slow ones were straight up torture.

We had no patients and were bored out of our minds when Kennedy and I started spinning in our chairs. One thing led to another and before long I was sitting criss-cross applesauce in a chair at the nurse's station while Kennedy spun me around as fast as the chair would go. She stopped the chair and shouted, "Go!"

I stood and walked in a straight line to the other side of the nurse's station. I turned around with a proud smile on my face and my steps faltered when my eyes met Jonah's. He grinned, "Huh, spinning in circles doesn't bother you, but the sight of me makes you stumble."

"Oh, shut it. What're you doing down here? Did something happen with your mom?"

"No, nothing happened. I, uh, couldn't sleep and was wondering when you took your lunch break, or whatever you call it when you eat in the middle of the night."

Kennedy and I both laughed. "Sorry, when you're an ER nurse, you eat when you can, not at a designated time."

"Doesn't seem like you guys are very—"

"No!"

"Don't say it!" we screamed at the same time.

Jonah's eyes widened at our outburst. "I can take my break now. Let's go," I said and headed for the break room.

"What was that about?" he asked.

"I'll explain it when I'm not working," I said and grabbed my salad out of the fridge. When I stabbed some lettuce with my fork and shoved it into my mouth, I looked up to find Jonah staring at me. "What?"

"Did you already put dressing on that?" he asked.

"I don't ever put dressing on my salad," I explained and continued to shovel food into my mouth.

"And you like it like that?" he asked skeptically.

"No, but I like being fat even less."

"You're not anywhere close to being fat."

"Not anymore," I said and pointed to the salad with my fork. "And this is why. I'm not this size by sheer luck."

"River—" he started but I didn't want to hear it.

"Please, don't. I was a fat kid; I'm not now. There's really no need to discuss it," I said firmly.

"I was going to ask how you got your protein," he said carefully.

"Sorry," I said and pointed my fork at my drink. "I don't like fish, and I'm not a huge fan of poultry, so I have one or two shakes a day. I also get most of my vitamins from the shakes, so two birds, one stone."

We sat in silence while I finished eating, which wasn't long because I inhaled my food when I was working as most, if not all, nurses did. When I finished my shake and wiped my mouth, I noticed Jonah was staring at his clasped hands.

"Hey, you okay?" I asked, wondering if he'd come down for another reason and not because he simply couldn't sleep.

He cleared his throat and looked up. "Yeah, I'm just, I guess I'm a little worried about tomorrow and how things are going to go. I can't lose her, too."

I stood from my seat and moved to sit beside him. "When did you lose your dad?"

He put his arm around my shoulders and pulled me close. "When I was fifteen."

"May I ask what happened?"

"You don't know?" he asked sounding surprised.

"I don't think so."

"My father was Jonas Jackson, the sheriff who was killed during the high-speed chase that ended on Main Street in Devil Springs."

I gasped as realization dawned. "I remember when that happened. He pulled out in front of the car they were chasing to stop it from crashing into the elementary school's playground."

Jonah swallowed thickly. "Yeah, he saved a lot of kids' lives that day."

"But that didn't make it any easier for you," I observed.

"No, it didn't. But, as I got older, it made it easier to accept. I would've still lost my dad that day because he wouldn't have been able to live with himself if he hadn't put himself in front of that truck," Jonah said.

I stayed snuggled against him for several minutes hoping I was silently comforting him when I had an idea. "You want me to stop by your mom's room after my shift?"

"I've seen you walk in the door and practically fall asleep walking to your room. I don't want you staying any longer than you have to and risk falling asleep on your way home," he said seriously.

"Okay, how about this? I'll go home and sleep, then I'll come back to see how things are going," I offered.

"You don't have to do that. I'll be okay," he countered.

"All right. Let me know if you change your mind," I said. I wasn't going to argue with him, but I was going to come back to check on him after I got some sleep.

And that's exactly what I did almost twelve hours later.

I didn't expect to find Jonah alone in his mother's room. His head was resting on the bed, and he had one of her hands clutched in his much larger one. Even in his sleep, lines of worry were etched on his face.

I stood in the doorway for several minutes wondering if I should leave and come back later, but ultimately decided to quietly slip into the room and wait for him to wake up, which he did around an hour later.

His eyes landed on me the moment they opened, and the corner of his lips tipped up into a smile. "Hey," he rasped. "How long have you been here?"

"About an hour or so. I didn't want to wake you. Figured you needed the sleep."

He stood and stretched, causing his T-shirt to reveal a hint of his toned stomach. He totally caught me staring and laughed. "You make me feel like a piece of meat."

I rolled my eyes. "Please. Like you don't know you're hot."

"I didn't say it was a bad thing," he grinned and came over to sit beside me on the small sofa in the room.

"How's your mom?" I asked, changing the subject intentionally.

He sighed and pinched the bridge of his nose. "No changes. I didn't realize how long and drawn out the cooling and rewarming process would be."

"They didn't explain that to you?"

"I don't know. Somebody probably did along the way, but it wasn't knowledge that I retained. Initially, I only wanted to know if she was expected to live and, if so, would she make a full recovery."

"For future reference, if you have any medical related questions, please don't hesitate to ask me," I offered, and then I explained the rewarming process to him and what to expect.

"Thank you. I've been waiting for her to wake up, and I've been growing more and more concerned as each hour passed."

I patted his thigh. "Glad I could help."

He scooted closer and put his arm around me. "Me, too, and I'm glad you're here," he said softly and kissed the top of my head.

I relaxed into him, and we fell into a comfortable silence until more visitors arrived some time later. I hadn't realized that they had other family members that might be coming by to visit, so I was surprised when three people and a very large dog entered the room.

My eyes widened and I turned my head to Jonah. "It's okay; Titan's a service dog."

I turned back to the dog and realized he was wearing a service dog harness. "I know he looks scary, but he's harmless...unless you're trying to attack me. Then, he'll hurt you," a girl who looked vaguely familiar said.

"Not helping, sister cousin," Jonah chuckled.

"Any news, brother Judge?" she asked.

"No, and there probably won't be until sometime tomorrow. The rewarming process can take close to a day, and she probably won't wake up right away once she reaches the regular temperature," he explained, just as I'd explained to him.

The girl smiled sadly. "Well, I guess no news is good news then." She cleared her throat and made a show of looking from Jonah to me and back.

He chuckled, "This is my friend, River. River, this is my nosy little cousin, Harper. That scary looking fucker is her fiancé, Carbon, and the one who looks like me, but not as handsome, is her brother and my cousin, Duke. And, of course, Titan."

"Hi," I said shyly and waved awkwardly.

The guys nodded, and Harper waved back with a smile, "Hello. So—"

Jonah removed his arm from around me and stood. "So, we're going to head out and get some dinner. You guys going to be here for a bit?"

"I was going to offer to spend the night. You've been here the last two nights," Harper said.

Jonah walked over and enveloped her in a hug. "Thank you, sister cousin. You'll call if anything changes?"

"Of course. Love you, brother Judge."

"Love you, too, Harpy. River, you ready?"

"Yep, let's roll," I said and waved goodbye to the group as I followed Jonah to the elevator.

CHAPTER SIXTEEN

JUDGE

The next few days were a whirlwind of activity. Mom went from being on the breathing machine and completely unresponsive to awake and ready to get out of the hospital.

For some reason, I assumed she would just wake up all of a sudden and start acting like herself, but that's not what happened. It was a slow, gradual process, and I was grateful to have River by my side to explain things to me. I felt bad about her spending her days off at the hospital, but she said she didn't mind being there, so I didn't argue with her because I needed her there with me.

After going back to my house so both of us could shower and change, I drove us back to the hospital in her car. I knew she had to work, but I hated to let her go, which I told her right before I kissed the hell out of her in front of the elevators.

"Jonah," she breathed. "I work here."

"Yeah, but you're not on the clock just yet," I said and gently tugged on her bottom lip with my teeth. I groaned and pressed my body against hers. "Knew I should've fucked you again before we left."

She playfully slapped my chest and stepped back. "I really have to go. I'll see you in the morning," she said and winked at me before disappearing through the double doors that led to the Emergency Department.

I readjusted myself while I waited for the elevator to take me up to Mom's floor. If all went well, she would be discharged the following morning.

"There's my boy," Mom said with a wide smile when I entered the room. "Where's your girlfriend?"

"She's not my girlfriend, Ma, and she had to

work tonight," I explained.

Mom rolled her eyes. "That shimmery lip gloss smeared across your lips says otherwise."

Harper started laughing from her perch in the corner of the room. I immediately looked away and wiped my hand over my mouth. Damn River and her fucking lip gloss that tasted like cotton candy.

"You must be doing okay if you're feeling well enough to give me shit the moment I walk into your room," I grumbled.

Mom smiled brightly, "I am. I'll be even better once I get home."

Despite her insistence that I go home, I stayed the night with her again. I didn't want to leave her by herself, and I liked being in the same building as River.

I did manage to slip out of the room without waking Mom and go downstairs to join River for her break. They seemed to be pretty busy, but she assured me she had plenty of time to eat.

"So, I'll just plan on coming up to your mom's room and hanging out until she is discharged, which will probably be around lunch time, give or take an hour or two," she said around a mouthful of lettuce.

"Yeah, that'll work," I said and fidgeted with

my hands.

"You okay?" she asked.

I chuckled nervously, "Yeah, I, uh, wanted to ask you if you would be willing to stay at my mom's house for the next week or so. Not as her nurse or anything, but I'll be staying there, and it would make me feel a lot better if you were there, too."

She paused with her forkful of food in mid-air. "Does she have room for me?"

"She does. She lives in a farmhouse that has always been too big for our little family." As it was told to me, when my parents were house hunting, Mom saw the house and fell in love with it, so Dad bought it for her. They had hoped to fill it full of children, but it wasn't in the cards for them. Mom had a traumatic delivery with me, and though neither one of us lost our lives, she did lose the option of having more children.

River waved her fork in front of my face and pulled me from my thoughts. "Did you hear me?"

I shook my head, "No, sorry, what did you say?"

"I said it was fine with me as long as your mother doesn't mind having a houseguest."

"She won't mind. She likes having people stay at her place. I've been trying to convince her to turn it into a bed-and-breakfast for years, but she won't do it. She said she likes having friends and family stay with her, but she has no interest in opening up her home to strangers," I explained.

River nodded in agreement. "Can't say I blame her there. It'd be one thing if she was staying in a different place, but I wouldn't be able to sleep if there were people I didn't know staying in my house."

"Yeah, that makes—" I was cut off by an electronic tone blaring through the room followed by a loud commotion in the hallway.

"Code Blue, Room Two. Code Blue, Room Two," was announced overhead.

"Gotta go," River said and placed a quick kiss on my lips before she ran out the door and into the fray.

***

River arrived in my mother's room a little after eight o'clock in the morning looking like she was ready to drop.

"Busy night?" I asked.

She sighed and dramatically fell into the reclining chair in the corner of the room.

"Yes," she groaned. "I don't know why, but stuff always happens in threes in the hospital. Without fail. It's three car accidents, three broken bones, three strokes, three deaths. We had three respiratory arrests last night. One right after the other."

She paused and slapped her hand over her mouth. "Mrs. Jackson, please forgive my rudeness. I blame it on exhaustion. How are you feeling?"

Mom grinned and waved her hand dismissively, "I'm fine, sweetheart. And more than ready to get out of here."

"Has your doctor already been by to see you?"

Mom nodded. "You just missed him. He said I was good to go as soon as he finishes with the paperwork."

River nodded and glanced at the clock on the wall. "It'll be at least another hour or two, if not more."

Mom sighed. "Yeah, that's what he said, too."

The room fell silent for several minutes until it was filled with River's soft snores. Without thought, I raised the footrest on the chair and covered her with a blanket so she'd be more comfortable.

When I returned to my seat, Mom was watching me with a goofy smile on her face. "What?" I asked.

Her grin morphed into a broad smile. "You two are going to make me some beautiful grandbabies."

I turned away from Mom. "Nope, not going there," I stated causing her to snicker.

"Keep telling yourself that, Son."

When we arrived at my mother's house in River's car, I helped Mom inside while she continuously tried to swat my hands away. "Mom," I snapped, a bit harsher than I intended. "You're lucky I'm not carrying you inside. Pay attention and let me help you."

She grumbled something under her breath and moved closer to River, who she did let help her up the few stairs in front of the house. I held the door open for them while they made their way inside. Mom was moving slower than I'd expected, and I made a mental note to ask River about it.

We entered the living room to find Harper, Carbon, and Titan, as well as Duke, Reese, and their son James. Harper motioned with her hand, and they all whispered, "Welcome home."

Mom's brows furrowed and she looked back and forth between me and them. Harper stood and engulfed Mom in a hug. "We didn't think it would be a good idea to startle someone who'd just had a heart attack," she explained causing Mom to laugh.

"Well, I appreciate that. Now, let me sit down so I can hold that sweet boy," she said referring to James. Reese and James had come up a few days ago, but Reese didn't want to bring him to the hospital while the flu was still prevalent.

While Mom played with James, I showed River to the room she'd be staying in. "Go ahead and lay down," I said and gestured to the bed. "When you wake up, I'll take you back to the house so you can get your clothes and whatever else you need before work tonight."

"My car's here, Jonah. I can just run by there on my way to work," she countered.

"Yeah, but my bike's not here, and I'm not driving Mom's car if I need to go somewhere."

"What's wrong with your mom's car?"

"It's a bright red Mazda Miata. Even if I could fit in it, I wouldn't because it's a chick car," I explained.

"A chick car?" she asked, sounding like she

was gearing up to argue with me.

"I didn't mean it like that. Mom has girly stickers and shit on it, not to mention all the crap hanging from the rearview mirror. The point is, I'm not driving it. If you don't want to take me to get my bike, I'm sure Duke or Carbon will."

"Sorry, my mind doesn't work all that well when I haven't had enough sleep. We can go when I get up. I usually set my alarm for three o'clock. Does that work for you?" she asked.

"Sounds great," I said and softly kissed her lips. "Sweet dreams."

CHAPTER SEVENTEEN

RIVER

I spent a week at Leigh's house with Jonah before she convinced him she didn't need anyone to stay with her. She was right, but Jonah wasn't happy when I agreed with her.

He didn't say a word the entire way back to his house and the vibes rolling off him were anything but pleasant.

He headed down the hallway to his bedroom while I went to mine. Before I closed my door, I stuck my head out into the hallway and said to his back, "Your aura is brown."

I silently counted. One. Two. Three.

Jonah appeared in the doorway. "My what?"

"Your aura," I said and waved my hand in his direction. "You know, your mood or attitude."

He crossed his arms over his chest. "Is that so?"

"It is. You should cleanse it," I suggested.

He pushed away from the door and slowly advanced on me. "And how exactly does one cleanse their aura?"

I shrugged. "Not sure, but I think you're supposed to try to relax and find a way to release the tension from your body," I said and reached for his belt. My fingers worked the leather through the buckle and popped the button on his jeans. "I might know a way to help you with that."

I slid his zipper down while I sank to my knees. He sucked in a sharp breath when I pulled his boxer briefs down and freed his cock, but the groan he released when I took him into my mouth was music to my ears.

I knew what I was doing and I wasted no time in getting started. I used one hand to cover what wouldn't fit into my mouth and started moving while I massaged his balls with my other hand.

He carefully laced his fingers through my hair and cupped the back of my head, but he made no attempt to control my movements, which told me he was holding back. While I appreciated the thought, it wasn't what he needed.

Moving my hands to his ass, I pulled him closer as I took him deeper. When I flicked my eyes up, he was watching me intently with a look of utter awe on his face. Without breaking my rhythm, I kept my eyes locked with his and waited for the inevitable.

"Fucking hell, woman," he groaned and tugged on my hair. I shook my head and increased my pace. "River," he warned with a hint of panic. "River, I'm gonna come."

With that, I inhaled through my nose, pushed forward, and swallowed, repeatedly. Jonah uttered a string of colorful expletives as he came down my throat.

When I was sure he was finished, I let him slip from my mouth and carefully tucked him back into his boxer briefs. He snorted and pulled me to my feet. "My turn."

I shook my head. "No, that was just for you. But I wouldn't say no if you wanted to climb into bed and take a nap with me."

He grinned and pulled his shirt over his

head. "I can do that." I stripped off my shirt and pants while he shucked his jeans. As soon as we were snuggled together under the covers, he asked, "Is my aura still brown?"

"No, but mine will be if you don't let me sleep."

"One more thing and then you can sleep," he said and paused. "Don't take this the wrong way, but you are really fucking good at, uh, cleansing auras."

I couldn't help but laugh at his choice of words. "Yeah, I know."

"You know?"

"Yes," I repeated. "When I was in college, one of my friends asked me to give her pointers because she'd never gone down on a guy and wanted to give it a try with her boyfriend. Anyway, I'd never done it either, so we watched some porn videos and practiced on zucchinis." When Jonah remained silent, I rolled over so I could see his face. "What?"

"You're serious? Zucchinis?"

I shrugged. "We didn't have any other phallic shaped produce handy."

He threw his head back and laughed before kissing me on the forehead. "That is the best fucking thing I've heard in a long time."

"Ha ha ha. Can we sleep now?"

"Yeah, baby," he said and tightened his arms around me. Within minutes, I was fast asleep.

***

Jonah and I seemed to wake at the same time. He smiled softly but made no move to get up. I had no desire to get out of bed either, but I'd thought of something I wanted to ask him just as I was drifting off to sleep.

"Have you heard anything about my rental house? I know you said you didn't mind, but I don't want to overstay my welcome. If it's going to be much longer, I can always check into a hotel," I said.

I wasn't sure about it at first, but I sort of liked staying with Jonah. Even still, I felt compelled to let him know that I didn't expect him to let me continue to stay there just because we had started sleeping together.

He scoffed. "How'd that work out for you last time?"

I slapped his bare chest. "Don't be an asshole."

He sighed. "I haven't heard anything about

the rental house, but I'll give Copper a call and see what's going on. As for you staying here, will you agree to not bring it up again if I promise to tell you if I want you to move out? Though I really don't see that happening before my house is finished or your contract is up, whichever comes first."

I thought about it for a few minutes before agreeing with him. "Yeah, okay. I guess I didn't realize I only have a few weeks left on my contract. Time is definitely going by faster than I thought it would."

He grinned and rolled over on top of me. "That happens when you're having a good time."

He brought his lips to mine in a gentle kiss that would have turned into more if we weren't interrupted by a ringing phone. Jonah snatched his cell off the nightstand and answered with a clipped, "What?"

"Shit. Sorry, Prez. I'll be right there," he said, already on his feet and reaching for his shirt.

"I have to go. I have a meeting at the clubhouse that I was supposed to be at ten minutes ago." He paused to shove his feet into his boots and then met my eyes. "Come with me."

"What?"

"Come with me to the clubhouse. There's usually a party after Church. You can meet the rest of the brothers. And I'm pretty sure Batta said he was bringing Kennedy."

Kennedy had been after me to hang out with her again, and I did want to; I just didn't want to do it at a bar or somewhere I could potentially run into ex-boyfriends, relatives, or any of the other scum of Devil Springs. "Okay, but I need a shower first. Text me the address and I'll head over once I'm ready."

"Will do," he said and kissed me. He released me and pushed me toward the bathroom with a light slap to my ass. "Don't be too long."

After hemming and hawing about what to wear, I finally decided simple was best. I chose a long-sleeved black shirt paired with ripped jeans and high-heeled ankle boots. After adding a few pieces of jewelry and lightly applying my makeup, I got into my car and followed the GPS directions until I came to a locked gate.

I looked around for a button or something to either open the gate or call someone who could. When I didn't see anything, I began to wonder if I was in the right place. I grabbed my phone and sent a text to Jonah.

River: Is your clubhouse behind a locked gate?

Jonah: Yes. Prospect will let you in.

River: What?

Jonah: Give your name to the prospect.

River: Is that a person?

Jonah: Yes. The guy at the gate.

River: There's no guy at the gate.

Jonah: I'll be right there.

A few seconds later, the gate magically parted allowing me to enter what looked like a compound of sorts. There was one large building with a bunch of motorcycles parked out front. I could also see several smaller buildings scattered around the property. I parked my car beside the handful of other cars in the lot and walked toward the big building's doors.

The music inside the building got louder and louder with each step I took. Suddenly, I was unsure about walking inside by myself. I was standing right outside the doors trying to gather my courage, when one of the doors flew open and narrowly missed me.

Jonah looked at me in surprise. "What are you doing out here?"

"I was on my way inside," I said.

He shook his head. "No, you were standing

out here looking like you were about to run back to your car and get the hell out of here," he said slowly and pointed to the security camera mounted over the door.

"Can you blame me? It's not that easy to just walk into a biker clubhouse all alone," I blurted.

"River, you've already met most, if not all, of the brothers. You know there's no reason to be scared," he reassured me.

"Whatever. Can we go inside now?"

"Follow me," he said and led the way.

The inside was not what I expected. I'm not sure what that was, but a clean, smoke-free room filled with tables and chairs was not it. There was also a bar along the back wall of the room and a few pool tables off to one side.

Jonah walked over to a table near the bar where Kennedy and Trey were sitting. "River!" Kennedy squealed and jumped to her feet when she saw me. "I didn't know you were coming!"

I smiled as she hugged me. "It was a last-minute decision," I said.

"You want something to drink?" Jonah asked.

"Shots!" Kennedy yelled excitedly leading me to believe she'd already had one or two before I arrived.

Jonah winked. "Be right back."

He returned with two large shot glasses filled with a dark, almost black liquid. "Here you go," he said and handed one to me and one to Kennedy.

I tentatively sniffed the concoction. "What is this?"

"It's called a BWOL," he said. When I cocked my head to the side, he added, "Blackwings Old Lady. It's something Layla came up with."

"Why'd she same it that?"

"Because it's sweet and mouthwatering, but will knock you on your ass," he explained.

"What's in it?" I asked, still eyeing the shot warily.

He shook his head. "I have no idea. I think Layla's the only one who does know."

"Where is she? I'll ask her."

"I don't think she's here yet. She mixes up a batch for the bartenders to pour on the nights we have parties. It's nothing gross or illegal. She made it with whatever we had behind the bar at the time, and you can see for yourself, we only keep the basics in stock," he said and gestured to the shelves lining the wall behind the bar.

"Come on, River, have some fun," Kennedy said and held her shot glass out. I shrugged and thrust my glass out to clink with hers then promptly downed the liquor. I was expecting it to be horrible, as most shots were, but I was surprised when the taste of chocolate covered strawberries filled my mouth.

"Holy shit! That was good. Can I have another one?" I asked eagerly.

"Ditto," Kennedy chirped causing Jonah and Trey to laugh.

Jonah returned with four more shots, two for each of us, which Kennedy and I quickly made disappear.

"Would you like more?" Jonah asked.

I shook my head. "I would, but I'm not going to have any more since I don't know what's in it. Plus, I probably should eat something before I have any more alcohol of any kind."

Jonah pulled out his phone and pecked at the screen before returning it to his pocket. "Would you ladies like to play a game of pool or maybe some darts while we're waiting for the pizza to be delivered?"

"Ooh, darts! I love darts," Kennedy said excitedly.

With that, everyone stood and moved to the dartboards set up behind the pool tables. I reluctantly followed the group. I hated darts—

because I sucked at them—but no one asked me and I didn't want to spoil everyone else's fun.

We took turns throwing the darts with Kennedy going first. I'm not even sure if we were playing on teams or keeping score. I just went when they said it was my turn.

"I'm guessing you don't like darts," Jonah rumbled beside my ear.

"I don't, but it's fine. Kennedy seems to be having a great time," I said and then asked, "Can I have another one of those shots?"

I had started to feel a little bit of a buzz, but it had since worn off, which led me to believe whatever was in them wasn't that strong.

"Sure thing, babe," he said and swatted my ass.

He returned with two shots for me and I thought, "What the hell?" and downed them both. This time, they tasted the same as far as flavor, but the taste of alcohol was much stronger.

"Is there something you would rather do instead of playing darts?" Jonah asked after I took my turn and only managed to get one dart to hit the target.

"Yep," I said and popped the p. "I would much rather throw knives."

He started to laugh, but quickly stopped

when he saw my face. "You're serious?"

I reached into my purse and pulled out a set of throwing knives that were in there solely because I continuously forgot to take them out. "I am. Can I?" I asked and wiggled the sheathed blades.

He looked around the area and shrugged. "I don't see why not. Just don't hit anybody."

I smirked. I wasn't going to hit anything except the target. I was fucking good, and I knew it. With no fanfare, I pulled the blades out and proceeded to hit dead center with the first one. I followed up with the second and third in quick succession—one going to the immediate left and the other to the immediate right. They were so close to the blade in the center that they were touching.

I turned around and smiled proudly. "Ta-dah!"

Jonah was staring at me with heated eyes. He reached down and adjusted himself. "Oh, baby, you just made my dick hard. That's fucking hot."

"Want me to do it again?" I asked huskily.

"Fuck, yes," he breathed.

I plucked my knives from the target and decided to show off a little. I stuck the first one in the center again. However, it fell to the floor when it was dislodged by the second blade knocking it out of place. The second blade followed the fate of the first when my third knife hit the bull's eye.

When I turned around to smile at Jonah, he was so close my nose bumped his chest. He roughly fisted my hair and yanked my head back so he could crush his lips to mine.

While he devoured my mouth, he hoisted me up by my ass so my legs wrapped around his waist. Then, he slammed my back against the wall as he pressed his big body against me. It was an all-out frenzy of hands, lips, tongues, and teeth as we tried to consume one another.

The sounds of raucous cheers had Jonah breaking the kiss and burying his face in my neck. "Fuck. Sorry, babe," he mumbled against my neck.

I giggled. "You gonna put me down?"

He groaned. "In a minute."

The pizzas arrived a few minutes later and took the focus off of our little show. Normally, I would have been embarrassed, but for some reason, I wasn't. I don't know if it had to do with the alcohol I'd consumed or if it was because it was Jonah, or a little of both.

While we were eating, Kennedy asked the question I'd been waiting on, though I thought it would have come from Jonah. "How is it that you can throw knives like a fucking ninja, but you can barely hit the target with a dart?"

I had wondered that myself several times, so I gave her the only answer I'd been able to come up with. "Each one uses a completely different technique to get the projectile from your hand to the target. I'm good at one and terrible at the other."

She nodded like what I was saying made perfect sense to her. "So, can you teach me how to throw knives? I want to be a ninja badass like you."

I laughed, a full-on belly laugh. "I can try, I guess. It's not something I learned to do or something that someone taught me. It's just something I can do."

"How'd you find out you could do it?" she asked.

I wiped my mouth with my napkin and reached for another slice of pizza. "Funny story. I grew up poor, and we didn't live in the best conditions. After school one day, I was in the kitchen doing my homework, and I saw this big ass bug crawling up the wall. For whatever reason, a steak knife was on the table, and without thinking about it, I picked the knife up and threw it at the bug. I didn't really expect to hit it, but the knife pierced through it with a disgusting crunch and stuck into the wall. That's when I grabbed my shit and ran to my room. When the bug was discovered later that evening, I pretended I didn't know anything about it."

"So, you were just good at it from the get-go?"

I shrugged. "Sort of. That lucky shot sparked my interest, so I started practicing," I said and went back to my pizza.

Jonah leaned close and nipped at my ear, "My badass little ninja."

CHAPTER EIGHTEEN

JUDGE

It was all I could do to keep myself from carrying River to my room to finish what we started before the pizza arrived. The more time I spent with her, the more intrigued I was by her.

She giggled when I nipped at her ear and turned her head to kiss me before grabbing another slice of pizza.

"I've never seen someone so small eat so much," Kennedy casually observed and I felt River stiffen.

She swallowed and wiped her mouth. "Yeah, I only allow myself to splurge every once in a while. I'll have to get an extra run in to work off all these extra calories sometime this week," she said and placed her half-eaten slice of pizza on her plate.

"Eat, sweet cheeks. I'll help you work that off later," I said low enough for only her to hear.

I reached for another slice of pizza and nudged River with my elbow. She had just taken a bite when Copper walked into the common room and motioned for someone to turn off the music.

He whistled loudly to get everyone's attention. Grinning widely, he shouted, "Brothers, it brings me great joy to announce the arrival of another Blackwings family member. Mere moments ago, Dash and Ember welcomed Raven Rose Lawson into the world. Mom and baby are both doing great."

Copper raised his beer in the air and the room erupted in shouts and cheers. I raised my own drink and clinked bottles with Batta before we both shouted our own congratulations into the air. I turned to tap my bottle to River's glass to find her seat empty.

My head shot up and I started to scan the

room for her when Kennedy waved her hand in front of my face. "She went that way," she said and pointed in the direction of the bathrooms. "She looked upset."

"Thanks," I said and wasted no time going after her.

When I reached the door to the bathroom, I stopped and took a minute to think about what I was going to say to her. She was obviously upset about the news of her brother's baby, but since she hadn't told me what happened between them, I had no way of guessing why the news upset her.

But the why didn't matter. So, I took a deep breath and knocked on the door.

"Go away, Judge," River said followed by a quiet sniffle.

Fuck that. "Not happening," I said as I opened the door and stepped inside.

She rolled her eyes. "Good thing I wasn't actually using the bathroom," she mumbled and tried to covertly wipe the few tears from her cheeks.

I reached for her hand and brought it to my lips before I gently pulled her to her feet and circled my arms around her. With her head resting against my chest, she said, "I'm sorry, I ju—"

"You don't have to explain yourself to me. I'll gladly listen to anything you want to share, but don't feel like you have to."

She remained silent for several minutes before finally saying, "I don't want to talk about it right now, but maybe one day. And thank you for not pushing me about it."

I kissed the top of her head and gently squeezed her. "You want to get out of here?"

"No, I don't want to leave. I was having fun; the news just caught me by surprise. I'm fine, really," she insisted.

"The entire club will probably head to Croftridge tomorrow to see the baby. You can come with us if you want," I offered even though I knew she wouldn't want to go.

Her forehead scrunched and she shook her head. "Why would the whole club go see my brother's new baby?"

"Because he's married to Ember, who is the daughter of the President of the Original Chapter, who happens to be Copper's and Bronze's first cousin. Ember's mom, Annabelle, is also Layla's sister," I explained.

"Okie dokie. You guys have fun, but I'll pass. I have to work tomorrow night anyway."

"Oh, and River, you call me Judge again and I'll spank your ass. I'm Jonah to you."

"Yes, Your Honor." With that, she opened the bathroom door and sashayed her way back to the table with Batta and Kennedy.

"Is everything okay?" Kennedy asked as soon as we reached our seats.

"I wasn't feeling good all of a sudden, but I'm fine now. Guess I drank a bit too much too fast," she lied.

I leaned back in my chair and subtly shook my head hoping Batta and Kennedy understood to drop it. But it was a moot point when, once again, the music stopped and Copper was standing in the middle of the room.

"One more thing—"

"Do we have to find the snakes again, Prez?" Batta shouted causing River to stiffen while Kennedy's mouth dropped open.

"He's kidding," I lied.

Copper glared at Batta. "No, dickhead. My girl and Judge managed to get a projection screen installed a few days ago so we can all watch Nathan's fight tonight!"

The room erupted in cheers as the screen began to descend on the far wall. "We should probably go ahead and grab a seat if we don't want to be stuck in the back," I suggested.

"Who is Nathan?" River asked.

"He's Copper's cousin," I said and then leaned down to whisper in her ear, "And he's Ember's younger brother."

She nodded but didn't seem affected by my words. "So, why are we watching him fight?"

"He's a professional MMA fighter," I explained.

We spent the next few hours watching the preliminary fights leading up to the main event featuring Nathan in his first televised event.

Silence fell over the room when it was time for the main event, but erupted in cheers when the announcer called, "Nathan 'Night Night' Davis!" Nathan burst from the locker room with his entourage surrounding him. I was not at all surprised to see Wave and Token flanking the trainers all the way to his designated corner.

River leaned in close and asked, "Why do they call him 'Night Night'?"

"You'll see."

I hadn't seen Nathan in well over a year, and I was shocked to see how big he had gotten. "Damn, Batta, you and Carbon might not be the biggest ones around if he gets much bigger."

Batta snorted, "No shit, man. I can't believe that's the same boy we helped rescue last year.

Ain't nobody gonna get the drop on him now."

And he proved that statement to be true when he knocked his opponent out a little over halfway through the first round. The fight was called, and like the good man he was, Nathan waited until his opponent was awake and sitting up before he allowed them to thrust his hand into the air to celebrate his victory.

Wave appeared beside Nathan in the center of the ring and whispered something into his ear. Nathan nodded, kissed two fingers, and held them up in the air while looking directly at the camera. "For Ember and Raven," he shouted.

River flinched beside me, but quickly hid her discomfort by clapping and cheering along with everyone else in the room.

"Well, that was interesting," she said. "I've never watched an organized fight before."

"We'll be watching all of his televised fights, but if you ever want to go to one, I'm sure I can get tickets," I offered.

"I'll keep that in mind," she laughed.

"Time for bed," I said and hoisted her over my shoulder causing her to squeal in protest.

Batta laughed while Kennedy waved at her. "Night, River. See you tomorrow."

I carried her down the hall to my rarely used

room at the clubhouse. Pushing the door open, I froze at the sight before me. It was all I could do to contain my rage and back out of the room hoping River wouldn't see.

Of course, that would have been too easy. Before I could close the door, Didi climbed off the bed and pranced her naked ass toward the door. "Where are you going, Judge? She can stay and watch."

"Wrong, bitch. He can stay and watch me kick your skanky ass. Again! We'll call it 'Return of the Thunderous Cunt: The Final Smackdown'!" River screamed and started thrashing against me.

I clamped my arms around her legs and moved down the hall as she beat her fists against my back.

"Put me down! I have some fake tits to pop!"

"Not happening, lil' ninja. Batta, can you get the trash out of my room?" I asked, though it wasn't a question.

We all turned at the growing sound of a woman screeching. Layla had somehow gotten a sheet wrapped around Didi and was using it to slide her across the floor.

"Could one of you get the door for me?" Layla asked sweetly.

Batta jumped up to get the door while Layla continued dragging and berating Didi. "I told you myself that you were banned from the club. Did you think I was joking? Did you think the President was just fucking with you? Banned means banned, bitch. You don't get to come here or to any of our establishments, and because you royally pissed me off, you better run the opposite direction any time you see anyone affiliated with the club anywhere. Now get gone!"

When Layla continued dragging Didi out the door, Batta took the sheet and used it as a sort of sling to carry Didi to the gate. He unceremoniously dropped her on the ground and slammed the gate shut while the rest of us watched in stunned silence. That was, until Layla and Batta came back inside. Then, everyone burst into fits of laughter. Even River.

Copper grabbed Layla around her waist and whispered something in her ear that made her blush before he buried his face in her neck.

I placed River on her feet and tilted her chin up with my thumb. "I'm sorry about her. I don't know how she managed to get into the clubhouse, let alone my room, but I'll make sure it doesn't happen again."

"The only thing you need to apologize for

is not letting me kick her ass again," she said seriously.

I shook my head. "Not going to apologize for that. I wasn't about to risk your safety. Not that I don't think you could take her, but she's obviously not in the best frame of mind if she thought she could show up here after being banned."

"Blah, blah, blah. I hope you don't think I'm going to sleep in that bed after she rubbed her hoochie hooha all over it," she said and wrinkled her nose in disgust.

I laughed. "What if I flip the mattress and put new sheets on it? Will that work for you?"

"Throw in some Lysol and you've got a deal," she returned.

CHAPTER NINETEEN

RIVER

I walked into a madhouse when I arrived at work. Nurses and techs were darting in and out of rooms. Phones were ringing while call lights and IV alarms sounded in the background. I quickly shoved my stuff into my locker, tossed my lunch into the fridge, and made my way into the mayhem.

"River, thank goodness you're here. I need you to be in charge tonight," Stacie, the day shift charge nurse, told me.

"Why? Where's Kennedy?" I asked. It was

rare that I ever worked a shift without Kennedy, though I supposed that was Kennedy's doing.

"I have no idea. The director said she called in earlier today and that was all I needed to know."

"I hope everything's okay," I said, more to myself than to Stacie.

"Yeah, me, too. Kennedy never calls in sick."

I decided I would call and check on her when I got a chance. After getting the shift report from Stacie and making sure we had enough staff to handle the full house we had, I hit the ground running and didn't stop for hours.

I stepped into the break room and grabbed my protein shake from the fridge. After taking a few sips, I pulled out my phone to call Kennedy.

"River, I need you out here," Dr. Daniels said from the doorway. "We've got an MVA coming in as well as a possible drug overdose."

I put my phone back into my pocket and downed the rest of my shake before returning to the fray just as the paramedics were pushing a stretcher into one of the empty rooms. I followed behind them and reached for a pair of gloves wondering why they weren't spewing off the patient's vital signs and a quick history of what happened.

"We declared death two minutes ago. We just need someone to officially pronounce," one of the paramedics said.

"Oh, let me get one of the doctors for you," I said and stopped dead in my tracks when my eyes landed on the lifeless woman on the stretcher.

Imposter Barbie.

Didi.

I shook my head and stepped out of the room. "Dr. Daniels, room six is a DOA. They just need you to pronounce."

"Got it. Can you check on the new arrival in room three?"

"Yeah, sure," I said, still feeling a bit dazed at seeing Didi's dead body. I didn't know her, and I damn sure didn't like her, but that didn't mean I wanted her to die. I just wanted her to go away. Though, her strange behavior made more sense. She was probably high on something the day she was watching porn at Jonah's house and when she showed up in his room at the clubhouse.

I knocked on the door and entered the room without waiting for permission. "Hi, I'm River and I'll be your nurse tonight," I said and began assessing my newest patient.

The night continued on at the same pace.

Before I knew it, my shift was over and I happily handed the reins back to Stacie.

When I pulled into Jonah's garage, I was disappointed that his bike wasn't parked in its usual spot. He said they might spend the night in Croftridge, but I'd hoped he would come back to Devil Springs.

Sighing, I drug my ass out of the car and into the house where I stripped off my filthy scrubs and took a quick shower before crawling into my bed and falling into a deep sleep.

I woke sometime later because I was uncomfortably hot to the point I was sweating. It took me a few seconds to wake up enough to figure out why I was overheated. Jonah had come in at some point and gotten into bed with me. The man was like a furnace with the amount of heat he put off.

I kicked the covers off of me and rolled over to face his chest. "I tried not to wake you," he rumbled and placed a kiss on top of my head.

"What time is it?" I asked.

"Around three o'clock."

"Oh, well, it's time for me to get up anyway," I said and made a big production of stretching and yawning. "When did you get back?"

"Around noon. How was work last night?"

"Crazy busy," I said and paused for a moment to gather my thoughts. "Listen, I can't tell you any details, but Didi was brought into the ER last night. She, um, she was dead on arrival."

"Say what now?" Jonah said as he shot up in bed.

"She was already gone when they got to the hospital. Like I said, I can't tell you any details, but I thought you would want to know," I said softly.

"River, nothing ever happened between her and I."

"I know. You've already told me that and I believe you, but she was at your club two nights ago and I felt like it was something you would want to know. I didn't know if any of the other guys knew her or whatever."

He shrugged, "I don't know either. She only came around a few times that I know of. I don't know why she seemed to be fixated on me. I shot her down the first time she was at one of the parties and haven't spoken to her since." He paused for a moment and asked the question I was expecting. "You can't tell me what happened?"

I shook my head. "No, I can't. Even though she's deceased, the privacy laws still apply."

He nodded and reached for his phone.

"What are you doing?"

"Texting Spazz," he answered distractedly as his fingers rapidly tapped against his phone.

"Why?"

"So he can tell me what happened to Didi. That man can find anything within a few minutes."

I plugged my ears with my fingers. "I can't hear this kind of stuff!" I shouted and proceeded to hum loudly.

Jonah reached out and snagged me by my waist, pulling me onto his lap. "I won't say anything else about it," he promised as his hands slid down to cup my ass.

I don't know why I asked, but the words were out of my mouth before I could stop them. "Did you have fun in Croftridge?"

He gave me a curious look. "I did. If you really want to know, I'll tell you about it."

"Nope, I'm good."

"She looks like you," he said quietly.

"Who?" I asked, even though I knew who he meant. I needed those extra seconds to push down the hurt that was trying to force its way to the surface.

"Raven. She looks like you." He ran his finger

along my jawline and circled my lips. "She has your lips and chin."

I rolled my eyes. "I think you were just seeing what you wanted to see."

The next thing I knew, his phone was in front of me with a precious, chubby little baby face filling the screen. I inhaled deeply. She was beautiful. And she did have my lips and chin.

"Yeah, I guess you're right," I admitted.

"Shit, I'm sorry. I wasn't thinking."

"It's all right. I don't wish my brother any ill will; I just prefer to pretend like he doesn't exist. Let's talk about something else," I suggested.

"I don't want to talk," he breathed right before captured my lips with his.

I moaned when he squeezed my cheeks and rocked my hips against his prominent erection. "Me either," I mumbled against his lips.

Within seconds, we were a frenzy of need. Our hands were all over the place while we tried to get impossibly closer. "Fuck, baby," he breathed and proceeded to knock everything off the nightstand while he blindly searched for a condom.

He pushed his boxer briefs down far enough to free himself and quickly put on our protection. Then, he shoved my panties to the side and almost savagely pulled me down on his cock while he thrust his hips upward.

There was no adjustment period. No calm before the storm. We were all out fucking from the moment he entered me.

He yanked the cups of my bra down and bared my nipples for his mouth and fingers.

I was on the verge of a major climax within minutes. As if he sensed it, he demanded, "Fucking come, River."

And I exploded into a million tiny pieces of utter bliss.

When I regained some semblance of reality, I was on my back with Jonah furiously slamming his hips into me. His arms were braced on the bed beside my head giving me the perfect view of every straining muscle as he worked us both over.

He leaned forward to gently kiss my neck and my arms automatically circled around his shoulders. "Give it to me," he said gruffly before he bit down on the tendon between my neck and shoulder.

I'm not sure what happened next. I know I dug my nails into his back, I think I screamed, and I may have briefly died when my body was forced to the brink of pleasure and shoved over the edge.

Jonah chuckled and smiled down at me. "You okay?"

"Fuck, yes. Can we do that again?"

CHAPTER TWENTY

Judge

The following week was uneventful, which pissed me off. How in the hell could two junkies like Spring Lawson and Roy Mayfield completely disappear without a trace?

Despite our best efforts, as well as those of the Devil Springs Police Department, no one had seen hide nor hair of River's mom or her boyfriend.

My phone buzzing on my desk pulled me out of my thoughts. I glanced at the screen to see Spazz's name and quickly answered. "What's up, brother?"

"Got some info on your girl. She—"

"—is not my girl," I interrupted.

"The girl you asked about. Is that better?" he snapped, which was very out of character for him.

"What did you find?"

"Like River said, Didi died from an overdose. Preliminary testing showed a variety of things in her system, including opiates, marijuana, and cocaine. According to hospital records, she had track marks on her forearm, so it sounds like it was a heroin overdose, but they can't officially say that until the toxicology reports are back."

"Do you think that's why she started hanging around the club?" I asked.

Spazz made a noncommittal noise. "I wouldn't think so. Everybody in this area knows we're not into drugs."

"Maybe she's not from around here."

"She is. Born and raised in Fountain Mill."

"Really? Did she go to school in Devil Springs?"

"Nope. Mountville. Not that it matters. None of us would've known her. She was only twenty-one years old."

She certainly didn't look twenty-one. She

looked much older, but repeated drug use will age you faster than anything else.

"There is one other thing," Spazz said and paused. "She was last seen at Precious Metals. Apparently, she left the bar, drove herself home, and was found unconscious in her car by whoever anonymously called 9-1-1."

"Does Prez know?"

"Told him the second I found out. He said he'd discuss it in Church tomorrow."

"Thanks, Spazz," I said and disconnected the call.

What in the hell was Didi doing at Precious Metals the night after she was banned from the club and any club owned establishments? And more importantly, did she already have the drugs on her, or did she get them from someone at Precious Metals?

***

I barely made it to Church on time after spending the morning with Mom. Knowing how hard-headed she could be, I wanted to make sure her floors were mopped and vacuumed so she didn't try to do it herself. I also mowed the front yard and even pulled the few weeds from her flower beds. By the time I was finished, I was covered in dirt and sweat, so I had to go back home to take a shower and change.

"Nice of you to join us," Copper teased as I dashed into the room and took my seat.

I made a show of looking at my watch. "I'm not late."

He laughed. "No, but you're the last one to arrive, and you're almost always the first. But, since everyone is here, we'll get started a few minutes early."

We went through the usual stuff we discussed at the beginning of every meeting before we brought up any new business.

"Any word on the repairs for the rental house?" I asked.

Copper grimaced while Bronze answered. "We've had a few issues passing the inspection. We've got another one scheduled for the end of next week."

"What was the issue?" I asked.

"The first time it was because the steps leading from the kitchen to the garage didn't have a handrail, which is required for anything over thirty inches."

"The first time?" I asked in surprise.

"Yeah, we've failed two. I distinctly remember there being a handrail on the garage stairs when we first purchased the house. We fixed it and had them come back out. This time, apparently, the wiring wasn't up to code," Bronze offered.

"How is that possible? And why wasn't it mentioned in the first inspection?"

Bronze leaned forward on his elbows. "We don't know. Splint's dad's company did the work. When we didn't pass the second inspection, his dad came out and inspected the wiring himself that same day. He says there's nothing wrong with it. So, we've hired an independent company to do an inspection the day before the city inspector comes. We'll see what happens this time and go from there."

There wasn't anything I could add, so I nodded and sat back in my chair while Copper moved on to the next topic.

"This may or may not be anything, but it's worth bringing to your attention. The girl who was kicked out of the clubhouse last weekend, Didi, died from an apparent overdose the following day. The part that concerns me is that she was seen leaving Precious Metals before she was found dead in her car in her driveway," Copper shared.

"What are you getting at, Prez?" Tiny asked.

"Hopefully, nothing, but I want to have more brothers present at Precious Metals for the next few weeks. We need to be absolutely certain no one is bringing drugs into our place of business," Copper ordered.

"I'm all for being more present, Prez, but I seriously doubt anyone would be stupid enough to try something like that in our presence," Batta added.

Copper grinned. "You're right. And that brings me to the next topic of discussion. Coal and Savior arrived in Devil Springs this morning. They're getting settled, but we'll welcome them with a party tonight. Anyway, I was thinking they would be the perfect ones to hang around Precious Metals. Without their cuts, no one will know who they are."

After we all voted in favor of the plan, Copper dismissed Church and reminded us to be back at the clubhouse by seven o'clock so we could welcome our new brothers, which left me plenty of time to catch up on some work, shower, and have dinner.

I was surprised to find River sprawled on the sofa with her eyes fixed on the television when I arrived at my house. She usually slept until three or four when she'd worked the night before.

"What are you—?"

"Shh!!" she demanded with one finger pressed against her lips. She quickly sat up and grabbed the remote to pause her show. "Sorry, I'm trying to catch up before the new season starts. Everyone talks about this show, but I'd never seen it because I didn't see the point in paying for any kind of television service, let alone paying extra for a specialty channel."

"I see. So, you're planning on living here for at least the next six weeks?" I asked.

"Not necessarily. If I'm not still living here, I'll come over to watch it on Sundays, or the following morning if I had to work," she explained.

I chuckled and noted the scene paused on the screen. "Looks like you're almost caught up. When did you start watching it?"

Her cheeks flushed and she looked away from me. "Um, last week."

"You've watched almost all seven seasons since last week?" I teased.

"Shut it. I'm skilled at binge watching. Now hush up so I can finish."

I kicked off my boots and made my way over to the sofa where I spent the next two hours watching the last two episodes of season seven with her.

"So, what do you think's going to happen next?" I asked.

"If they pull another bullshit move like they did with *The Sopranos*, I think it will be the end of *HBO*. You don't think they'll kill everyone, do you?"

I shrugged. "I honestly have no idea. I would hope not, but it seems to be a common theme for finales of hit series to go very wrong."

She slapped my chest playfully. "You were supposed to say, 'No, River, of course they won't kill everyone.'"

"Sorry, babe, if you want false reassurances, you came to the wrong man," I told her honestly.

"I suppose that's not a bad thing."

I grinned. "Listen, we're having a party at the clubhouse tonight to welcome two new members. You wanna come with me?"

"Sure. Do you know if Kennedy or Layla are going to be there?"

"Layla will definitely be there, and probably some of the other Old Ladies, but I don't know about Kennedy. Come on," I said and extended my hand, "I need a shower, and you will, too, after I fuck you against my bedroom wall."

CHAPTER TWENTY-ONE

RIVER

When we arrived at the clubhouse, I took a seat at the bar beside Layla while Jonah went to meet with the other club members.

"I didn't get a chance to thank you for stepping in last weekend," I said.

"Oh, you don't have to thank me. It's my job as the President's Old Lady to make sure the girls that come around know their place. But, I kind of felt bad about it when I heard she died the next day," Layla replied.

I cleared my throat and shifted uncomfortably. "I can't say anything about it because I work at the hospital, but, yeah, it was sad."

"No worries. I already know what happened."

"You do?" I asked in surprise.

"Yeah," she laughed. "I guess this is where I can't say much of anything, but the guys thought they should look into what happened since she'd been hanging around the club."

We fell into an awkward silence and I studied the drink in front of me trying to think of something to say.

"Is Kennedy—?" "Have you met—?" we started at the same time.

"Sorry, you go first."

"Have you met the new members?" she asked.

I shook my head. "No, Jonah hasn't said anything about them."

"They're from the Croftridge chapter. One is..." Her words faded into the background as my mind was consumed with one thought that played over and over.

Not Reed.

Not Reed.

Not Reed.

Jonah would have told me if it was Reed.

Wouldn't he? He wouldn't spring something like that on me in front of so many people. Right?

"River!" Layla said loudly and clapped her hands bringing me back to the present.

"I'm sorry. What were you saying?"

She looked at me quizzically but continued talking. "I said one is my nephew, Coal, and the other goes by Savior. Coal is about to turn twenty and Savior is a few years older than him, I think. I actually don't know either one of them very well, but the guys speak highly of both."

I cocked my head to the side. "You don't know your nephew very well?"

She shook her head. "No, I don't. I recently found out my biological father, who was never in the picture, had two other children. It's a long, twisted story, but it ended well."

"You can say that again," a familiar voice said from behind us.

We both turned around and Layla let out an ear-piercing shriek. "Leigh!! What are you doing here?"

"I wanted to be here to welcome the new members. Don't worry; I'm not staying long."

"Did you drive?" I asked.

Leigh chuckled and shook her head. "No, I didn't. I have some friends visiting for the weekend and I rode with them."

"I thought they were having a party," a male voice rumbled.

"Boar and Shannon!" Layla gasped and flew across the room to hug the man and woman standing just inside the door.

"Boar is the President of the Manglers MC in Reedy Fork and Shannon is his Old Lady and wife," Leigh told me as they made their way over to the bar. "Boar, Shannon, this is River Lawson."

I extended my hand to each of them. Boar shook my hand and turned to Leigh, "This is your boy's girl?"

Leigh smiled broadly, "Sure is."

"Well, it's a pleasure to meet you, River."

"Nice to meet you, too."

We continued talking until the club members were finished with their meeting. By that time, some other women and a few men had filtered in.

Copper whistled loudly to get everyone's attention. "Please welcome our newest brothers, Coal and Savior!"

After the members were congratulated and the noise died down, Jonah came straight to our table. "Mom, what are you doing here?"

"I feel so wanted," Leigh said and rolled her eyes.

"That's not what I meant and you know it," Jonah said in a voice filled with concern.

"I'm not staying long, Son. I just wanted to stop by to welcome the new members and then Shannon and I are going to head back to my house."

Jonah's eyes moved to Boar and Shannon. "I didn't know you two were coming."

"It wouldn't have been a surprise if you did," Shannon said as she gazed at Jonah. "Your hair's darker, but you really do favor your cousin."

"Hey! I'm right here," Boar said, though his tone was light.

"Oh, hush, you big galoot. You know I love you and only you," Shannon said playfully.

"What're they talking about?" I asked.

"Shannon was married to my cousin a long time ago. She's just messing with Boar."

When I glanced over at the two, Boar had his face buried in Shannon's neck and she was giggling like a school girl. It was obvious to anyone in the vicinity that they were deeply in love with one another.

I realized I was staring at them when I felt Jonah's warm breath on my neck seconds before he nipped my ear. "Jealous?"

I turned my head to capture his lips. "No, respectfully craving."

Jonah laughed loudly and pulled me against his chest. "Fuck, I love...your witty remarks," he said, but there was a distinct pause between love and your which I chose to completely ignore.

The rest of the night was spent sharing good conversation over food and drinks. I enjoyed spending time with Layla and getting to know the other club members. I couldn't help but notice how much of a family they were to each other, and I couldn't ignore how much I wished I had that in my life.

"Do you mind if we give Boar a ride to my mom's house before we go home?"

"Of course not. Are you ready to go now?" I asked.

"Yeah, we should get going. It's getting late and this is when the atmosphere tends to change," he said cryptically. I fully understood his meaning as Slutty McSlutterson and her skankettes walked through the door as we were leaving.

"Hey, Judge," Slutty said and reached out to place her hand on his chest, but I caught her wrist before she could make contact.

"Bad dog. Don't touch," I snapped and continued on my way outside.

"He doesn't have an Old Lady. I can touch him if I want," she said.

I rolled my eyes skyward. "Why must they all be stupid? Is it asking too much to have a few smart sluts sprinkled around?"

I turned to stand my ground, but kept my mouth closed when Copper spoke. "We have different rules at this clubhouse. Whores don't mess with any brother who has a wife, Old Lady, or a girlfriend. River is his girlfriend. Best you remember the rules, because I won't be telling you again. Now, go play nice or get the fuck out."

"Thanks, Prez," Jonah said and ushered me to his truck.

As soon as we were on the road, Jonah asked, "So, Boar, how'd you end up staying at my mom's house?"

Boar chuckled. "Her and Shannon took a liking to one another when y'all were up in Reedy Fork. She wanted to come for a visit when Leigh was well enough and I wanted to be there when Coal transferred chapters. Taking a bullet with someone creates a unique bond between them."

"You two were shot? When? How?" I asked and turned around in my seat.

Boar nodded. "We were. It's been almost a year ago now. Can't tell you the why or how, but I took one to the chest and Coal took three to the stomach. We're both lucky to be alive."

"Did it hurt?" I asked stupidly.

"Funny you should ask. I have no idea. I don't remember much of anything that happened right before or right after. But when I woke up in the hospital days later, my chest hurt like hell," he said and absently rubbed at what I presumed was the scar on his chest.

"Did they catch the person who shot you?"

Boar grimaced and Jonah reached over and gently squeezed my thigh. "Yes, they did," Boar said solemnly.

"So, how long are you and Shannon staying?" Jonah asked, effectively changing the subject and leaving me wondering what happened.

CHAPTER TWENTY-TWO

JUDGE

Coal and Savior were more than happy to hang out at Precious Metals as their first assignment, and they got started on it right away.

When Copper called me three days later, I was sure it was to tell me they'd seen or heard something at the bar. I did not expect to be called in for Church. Copper never called us in unless something was seriously wrong, so I dropped what I was doing and pointed my bike straight for the clubhouse.

Copper was in the front of the room pacing back and forth and he didn't stop until every officer had arrived. "We've got a problem, brothers," he announced. "While Bronze and I were at the rental property with our private inspector, Precious Metals was just raided by the police."

"Say what?"

"What the fuck for?"

"Why?"

Copper held his hands up to quiet the room. "They claim they received an anonymous tip that we were using the bar as a front for dealing."

"That's bullshit," Batta spat.

Copper nodded and grinned, "Yeah, it is. And now they know it because they didn't find shit."

"So, what's the problem, Prez?" Tiny asked.

"The problem is the anonymous tip. We've never been into drugs and everyone around here knows it. So, we've either pissed someone off or we're being targeted for another reason. Either way, I fully expect the cops to show up here and possibly any other businesses associated with the club. Just make sure there's absolutely nothing for them to find."

"Well, that should be easy, since there isn't anything for them to find," I added.

"Exactly. Stay vigilant and keep your eyes and ears open, brothers," Copper ordered and banged the gavel on the worn wooden table.

As everyone was leaving, Copper asked me to stay behind. "I want to talk to you about the rental house."

"How did the inspection go?" I asked.

Copper's eyes narrowed. "We don't have the official report, but the inspector we hired said there was nothing wrong with the property."

"He actually commented on several extra safety measures we'd taken that were above and beyond the minimum requirements," Bronze added.

"So, where were the frayed wires?"

"That's what we'd like to know. This is exactly why we hired an outside inspector. I don't know what's going on, but something is definitely off. Can you get some discrete cameras up on the inside of the house? I would like to see first-hand what is and is not being inspected."

I nodded. "Not a problem. When do you need them installed?"

"Before tomorrow morning," Bronze said.

"Shit. I'll have to see what I have on hand. I might have to get creative, but I'll figure something out," I said.

Copper clapped me on the shoulder, "Thanks, man."

With that, I left the clubhouse and headed back to my office to dig through my inventory. I always kept the basics readily available, but I didn't keep much of the high-tech equipment on hand because most of it was expensive and could easily go out-of-date before it was installed.

Once I found what I needed, I headed over to the rental house to get started on the install. I decided to start in the living room by hiding a camera in the ceiling fan.

I climbed up the ladder and damn near fell on my ass when I caught a glimpse of what looked like feet sticking out from under the kitchen table.

Quietly climbing down, I pulled my gun from its holster and silently crept into the kitchen. I rounded the table with my gun aimed and ready. "Don't fucking move," I ordered.

My command was obeyed and met with an eerie silence. I cautiously squatted down to get a better look at the person and immediately fell back on my ass when my eyes met those of a very dead man.

"Fuck!" I cursed and pulled my phone from my pocket.

"Prez, need you at the rental house, right fucking now!" I barked and disconnected the call.

Copper, Bronze, and Batta rolled up less than fifteen minutes later. "What the fuck is going on, Judge?" Copper asked before he'd even gotten his helmet off.

I shook my head and said, "Come inside and see for yourself."

The three of them followed me into the kitchen and followed my finger as I pointed to the dead body sprawled on the linoleum floor.

"Who the fuck is that?" Copper asked.

I looked at him incredulously. "I don't know, Prez. I didn't think it would be a good idea to check his wallet for an ID."

Copper glared at me. "Do any of you fuckers recognize him?"

"No," the three of us said in unison.

"Wait a sec," Batta said and stepped closer to the body. "Isn't this the guy who was bothering River that night at Precious Metals? Brett something?"

I moved closer and took a better look at the man's face. "I'm not completely sure, but I think you might be right."

"Fuck me," Copper said and pinched the bridge of his nose. "Bronze, call it in."

I held my hand up. "Let me see if Dunk's working and can take this call."

Lucky for us, Officer Dunk and Officer Underwood were on duty and showed up at the rental property ten minutes after I called.

"All right, boys, I'm going to need y'all to clear out while we secure the crime scene. Then, we'll need to ask you some questions."

"Would it be all right with you if we went to my house next door?" I asked.

Officer Dunk's forehead scrunched in confusion. "Since when do you live next door?"

"For a few weeks now. I'm only staying there until my new house is finished being built," I explained.

"Yeah, you guys can go wait over there, but let me make sure I have the basics. You came over to upgrade the security system and make some additional repairs and found the body in the kitchen. Is that correct?" she asked.

"Yes. We have an inspection scheduled for tomorrow and wanted to go over the list one last time to make sure we hadn't missed any of the items needing attention," Copper answered.

"Got it. We'll be over in a bit," Officer Dunk said and made her way back into the kitchen.

Once we were inside my house, Copper went

straight for the fridge and pulled out four beers. "What in the hell is going on around here? I'm starting to think that damn house is cursed."

River came around the corner and plopped down at the kitchen table. "What house is cursed?" she asked and took the beer from Batta's hand.

Batta laughed. "Which one do you think?"

River looked from Batta to me. She must have seen something in my eyes, because she immediately asked, "What happened?"

I sighed and sat down in the chair beside her. "I went over to the house to upgrade the security system and found a dead body in the kitchen."

River choked and sprayed beer everywhere. "Shit! Are you okay?" I asked as I patted her on the back.

When she got her coughing under control, she glared at me. "First of all, the back patting doesn't do anything but make you feel better. As long as I'm making noise, I'm moving air. Secondly, never, ever say anything like that when someone is taking a drink. And lastly, what in the actual fuck did you just say?"

We all waited as she took another sip of her beer. "He said he found a dead body in the kitchen," Bronze repeated.

River cocked her head to the side. "Are you sure they were dead? I can go check."

"Oh, we're sure," I said. "Besides, the police are already over there doing their thing. They were nice enough to let us wait over here until they're ready to question us."

We made small talk for the next hour or so until Officer Dunk and Officer Underwood knocked on the front door. River excused herself to her room after offering both ladies something to drink.

They went through all the usual questions and took notes. When did we arrive? What were we doing there? When was the last time someone was at the house? Was the door locked when we entered? Was the security system on?

"I came in through the front door and yes, it was locked. The security system was also on. I can print out a log of the times it was armed and disarmed for you," I said.

"Yes, we'll definitely need that."

"I'll have it for you in just a moment," I said as I logged into the system from my phone and sent the document to my wireless printer in my home office.

"Did any of you know the man?" Officer

Underwood asked.

"None of us knew him, but Batta thought he might be the same guy who was causing problems at Precious Metals a few weeks ago," I said.

"And who was that?" Officer Dunk asked.

"Brett Owens," Copper said and Officer Dunk's head shot up confirming what we already suspected. "Him and his buddy attempted to assault a female in my establishment. Judge and Batta were on staff as security that night and intervened. The boys weren't cooperative and had to be physically removed from the premises. We filed a no trespass order the next morning for both individuals."

"I see. And who was the female involved in the assault?"

Fuck. I didn't want to tell her because I didn't want River involved, but if I didn't name her, it would come out later and look like we were trying to hide something. "River Lawson," I said.

"We'll need to speak with her and check into a few more things before we can close out this case."

I cleared my throat. "Uh, if you'd like to speak with her now, I can go get her. She's my roommate."

CHAPTER TWENTY-THREE

River

I was playing a game on my phone when someone knocked on my door and startled me. Before I could respond, the door opened and Jonah stepped inside.

"Are they finished?" I asked.

"No, not exactly. The officers would like to speak with you," he said hesitantly.

"Me? Why?" I asked in surprise.

"Because the dead body next door belongs to Brett Owens and they know about what happened at Precious Metals a few weeks ago.

They just want to ask you a few questions," he said.

My eyes widened and I sucked in a sharp breath. "They don't think I had something to do with his death, do they?"

I couldn't help it. I always assumed I was in trouble when I was being summoned by a person of higher authority.

Jonah reached out and cupped my cheek. "Hey, there's nothing to worry about. Just answer their questions with short, truthful answers and don't volunteer any information."

"What is that supposed to mean?"

He sighed. "It means don't tell them anything that isn't a direct answer to the questions they ask. For example, if there was any kind of history between you and Brett, don't mention it unless they specifically ask."

I gasped and pressed my hand against my chest. How in the hell did Jonah know anything about my past with Brett?

Jonah grabbed my hand and tugged me out the door. "Come on. We don't want to keep them waiting."

I took in a deep breath and put on my work face—the one I used when I couldn't make faces at how disgusting something was.

When I entered the kitchen, Jonah pulled out a chair for me. "Hello, again. Jonah said you had some questions for me."

Officer Dunk smiled kindly. "Just a few. Can you tell me what happened between you and Brett Owens at Precious Metals a few weeks ago?"

"Yes," I said and swallowed thickly. "I was walking to the restroom when he grabbed me and pushed me against the wall. I told him to let me go, but he didn't. He moved his hand up to my throat and started to squeeze, but he was suddenly pulled away by Jonah."

"I see. Why didn't you file a police report?" she asked.

"I didn't feel it was necessary. I would have if things had escalated, but Jonah stopped him and made him leave. I went home shortly after that," I explained.

"And have you had any other issues with Brett Owens?" she asked.

"No. I've only been in town for a few weeks. That was the one and only time I've had any interaction with him since I arrived in Devil Springs," I explained carefully. Yes, I was omitting certain details, but my farce of a relationship with him in high school had nothing to do with the current situation.

"It's rather odd that he attempted to assault you and was found dead in the house you were renting a few weeks later," Officer Dunk said, though her statement wasn't directed at anyone in particular.

"Do you think he may have been looking for you? Possibly to get back at you?" Officer Underwood asked.

"I honestly have no idea. Like I said, I've only had one encounter with him. There's no way I could presume to know what he was thinking," I said.

"Well, I think we have all we need. You guys are free to go, but you'll need to reschedule your inspection. They're still working the scene. I'll give you a call and let you know when it's been cleared."

"Thank you, officers," Jonah said and walked the ladies to the front door while I sat in stunned silence contemplating what they'd said.

"You okay?" Jonah asked.

I looked up and noticed everyone else had left when the officers did. "Uh, yeah, I'm fine. I'm just a little shocked, I guess. Do you think he was coming after me?"

Jonah shrugged. "It's feasible I suppose."

"If he was coming after me, how did he end up dead? Did you notice anything obvious when you found him? Was there blood or obvious trauma?" I asked.

Jonah shook his head. "Nothing like that. I would've thought he was passed out if his skin hadn't been a bluish-gray color."

"I thought the house was wired with a security system. How did he get in?"

"That's what I want to know. Every entry point to that house has a sensor. The only way to get by them is to disable the alarm, which was set from the time Copper and Bronze left earlier today until I returned a few hours ago."

Jonah's face lit up like he'd just realized something and he was on his feet moving down the hall the next second.

"Where are you going?" I asked as I followed him.

"To pull up the diagram of the house and see if all the sensors are on and active," he said as he furiously typed and clicked while staring at the monitor.

"Motherfucker!" he shouted causing me to jump.

"What?" I asked.

He turned the monitor around for me to see

and pointed at something on the screen. "This is the floor plan of your rental house. The green lines indicate security sensors. Every entry point should have a green line, including the windows and the attic door." He tapped his finger against the screen, "See this right here. This is the kitchen door."

"And there's no green line," I observed.

"Exactly. Now I want to know who in the fuck tampered with my system," he spat.

"Wouldn't you get an alert of some kind when that happened?"

"Yeah, unless it happened when the system had been disarmed by the master code," he explained.

"Who has access to the master code?"

"Only me, Copper, and Bronze," he said.

My mouth dropped open and I covered it with my hand. "You don't think they had something to do with this, do you?"

He scoffed. "Of course not. I trust them implicitly. I don't know what in the hell is going on, but I can promise you, I will fucking find out."

"Is there anything I can do to help?" I asked hopefully.

He grinned. "Yeah, get your naked ass in my

bed. I'll be in there in just a minute."

Well, that I could do. I nodded and winked at him over my shoulder as I sashayed out of the room.

But Jonah took longer than a minute. In fact, Jonah took so long that I ended up falling asleep. If he came to bed, I never knew it because he didn't wake me and he was gone when I woke the next morning.

CHAPTER TWENTY-FOUR

Judge

After River went to bed, I started digging through the files on my computer. I had to know when the sensor was removed before I would be able to get any sleep. I fully expected to find out it was tampered with during the inspection earlier that day.

What I did not expect was to have to dig back through days and days of files to find the answer. It took much longer than I thought and, by the time I found it, Officer Dunk had called to let me know the scene had been cleared.

I intended to just go over and lock up the house, but when I noticed my equipment still sitting in the living room, I decided to go ahead and complete the installation I had originally started and replace the missing sensor. I also changed the master code to be on the safe side.

By the time all was said and done, the sun was up and it was well into the next morning. After making sure the house was locked and the alarm was set, I went straight to the clubhouse to update Copper.

"The fuck you mean somebody removed a sensor? How?" he asked.

"My best guess is they did it during the first inspection, which would explain the frayed wires," I said.

"But Splint's dad didn't find anything wrong with the wiring. Are you saying he lied to us?" Copper asked incredulously.

"No way; he's an honest man, but that doesn't mean everyone he employs is. The wires were capped, so whoever did it, knew exactly what they were doing."

Copper picked up his phone and gave me a pointed look. "No sense in beating around the bush; let's get him in here and ask him."

Thirty minutes later, Dean Montgomery

walked into Copper's office with a worried look on his face. "What's going on, fellas?"

Copper explained the situation and asked, "Do you think any of your guys would have done something like this?"

He rubbed the back of his neck and exhaled slowly. "Honestly, Copper, I don't think it was one of my guys," he said and paused for a moment. "I didn't think anything of it at the time, but the day you called us out to the property, there was a guy hovering around the door in the kitchen. I assumed he was with the city inspector, but maybe I was mistaken."

"What did he look like?" Copper asked.

"Uh, he was kind of scraggly looking. Messy brown hair. Average height. Clothes were wrinkled and kinda ratty looking."

His description ruled out Brett, but it did match his friend from the bar. I looked to Copper. "You have the copies of the IDs from the two guys we kicked out of Precious Metals?"

Copper nodded and pulled two sheets of paper from his desk. Placing them in front of Dean, he pointed to Brett's friend, Oliver, and asked, "Is this him?"

"Yep, that's the guy."

After Dean left, Copper looked at me with

a feral grin. "Let's go have a chat with Oliver Burgess."

We waited for Batta and Bronze to arrive before we pulled out onto the road and headed for Oliver's listed address. It was around a thirty-minute ride there, and I spent the whole time wondering what in the hell was going on. Why would this asshole intentionally fuck with us? Unless he wasn't fucking with us. Maybe his actions were aimed at River. But that didn't explain how his friend ended up dead in the kitchen floor. Unless they were planning to attack River once she returned to the house.

We pulled into the driveway of a small well-kept house. Copper looked back with an arched brow. "I bet this is his parents' place."

Before any of us could reply, the front door opened and a young woman with a baby on her hip stepped outside. She glanced between the four of us but didn't appear to be fazed by our presence. "Can I help you guys with something?"

Copper got off his bike and took a few steps closer. "We're looking for Oliver Burgess. Does he live here?"

She shook her head and let out an exasperated sigh. "No, he doesn't and hasn't for well over a year now. Before you ask, no, I don't know where he lives, where to find him, or how to get in touch with him."

Copper nodded and rubbed his chin. "But you do know him?"

"He's my stepbrother."

Copper pulled a card from his cut and handed it to her. "If you happen to hear from him, would you let him know I'd like to speak with him?"

She plucked the card from Copper's fingers and grimaced. "What in the hell has he done now to garner the attention of the Blackwings?"

"Sorry, ma'am, that's something I'll need to discuss with him."

"Don't hold your breath. I haven't heard from him in almost a year. If you can track down his buddy, Brett, you might be able to find Oliver."

Copper cleared his throat. "Well, that's not likely seeing as how Brett was found dead yesterday."

She pressed her lips together and twisted them to the side. "Can't say I'm sorry to hear that."

"Well, thank you for your time," Copper said and strode back to his bike. "Follow me, brothers."

With that, we walked the bikes out of her

driveway and took off down the road. At first, I thought we were heading back to the clubhouse but soon realized that was not the case when we pulled into a rundown trailer park.

Our arrival brought every resident to their front door. Every resident except the one we were there to see.

"This is Brett's listed address," Copper said as he got off his bike and walked to the front door.

After banging on it a few times with no answer, a man walked up to us and introduced himself as the owner of the property.

"He's late on his rent and I don't want any trouble. If you boys need to go inside, I'll be happy to let you in," he stammered causing all of us to laugh.

"If we wanted inside, we wouldn't need you to let us in," Batta chuckled.

Copper held his hand up to quiet Batta and nodded at the man. "Yes, we would like to have a look inside."

Copper, as well as the rest of us, regretted those words the moment the landlord opened the front door and we were hit with the unmistakable stench of death and decay.

Bronze backed up several steps while

shaking his head. "Nope. Not happening. We're not going in there."

Copper placed his hand on the owner's shoulder. "Thanks, but I think we should wait for the police before anyone goes inside. Smells like a crime scene in there."

And for some reason unbeknownst to me, we sat there and waited for the police to enter the trailer and tell us what was inside.

CHAPTER TWENTY-FIVE

RIVER

For the first time since I'd arrived in Devil Springs, I walked into work in a bad mood. Why? Because of Jonah "Fucking Judge" Jackson.

After not coming to bed, he wasn't home when I woke up and he didn't come home before I left for work. But what really pissed me off was that he didn't answer his cell phone when I called or reply to any of the texts I sent. I thought about calling Leigh, but decided that would be weird. Instead, I opted to seethe in silence.

My anger was momentarily forgotten when I saw Kennedy. I hadn't worked with her, or even talked to her, since the night she called in sick.

I rushed over to her and pulled her into a hug. "Girl, where have you been?"

She laughed lightly. "In the seventh circle of hell. My niece picked up that horrid stomach virus that's been going around and passed it to me. One time I thought I was going to have to come in because I was absolutely certain I shit out part of my rectum. I even made my sister check and make sure nothing was hanging out of my asshole," she said seriously.

I tried, I really did, to hold in the laughter, but it burst forth until I was doubled over and clutching my stomach while tears ran down my face.

"What's going on?" Dr. Alvarez asked.

"River thinks a prolapsed rectum is a laughing matter," Kennedy answered and managed to maintain a straight face for all of five seconds.

"Never mind. I don't think I want to know," she chuckled and continued on her way.

And that was how we spent the first part of the shift—laughing and talking in between patients.

But the night took a different turn when

Jonah and Copper walked into the ER with two police officers. "River, we need to speak with you," Jonah said flatly.

My previous anger returned with a vengeance. I nodded and glanced at my watch. "Okay, I'll be happy to speak with you in about, oh, let's say twelve hours," I said sharply and turned to walk away.

"River," Copper called in a tone that had me stopping, but I refused to turn around. "This isn't something that can wait."

I let out an exasperated sigh. "Fine. Follow me to the conference room."

Once inside, Jonah closed the doors behind him. The taller of the two police officers smiled kindly and suggested, "Maybe you should sit."

"Maybe you should tell me whatever it is you came to tell me so I can get back to work," I snapped.

The two officers exchanged a look and both turned their gazes to Jonah and Copper. Copper nodded and Officer Number Two began to speak. "Miss Lawson, I regret to inform you that your mother, Spring Lawson, was found dead yesterday evening from an apparent drug overdose."

I stood silently waiting for more. When no

one else said anything, I asked, "Is that it?"

Officer Number One nodded. "Yes, ma'am."

"Thank you for telling me. Can I go back to work now?" I asked.

"Well, yes, I suppose you can. We won't be able to release your mother's body until the investigation is complete, which could be several days or even longer. Someone from the coroner's office will be in touch with that information."

I placed my hand on my hip and faced him directly. "I will not be claiming, accepting, or whatevering my mother's body. Please make note of that right now."

"But you have to," Officer Number Two whined.

"I sure as shit do not, but if you want to make an issue of it, she has another child. Call and tell him he needs to deal with his mother."

"Do you have his contact information?"

I shook my head and pointed to Jonah and Copper. "No, I don't, but they do. Now, if you'll excuse me, I have patients to attend to," I said and pulled the door open.

"River, wait," Jonah blurted.

I whirled around and met him stare for stare. "You do not get to come into my place of business and cause a disruption. This isn't the kind of job where I can come and go as I please. I can lose my license if I don't take care of my patients, and I'll be damned if that's going to happen, especially over something that involves Spring. Now, get the fuck out of my way or I'll have security remove you."

Copper's hand landed on Jonah's shoulder and physically pulled him back a few steps so I could leave. Somehow, I had reversed our positions while I was telling him off. I gave Copper a nod of appreciation and returned to my shift with the intent to pretend like the previous thirty minutes never happened, but I should have known two Blackwings and two police officers entering the ER as a unit wouldn't go unnoticed.

"So, what was your little visit about?" Kennedy asked as she grabbed her stuff from her locker.

"You're probably going to find out anyway, so I'll go ahead and tell you, but I don't want to talk about it. Okay?"

Her eyes widened, but she quickly nodded in agreement.

"They came to tell me my mother died from a drug overdose yesterday. I told them to call my brother if they were looking for someone who cared because it most certainly wasn't me," I said and then added, "And that's all I have to say about it. You ready to go?"

Kennedy stared at me with her mouth hanging open for long moments. Finally, I said, "Okay, then. I'll see you next time," and turned to leave.

"Wait! I'm coming," she called out and was walking beside me a few moments later.

As we walked in silence, I started to feel bad for making her uncomfortable. I sighed. "I still don't want to talk about it, but I will say that I've never had a good relationship with the woman who birthed me. The last time I spoke to her was well over seven years ago. I'm sorry if I made you feel uncomfortable, but this is no different to me than a stranger dying."

"I understand, but if you ever do want to talk about it, I'll be happy to listen," she said sincerely.

"Thanks, Kennedy," I said and stopped to give her a hug before heading to my car.

I wasn't surprised in the least to find Jonah leaning against my car with his arms crossed. "Why are you here?" I asked, making no attempt to hide my annoyance with him.

"I need a ride home," he said and moved to the passenger door.

"And you just assumed I'd give you one?"

"Yeah, because even though you're pissed at me, I know you care about me. I've had less than five hours of sleep in the last forty-eight hours. It's not safe for me to drive home."

It pissed me off even more that he was right. I did care about him. A lot more than I cared to admit to myself, or anyone else for that matter. I started to relent, then had a sudden realization. "Why didn't you ride home with Copper?"

"He was on his bike."

"The officers could have taken you home."

"A biker never gets into a police car by choice," he smirked.

"You could've called a cab or an Uber."

He grinned. "You need to hear it, baby? Fine. I was waiting for you...in case you weren't okay. Now, can we go home?"

"Fine. Get in," I snapped and unlocked the car. How dare he say and do something sweet and thoughtful while I was trying to be mad at him?

I drove home in silence. When I pulled into the garage and got out of the car, I expected Jonah to do the same, but he didn't. I called his name twice, but he didn't answer me, so I walked around to the passenger side and quickly realized he was sound asleep. A small part of me wanted to leave him right where he was, but the larger part of me cared about him and couldn't do it.

"Jonah," I called again and gently shook his shoulder. "Jonah, wake up."

He mumbled something and turned his head away from me. I leaned across him and shook him by both shoulders. "Jonah! Wake up!"

Before I could even blink, he had knocked both of my hands from his body and had his hand around my throat. Just as fast as he'd done it, he released me and raised his hands in the air. "Fuck! I'm sorry. Did I hurt you?"

"N-no, you didn't. I was just trying to wake you up," I stammered as I backed up and put some distance between us.

He dropped his head and rubbed the back of his neck. "I was in the Marines for a few years and I spent a good bit of time in a combat zone. If you can't wake me up from the side, it's better to let me sleep."

"Okay," I said softly. "Come on; I'm tired, and obviously, so are you."

With that, he followed me inside the house and to my bedroom where we both fell face first into the pillows.

CHAPTER TWENTY-SIX

DASH

When the phone rang in the middle of the night, I was pissed. It wasn't because it woke me up since I was already awake thanks to my hungry baby girl. No, it pissed me off because of the look it put on my wife's face.

"You better get that," she said quietly. "Something must be wrong."

I snatched my phone off the nightstand and answered without bothering to look at the caller ID as I stepped out into the hallway. "What?"

"Dash, sorry for calling so late, but I have some bad news," Judge said without preamble.

"What is it?"

"Your mother was found dead earlier this evening. They think it was a drug overdose."

"What's the bad news?" I asked. I didn't give a shit about my mother anymore. I did, at one time, as all children do, but as I got older, I learned that she didn't care about anyone other than herself and my hopes and dreams of having a loving mother were nothing but hopes and dreams.

"Well, I guess the bad news is you'll need to deal with the body and any arrangements since your sister flat out refused to."

"Shit. How did Rain take the news?" I asked. Even though my sister hated me, I loved her very much—so much that I respected her wishes and stayed away from her even though it killed me to do so.

Judge snorted. "I think she would've been more upset if I'd told her she had a flat tire. She didn't seem to care that your mother was dead, but she was fucking pissed when the officers suggested releasing the body to her. She told them to call you and went back to work."

Fucking hell. I had more important things

going on than dealing with my crackhead mother's rotting corpse, but if it meant Rain didn't have to do it, then I would. "Yeah, that's fine. I'll take care of everything. Do you think Rain would want a service for her?"

"I think you should try to talk to her yourself, man. I don't know what went down between you two, but this is something that the two of you should deal with together," he said.

I sighed knowing he was right. "I know; I was just trying to do what she asked and leave her alone. Listen, I can have Byte get it for me, but it would save me a lot of time and trouble if you'd give me her phone number."

"As long as you don't tell her you got it from me," he said and rattled off the numbers. "She gets off work at seven and usually sleeps until two or three."

"Thanks, man. I'll give her a call later this evening."

I walked back into my bedroom to find my beautiful wife gently placing our sleeping little girl back into her bassinet. "What happened?" she whispered.

I pulled her against me and held her for a few moments before I took her hand in mine and walked us out of the bedroom. "Judge called to tell me my mother died."

"Oh," she said and started fidgeting with her hands. "Are you okay?" she asked. I hadn't shared much about my mother, because there wasn't much to share. She was basically nonexistent during my childhood and even more so during my teen years.

"I'm fine," I reassured her. "My mother was not a real mother. Not like Annabelle is to you or like you are to Raven. My mother loved herself and her drugs. She had no intention of ever changing her ways and I'm not sorry or saddened that she's gone."

Ember studied me in silence for a few moments before she carefully observed, "But something is bothering you."

"My sister," I said and cleared my throat. "She's been working in Devil Springs for the last few weeks and I—"

"What?" she shrieked. "Why didn't you tell me? How long have you known?"

"Shh! You'll wake Raven," I whisper-yelled causing her to give me squinty eyes. "I've known since a week or two after she arrived. I didn't tell you because a few years ago, she asked me to stay out of her life, and I presumed that request also included my wife."

"You still could've told me. I wouldn't have gone up there and sought her out," she insisted.

"You might not have, but I can guaran-damn-tee one of the other Old Ladies would've."

She looked to her feet and rubbed her hands together. "Yeah, I suppose you're right about that. So, what happens now?"

I reached out and pulled her hands apart, taking each into one of mine. "Right now, we're going to get you back into bed and get some sleep before my little princess wants to eat again. I'll make some phone calls in the morning and see what I need to do in regards to her remains. Judge said Rain works the night shift and sleeps until two or three, so I'll try calling her around five or so."

"No, you will not. You need to go up there. It will be harder for her to shut you out face to face."

I shook my head. "I'm not leaving you and Raven to drive to Devil Springs to have a door slammed in my face. She didn't have a problem telling me to fuck off in person last time."

"Dash, this is different and you know it. You can drop me and Raven off at Dad's before you go. Plus, you can check on my brother for me."

"Okay, baby," I said and placed a soft kiss on

her lips. "We'll talk more about it in the morning. You need to sleep while you can."

"I love you, Dash."

"Love you, too, Ember."

CHAPTER TWENTY-SEVEN

RIVER

I woke up when my alarm went off at three o'clock. I rolled to my side to find Jonah sound asleep. Quietly climbing out of bed, I tiptoed to the door and made my way to his room so I could shower without waking him. If he'd had as little sleep as he'd said, he needed the rest.

After I showered and dressed, I went out to the kitchen and got a pot of coffee going while I started perusing the fridge and cabinets for something to eat. Once I decided on omelets and pancakes, I went back to his bathroom to blow dry my hair and put on a little makeup.

I had just started on the second omelet when someone rang the doorbell. I moved the pan off the burner and quickly ran for the door before whoever it was rang it again and woke Jonah. Without even thinking about looking, I yanked the door open to find a man I most certainly did not want to see standing on Jonah's front porch.

Before I could slam the door in his face, Jonah appeared beside me and extended his hand. "Dash, good to see you, brother. Come on in."

Jonah strategically moved me to the side without me even realizing what he was doing until it was too late. My brother was suddenly inside *my* space and being friendly with *my* man and I couldn't take it.

"Get out," I said in a low and even tone.

Reed's eyes widened, but Jonah stepped in front of me and cupped my cheeks in his hands. "You need to talk to him. Your brother is not a bad man. He wouldn't be in the club if he was. He came here to see you; the least you could do is hear what he has to say."

"Did you know he was coming?"

Jonah shook his head. "No, I didn't. I never

would've sprung something like this on you."

I nodded and took a moment to think about what I wanted to do. Well, I knew what I wanted— to kick Reed out and devour the scrumptious breakfast I was cooking. But, what I wanted to do and what I should do were likely not one and the same.

"Okay. Let me finish cooking and I'll hear what he has to say while I'm eating. If he starts talking while I'm hangry, things won't end well for anyone in this house."

"All right, lil' ninja. Get back to cooking so we can keep your monster under control," he said and placed a soft kiss on my lips.

With that, I returned to the kitchen while Jonah went into the living room with my brother. Instead of trying to figure out why Reed had shown up or what he could possibly want to discuss with me, I focused on the food. In fact, I was so focused on it I didn't realize I'd made five omelets and twenty-three pancakes until Jonah stopped me from mixing up more batter. "That's more than enough, baby. Go sit down and I'll bring yours to you."

I picked up my cup of coffee and took a seat at the kitchen table. A few minutes later, Jonah placed my food in front of me and returned with two more plates of food just as my brother took a seat across from me.

An awkward and uncomfortable silence surrounded us, so I began shoveling food into my mouth, not even bothering to chew it before I swallowed and shoved in another forkful.

"All right, I've had enough of this shit. Y'all have some things to discuss. You want me to stay or go?" Jonah asked.

To my absolute horror, Reed and I both shrugged and said, "Meh, whatever."

Jonah snorted. "In that case, I guess I'll stay."

A part of me didn't want him to stay and hear the humiliating details of my past, but another part of me wanted him to hear just how much of an asshole his beloved club brother really was. And that part was what encouraged me to get the ball rolling.

"So, what brings you to Devil Springs, brother dearest?" I asked in a chipper tone that was clearly fake.

"Our dead mother," Reed deadpanned.

"I see. And what exactly does that have to do with me?"

He sighed and sat back in his chair. "Do you want to have a service?"

My fork dropped to my plate with a loud clank. "You can't be serious." When his only response was to blink at me, I continued, "No, I don't want to have a service for her. I don't want to have anything to do with her or whatever is left of her."

"So, you don't care what I do with her?" Reed asked.

"You could let her rot in a potter's field for all I care."

"If that's how you feel, why didn't you arrange for that to happen?" he asked.

"Because I truly don't care—dump her in a field, burn her, bury her—it doesn't matter to me whatsoever. This is no different to me than a complete stranger passing away. If that's the reason you came, you could've saved yourself a lot of time and called or asked Jonah," I told him.

"It's not the only reason I came, Rain."

"River. My name is River," I snapped.

"Sorry, the last time you spoke to me you went by Rain," he snapped back.

"Actually, the last time I spoke to you I went by River; I just didn't give you a chance to use it."

"Fine, sibling, I also came to make sure you were okay."

I couldn't even begin to hide the look of utter shock on my face. "Why do you care?"

"I've always cared. Our mother died, and regardless of how you feel about me, I wanted to see for myself that you were okay," he said.

"Seriously, Reed? You've always cared? What kind of bullshit is that?" I yelled and pushed back from the table to stand.

"It's not bullshit, Ra—River!" he yelled back and got to his feet.

"Enough!" Jonah roared and slammed his hand down on the table. "Both of you sit down and shut up." I immediately shut my mouth and dropped into my seat. Surprisingly, Reed did the same. "River, why are you mad at your brother?"

I turned my head toward Jonah and pinned him with my best death glare. "He knows why."

"I didn't ask if he knew why. I asked why you're mad at your brother. Answer the question," Jonah demanded.

I crossed my arms over my chest and fumed. "Because he paid our mother to humiliate me and make my life a living hell."

"What in the hell are you talking about?" Reed asked, seeming to be genuinely confused, but I didn't buy it.

"After I found out you paid Spring to have

sex with my boyfriend, I started digging through her stuff and found letters from you telling her to make sure I never found out or you'd stop paying her," I blurted.

Reed's eyes grew comically wide and he started shaking his head. "That's not at all what happened. I paid her to make sure you were taken care of. I sent money for clothes, shoes, food, school stuff, spending money, or whatever you needed. I did send extra money that was specifically for her to use, but I told her to make sure you never found out. I didn't want you to know that I was supporting her drug habit, but I knew she would take the money meant for you if I didn't. As for the boyfriend, I don't know anything about that. I didn't even know you had a boyfriend."

My mouth dropped open as I stared at my brother. At one time, I loved him more than any other person in the world. He was always there for me, especially on the nights when Spring was out doing who knows what and left us home alone. He would let me sleep in his bed when I was scared. He made sure I had food to eat and clean clothes to wear. In a way, he raised us both. But then he left and everything changed.

"Think about it, Raindrop, I would never do

any of the things you said. You know that. Spring was a master-manipulator and only cared about herself. She probably tried running you off so she could keep all the money I was sending for herself."

"Why didn't you write me or call me? You left and never came back. What was I supposed to think?" I asked and bit down on the inside of my cheek in a weak attempt to keep the tears at bay.

"I did write you. Every time I sent a letter to Spring, I sent one to you. You didn't get any of them?"

I shook my head. "Not a single one."

He sighed. "I couldn't call because you didn't have a phone. I paid all the bills for the utilities directly to the company, but I couldn't arrange for a landline to be installed without Spring's consent, which she refused to give. I didn't get many letters from her, but she always said you were doing well. One time, I asked why you never wrote to me and she said you were too busy studying and working hard to get a college scholarship. She said it was easier for her to update me on what was going on with you. I guess I fell for her lies, too."

"Why didn't you tell me all of this when you

found me a few years ago?" I asked.

"Because you didn't give me a chance before you told me to stay away. I didn't know why, but you were so adamant about it and even threatened me with a restraining order. I figured you had your reasons and would eventually change your mind, but that never happened."

I wasn't sure what to say or do next. I really wanted to believe him, but I was afraid to. What if he was the master-manipulator? What if he was just trying to hurt me?

"Spring said you hated me because I was the reason our dad left," I whispered.

"That fucking cunt!" Reed swore. "I don't have any memories of the man she claimed was our father, so how could I hate you for something I don't even remember?"

I sucked in a breath hoping to calm myself, but it had the opposite effect and a sob burst from me before I could choke it back. I covered my face with my hands and then I was wrapped up in familiar arms.

"It's okay. Everything's going to be okay."

"I'm sorry," I cried.

"Nothing to be sorry for. Just know, I will always love you, Raindrop," my big brother said and kissed the top of my head.

"I love you, too, Reed."

When I managed to get my emotions under control, I stepped back and looked around the room. "Where's Jonah?"

"He left the room a while ago," Reed said. "Judge! You can come back now!"

Jonah entered the room and looked between the two of us. "Y'all get things worked out?"

I nodded and Reed put his arm around my shoulders. "We did," he said and I could hear the smile in his voice.

Jonah smiled widely. "Good. Now, let's eat."

Reed stayed until it was time for me to leave for my shift at the hospital. He said he would take care of everything regarding Spring and asked Jonah and I to come visit him and his family in Croftridge over the weekend.

"I would love to," I exclaimed excitedly.

Jonah cleared his throat and placed his hand on my shoulder. "Sorry, I already made plans for us this weekend. Maybe the next weekend that you're off?"

"Just let me know when you guys are coming," Reed said. "If we're not at home, we're at Phoenix's house. Raven is still too small to really go anywhere else."

"I typically work every other weekend, so

maybe weekend after next?" I suggested.

"Sounds good. I better get going. Don't want you to be late for work," he said and headed for the door.

We hugged again before he climbed on his bike and rode off. I stood on the porch looking in the direction he'd gone until I could no longer hear his pipes. Sighing, I went back inside and got ready for work. Who would've thought my mother's death would be the thing to reunite my brother and me?

CHAPTER TWENTY-EIGHT

JUDGE

After River left for work, I went over to my mom's house to have dinner with her and make sure she was doing okay. I knew Layla had been spending a lot of time over there, but I wanted to see for myself.

I rang the doorbell with my hip since my hands were full of bags from her favorite restaurant. To my surprise, Splint's dad, Dean Montgomery, opened the front door.

"Hey, Judge. Oh, let me help you with that," he said and reached to take one of the bags.

"Hey, Dean. What're you doing here?" I asked, not bothering to hide the suspicious undertone in my voice.

He held his hands up in a placating manner. "The relay switch went out on the compressor of your mom's fridge. She called and asked me if I had time to replace it."

"Why'd she call you? I could've done it for her."

"Jonah Jackson, mind your manners in my house," Mom scolded.

"Sorry, Ma. My apologies, Dean. It caught me off guard when you answered the door." I held up the bag of food I was still holding and grinned. "I brought dinner."

Mom smiled. "Wonderful! Dean, would you like to join us?"

He glanced between Mom and me before saying, "I'll have to take a rain check. I've got a big job starting tomorrow that requires some prep work I'd like to get done tonight."

"Oh, okay. Maybe another time then. How much do I owe you?" Mom asked.

"If you'll make me a batch of your cookies sometime, we'll call it even."

"You've got yourself a deal," Mom said. "Thanks again for coming over on such short notice."

After Dean left, Mom and I sat down to dinner. She started yammering on about anything and everything, clearly trying to avoid a certain topic, but I wasn't going to let that happen. In the middle of her spiel about her flower beds, I interrupted her, "Why'd you really call Dean to fix the fridge? I could've done it for you. Hell, you could've done it."

Ma wiped her mouth with her napkin and looked down at her plate. "When I was still in the hospital, Splint and his dad came by to visit. I knew Splint worked the call, but I didn't know his dad was in the restaurant when I collapsed. He's actually the one who started doing CPR on me before the ambulance got there. Then, I ran into Dean when I was having lunch with Boar and Shannon and invited him to join us. He's a nice guy and I enjoy talking with him."

I reached across the table and placed my hand on top of hers giving it a gentle squeeze. "Mom, if you're worried about how I'll react to you seeing someone; don't. I know you loved Dad with all your heart, but he's been gone a long time, and he wouldn't want you to be lonely."

She placed her other hand on top of mine and patted it. "That's good to know, sweetheart, but Dean and I are just friends."

"Be sure to let me know if that changes," I said.

She laughed. "You don't have to worry about that. You boys gossip more than any girls I've ever known, so you'll probably know before I do."

"I highly doubt that," I chuckled and went back to my food.

"So, things still going good with you and River?"

I nodded and told her about River's mother dying, as well as Dash showing up for an unexpected visit.

"Spring Lawson. Why does that name sound familiar?" Mom asked and cast her eyes upward like she was trying to physically search inside her head.

I shrugged. "Don't know. She's lived in Devil Springs for at least thirty years, if not longer. According to Dash, she's been into drugs for the entirety of his life, so maybe you saw her name in the news. I'm sure she's been arrested a number of times."

"Maybe that's it," she said distractedly, clearly still trying to place River's mother.

I knew why she recognized the name, but I didn't feel right sharing the story about River's humiliating prom experience.

After dinner, I helped her with a few things around the house before heading home for the night. I was still exhausted from the last few days and desperately needed to catch up on some sleep.

***

I dropped into my seat and waited for Church to begin. I was hoping it would be a short meeting because I wanted to get on the road before it got too late. River had no idea what we were doing for the weekend, and I was anxious to get the ball rolling.

The words "rental house" pulled me back to the present. "The inspection has been rescheduled for next Wednesday. We are still trying to locate Oliver Burgess, who we believe to be the person who tampered with the sensors. Spazz will be sending his picture to each of your phones so you have something to reference if you don't know what he looks like. Also, continue to be on the look out for Roy Mayfield. If you do happen to see either one of them, grab 'em and bring 'em to the clubhouse. That's all I've got. Anybody else have anything we need to discuss?"

I sat forward in my chair and cleared my throat. "I'm taking River out of town for the weekend, so she won't need a tail. We should be back sometime Sunday evening."

"Let me know when you get back. Anybody else?" he asked. When everyone shook their heads, he banged the gavel effectively dismissing us.

CHAPTER TWENTY-NINE

RIVER

I was awake and ready to go by the time Jonah returned from Church. I hoped the bag I packed would fit in his saddlebag. I tried to pack light, but it wasn't easy since he wouldn't tell me what we were doing or where we were going.

"I just need to grab my bag and I'll be ready to go," he said with a broad smile.

"Will you please tell me what we're doing? It's driving me crazy," I whined.

"And ruin the surprise I've worked so hard

on? No way in hell, lil' ninja. You're just going to have to wait."

"Fine, fuckface. Have it your way," I grumbled causing him to laugh.

A few minutes later, I was on the back of his bike and we were on the road. As much as I wanted to pout about not knowing where we were going, I couldn't keep the smile off my face as the wind whipped around me while I clung to Jonah's body.

It suddenly hit me that I didn't have much time left in Devil Springs. In all the years I'd worked as a traveling nurse, I'd never let myself become involved with anyone beyond casual relationships. Even my friendships were superficial. I never opened up or shared anything personal because I knew my stay would be temporary, but somehow, Jonah Jackson managed to break all of my rules.

I tried to shake off the sense of sadness that washed over me and enjoy the ride, but my mind kept wandering back to how much I was going to miss Jonah, Kennedy, Leigh, and the other friends I'd made in Devil Springs.

The bike came to a stop and Jonah patted my thigh indicating for me to get off. I looked up to see we were in the parking lot of a small country store.

"What're we doing here?" I asked.

"Getting groceries."

"And where are you planning to put those groceries?" I asked. I knew he had storage compartments on his bike, but there weren't that many and the ones he did have were already full.

He grinned. "In my mouth."

I rolled my eyes and followed him inside the store.

"Hey, Bruce!" Jonah exclaimed and extended his hand to an older man behind the register. "How's it going?"

"Well, now, I suppose I can't complain. You boys keep me and Peggy in business. Good to see you, Judge. And who's this you've brought with you?"

Jonah introduced me to Bruce and I reached out to shake his hand. "She doesn't know where we're going, so don't let her try to get it out of you."

Bruce laughed. "You're a brave man, Judge— taking a woman away for the weekend and not telling her where you're taking her. How's she supposed to pack?"

"See! He gets it!" I shouted.

"I sure do, and I learned it the hard way,

too," Bruce shared.

"I'm still not telling you," Jonah declared. "Pick out what you want to eat tonight and for breakfast tomorrow and Sunday. And anything you might want for snacks."

"What about lunch and dinner tomorrow?"

"You don't need to worry about that," he said cryptically and went about gathering a few items.

After Jonah paid for the groceries, he carried the bags out to a truck parked in the lot. Before I could ask what he was doing, Bruce got into the driver's seat and said, "I'll follow you."

We got back on the bike, but instead of pulling out onto the road we'd been on, Jonah took a different road that started to look more like gravel and less like road the farther we traveled. Then there were sections of the road that were so steep I was certain I would slide off the back of the bike and Bruce would run right over me.

Finally, Jonah stopped in front of a beautiful cabin. The thing was massive and appeared to be sitting directly on top of the mountain.

"Where are we?" I asked as I turned my head from side to side trying to take in as much as possible.

"Let me get the groceries from Bruce before

he tries to unload them himself and then I'll tell you."

I followed Jonah to the truck to grab a few bags and thank Bruce for not running over me.

The inside of the cabin was just as breathtaking as the outside. I dropped the bags on the counter and ran to the huge glass window in the living room that looked out over the mountains.

"Will you tell me where we are now?"

Jonah chuckled. "We're at my friend's cabin. He's actually the VP of the Croftridge chapter. Anyway, he doesn't get up here very often so he lets other club members use it whenever he's not. Copper actually met Layla up here."

"But this place seems so remote. How did that even happen?"

"It's a long story and it's not mine to tell, but I'm sure Layla would be happy to share it with you sometime."

"I'll be sure to ask her about it when we get back."

"Do you want to eat now or go explore first?" he asked.

I chose to eat first because I knew I wouldn't want to stop whatever we were doing to come back and eat; plus, I was starving since I hadn't eaten much before we left.

Once we were finished eating, I sprayed any exposed skin with bug spray I found in one of the bathrooms. I don't know what it was about me, but mosquitos loved me. Had I known we were going to a cabin in the woods, I would've brought my own.

Jonah was standing by the back door waiting for me with a shotgun strapped to his back. "What're you doing with that?"

"There's a lot of wild animals up here, and technically, we're in their territory. I'd rather be prepared if we happen to run into anything."

"Hold up. What kind of wild animals?" I asked, thinking that maybe we should stay inside and explore the cabin. I had no interest in becoming bear poop.

"Cougars, black bears, boars, elk, and coyotes to name a few."

I was already shaking my head and backing away from the door. "Nope. No thank you. I'll be perfectly fine staying right here in the animal-free zone."

Jonah laughed. "There's nothing to worry about. If we happen to come up on any animals, chances are they'll run away when they see or hear us. If they don't and it comes down to it, I'll shoot them."

"Has anyone ever been attacked up here?" I asked.

Jonah grimaced and reluctantly nodded. "Yes, it's happened one time, but the circumstances were very different and she didn't have a gun or any other kind of weapon to scare them off."

I placed my hands on my hips. "She? Them? Explain."

He sighed. "Two wild boars chased after Layla and one of them got her leg before she could get away. She was unarmed and didn't even know she needed to be watching for them. Copper heard her screaming and came to her rescue. But, in all the years we've been coming to this cabin, that's the only time anyone's had a problem," he reassured me.

"You know how to use that thing?" I asked and pointed to the shotgun.

Jonah threw his head back and laughed. "My dad taught me how to shoot when I was five years old. Not only do I know how to use it, I can hit what I'm aiming for. Hang on a sec," he said and turned to open the closet behind him. After rummaging around for a moment, he handed me something that looked like a mini fire extinguisher. "That's bear spray. It's like pepper spray, but meant for animals."

"Do you have boar spray and cougar spray in there?" I asked as I studied the can in my hand.

"That works on other animals, too. If it doesn't, I have a gun, remember. We'll be fine," he insisted.

I wasn't so sure, but I sucked it up and followed him outside. "Which way do you want to go?" he asked.

I surveyed the area and started in the direction I wanted to go. Jonah snorted behind me and mumbled, "I should've known."

"Known what?"

"You'll see."

After walking a bit more, I turned and asked, "What's wrong with that rock?"

Instead of answering me, Jonah walked over to the rock and flipped open a hidden panel to reveal a keypad. He punched in some numbers and motioned for me to follow him to the other side of the rock. With his foot, he swept away a pile of leaves and uncovered a door. "Open it."

"Do I have stupid written on my face?" I trusted Jonah, but everything within me said opening a random door in the ground was not a wise decision.

"It leads to an underground bunker. Badger's

uncle was a prepper and had it installed years before Badger inherited the place. It's come in handy a time or two in recent years, so Badger keeps it stocked just in case it's needed."

I wasn't sure how a bunker could come in handy, especially more than once, but decided not to ask. Knowing Jonah, he wouldn't tell me anyway.

"Do you want me to go first?" he asked when I continued to stare at the door.

"Yes, please."

Surprisingly, he didn't give me shit about it. He just opened the door and climbed down the ladder. Against my better judgment, I climbed down after him.

"Holy shit!" I gasped.

I'd never seen anything even remotely close to Badger's bunker. I was expecting it to be similar to a storm shelter, but it looked more like a studio apartment. The place even had a shower and toilet.

"Not what you were expecting?"

"Not at all. You could live in here."

"Yeah, that was the idea—to be able to live in here for at least a year if necessary. Though I don't think Badger keeps it stocked with a year's worth of supplies anymore."

I looked around the bunker a little more before we climbed out. Jonah covered the door with leaves and used the keypad to lock it before we ventured off into the woods.

After walking for a while, we came to a fairly decent sized creek. The water didn't appear to be moving fast and I didn't see any rapids, but I could clearly hear the sound of rushing water.

"Do you hear that? The water?" I asked.

"Yeah, there's a waterfall a little ways down," Jonah said.

"Can we go? I want to see it," I said excitedly.

He grinned and reached for my hand. "Let's go."

The waterfall was gorgeous. The creek spilled down over several layers of rocks into a much wider creek at the bottom. "You know, I don't think I've ever seen a waterfall from the top."

"I've never really thought about it, but I guess you're right; most of the time people view them from the bottom."

"Are there any other—" I started, but Jonah cut me off.

"River, do not move. I mean it. Do. Not. Move," he said so sternly that I obeyed him without thought.

"Wh-why?" I whispered.

"Just keep your eyes on me. Everything will be okay if you stay calm and stay focused on me."

"Jonah, you're really freaking me out."

"I know, baby; I know, and I'm sorry. Just stay still for a little bit longer and keep looking at me."

My heart was pounding in my chest and it felt like I couldn't breathe. It was taking every ounce of my inner strength to stay still when all I wanted to do was jump into the safety of Jonah's arms.

I was on the verge of having a good old-fashioned meltdown when Jonah said, "Slowly, and I mean *slowly*, start walking to me."

I tentatively took one step and stopped. When he motioned for me to keep going, I took another step. "Good. Keep coming," he said.

Finally, I reached him and jumped into his arms. "What the hell was that all about?"

He placed me on my feet and turned me around. "Look right there," he said and pointed to the edge of the water. "That copperhead was slithering along and stopped right by your feet. He took his sweet ass time deciding to keep going."

"Holy shit! Those things are poisonous!" I

shrieked.

"No, they're venomous."

"What?"

"Snakes are not poisonous; they're venomous. Same with spiders and bees. Poison is ingested. Venom is injected. Didn't they teach you that in nursing school?"

"No, they didn't. But I did know that some snake bites require antivenom, so what you said makes sense. Can we go now? I think I've had enough of the great outdoors for the time being."

Jonah chuckled and took my hand. "Yeah, we can head back now."

CHAPTER THIRTY

JUDGE

I refused to tell River how we were spending our Saturday because I wanted it to be a surprise, and because I was afraid she wouldn't want to go.

"Uh, I have something for you before we leave," I said and handed her the two bags I'd managed to keep hidden from her.

She gave me a quizzical look, but took the bags. She reached into the first one and pulled out a pair of leather chaps. "Those go over your pants. You can slide the belt through the loop on your jeans, but you don't have to," I explained.

Without uttering a word, she reached into the other bag and pulled out a leather jacket. "I'm assuming you want me to put these on."

"Yes, and your boots."

"What if I didn't bring my boots?"

I grinned. "I know you did because I checked your closet before we left."

She shook her head and laughed. "I'll be right back."

When she came down the stairs in head to toe leather, I damn near dropped to my knees. The leather hugged every curve of her body in the most delectable way.

"I guess I don't need to ask if I look okay," she giggled.

"You look fucking hot. Come 'ere," I growled and yanked her to me so I could devour her mouth.

When she broke the kiss, we were both panting. "As much as I would love to continue this, I'm starting to sweat in places that shouldn't sweat."

With that, I locked up the cabin and we headed to my bike. We donned our helmets and climbed on. "I turned the Bluetooth on so we can talk," I said and felt her jump behind me.

"Fucking hell, Jonah! You scared the shit out of me!" she yelled and slapped her hand against my back.

I laughed. "Well, it's about a two-hour ride, so I thought you might want to talk."

"Works for me."

We chatted for most of the ride, which surprisingly didn't bother me. I usually liked to ride listening to nothing other than the wind and the sound of my bike, but I enjoyed having River's voice fill my helmet.

I pulled into the parking lot of the Harley-Davidson store and announced, "We're here."

"You drove two hours to bring me to a dragon Harley store?" she asked.

"Well, that's up to you. If we keep going, this road turns into what's known as the Tail of the Dragon, and I want you to ride it with me. But if you don't want to, we'll check out the store, grab some lunch somewhere, and go home," I said nervously.

"What am I missing, Jonah?"

I sighed. I had to be honest with her even if it meant she wouldn't go. "The Tail of the Dragon features three hundred and eighteen curves in eleven miles. It can be very dangerous if you don't know what you're doing."

"Do you know what you're doing?"

"I wouldn't have even contemplated bringing you here if I didn't," I answered honestly.

"Have you ever ridden it before?"

"I rode on the back of my dad's bike when I was five or six. That's the only time I've been."

I waited quietly while she mulled it over. I don't know if she spent all that time thinking or if she was trying to make me sweat it, but finally, she said, "I guess I'll give it a try, but if you get me killed, I will come back and haunt you any time you're about to have sex with someone."

I threw my head back and laughed. "I have no doubt about that." Once I stopped laughing, I asked, "You ready?"

She clapped her hands together and said, "Yep. Let's do this."

And we did. I'd been riding for many years and had a lot of experience under my belt, but I still took it slow. I wasn't there to test the limits of my bike or my skills; I was there to enjoy the ride with my woman.

I didn't turn on our Bluetooth because I didn't want any kind of distractions. The road was a bit busier than I expected, but we made it to the other end without incident.

I pulled into the parking lot of the iconic Tail

of the Dragon store and braced myself for River's response. She quickly climbed off the bike, removed her helmet, and started for the store.

"Where are you going?"

She looked back over her shoulder but never stopped moving toward the store. "To get a T-shirt. You coming?"

Twenty minutes later, River and I had matching "I survived the Tail of the Dragon" T-shirts. We rode the dragon three more times before we called it a day and leisurely made our way back to the cabin after we stopped for something to eat.

River walked inside and made a show of stretching. "I didn't realize riding would make your muscles so stiff and sore."

"Lucky for you, I have just the thing for that."

She laughed. "I'm sure you do, big guy."

"That's not what I meant," I said and grabbed her hand to pull her along behind me. I pointed to the six-person hot tub in the corner of the screened-in porch. "That's what I meant."

"Crap. I didn't bring a bathing suit, but I guess I could just wear a camisole and some shorty shorts."

I rolled my eyes. "Do you see anyone else here? You don't have to wear anything to get in.

I'm not going to," I said and started stripping off my clothes. Once I was completely naked, I stepped into the hot tub without hesitation and situated myself so I could watch River.

When I looked up, she was staring at me with her lips slightly parted. "See something you like?"

She blinked, and her cheeks flushed ever so slightly. "Yeah, you have a really nice ass. And I've seen a lot of bare asses. Yours is definitely one of the best."

I gasped and acted like she'd offended me. "One of? Have another look." I proceeded to stand and display my naked ass for her.

"I stand corrected; you have the best ass I've ever seen. But really, Jonah, fishing for compliments? I thought you were more confident than that," she said as she stepped into the water.

I whirled around and pulled her against me. "I'll show you confident," I said and covered her mouth with mine as I sank into the steamy water with her legs around my waist.

I leaned back in my seat and lifted her slightly to reposition her legs, but I inadvertently lined us up perfectly and my hard, bare cock slid right into her wet pussy.

"Oh, fuck," I hissed. I had never had sex without a condom, and she felt amazing. So amazing that I took a few moments to relish in the feeling before I gathered my strength to do the right thing.

I placed my hands on her hips and started to move her. "I'm sorry. I didn't—"

"Have you been tested?" she interrupted.

"Yeah, at my last physical. And I haven't been with anyone since," I told her.

"I haven't been with anyone since my last checkup and I'm on birth control, so it's okay, if you want to, uh, not use a condom," she said and looked down at my chest.

I gently tilted her chin up with my finger. "Are you sure? Because I'm not about to say no."

She smiled shyly. "I'm sure. I mean if you knock me up and leave me stranded, my brother will kill you and give me all your money."

I snorted and shook my head. "He wouldn't have to. You know I would never do that," I told her honestly.

"Yeah, I know," she breathed and pressed a soft kiss to my lips.

What started out as a mishap turned out to be one of the most profound sexual experiences of my life. Our bodies moved together slowly, deliberately. We took our time savoring every blissful sensation brought to life by each gentle caress.

With my hands in her hair, I brought her forehead down to mine. I needed her closer, needed to have her eyes locked with mine while our bodies said the words our mouths were too afraid to say.

"Jonah," she whispered and her chin quivered ever so slightly.

"River," I breathed and saw her eyes light up before we were both consumed with a pleasure so intense I felt lightheaded.

"Jonah," she said softly with a hint of concern in her voice. "We need to get out. We've been in here too long."

"You're right," I said and helped her step out of the hot tub. "But that's not what made you feel weak and breathless."

"Of course, it is," she said.

I grabbed several bottles of water from the refrigerator and followed her upstairs to the bedroom. "Why are you grinning like that?" she asked.

I tossed her a bottle of water. "Drink up, sweet cheeks. I'm about to prove you wrong."

CHAPTER THIRTY-ONE

RIVER

When we returned from our weekend at the cabin, I had to work Monday, Tuesday, Friday, and Saturday that week. I'd never cared about having to work the weekends before I met Jonah, but there I was not wanting to go to work because I wanted to stay with him.

What in the hell was I going to do when my time in Devil Springs was over? The agency I worked for had already called and asked me if I wanted to renew my contract for another year with them. Every other time they'd asked, I'd immediately said yes. This time? I told them I would have to think about it and get back to them.

Once I got to work, I forgot about not wanting to be there because we were extremely busy. To be a relatively small town, Devil Springs had a very active ER.

"We've got two en route from an MVA. You and Dr. Daniels will take the compound femur fracture while Dr. Alvarez and I take the head injury," Kennedy said.

"ETA?"

"Two minutes tops," Kennedy shouted as she hustled to the room designated for her patient.

I quickly moved to my room and started pulling out supplies I thought we might need. Broken bones used to really gross me out, but I had to get over it when I started working primarily in emergency rooms.

When the paramedics wheeled the patient into the room, I silently cursed to myself as they moved Roy Mayfield from their stretcher to our bed. Since Kennedy was busy with her own patient, there wasn't anything I could do except do my job for the next few minutes.

He already had an IV started and had pain

meds on board, so I hoped he wouldn't pay any attention to me, but I had no such luck. "You little fucking cunt," he sneered. "You better give me the good stuff and not try to stiff me like you did last time."

Dr. Daniels's head whipped around to me. "Do you know him?"

"Not exactly. He's my mother's boyfriend," I said.

"Was! I was her boyfriend! Until you killed her!" he screamed and tried to sit up but Dr. Daniels placed her hand on Roy's chest and gently pushed him down.

"Let's get him stabilized and then you and Kennedy can switch patients."

"Thank you," I said and breathed a sigh of relief.

"Mr. Mayfield, we're going to give you some medicine to help with the pain, but we're going to have to operate on your leg to fix it. Is there someone you would like us to call for you?" Dr. Daniels asked.

"Yeah, call my son. I need him to come get my shit. Are you getting my medicine? I want the good shit! You hear me?" he bellowed.

"We'll make sure you're taken care of, Mr. Mayfield. What's your son's name and phone number?" Dr. Daniels asked.

"You better or I'll sue every single one of you starting with that murderous bitch right there!" he screamed and jabbed his finger in my direction.

"River, maybe you better go ahead and trade with Kennedy," Dr. Daniels said and turned back to Roy. "How can we get in touch with your son?"

"His name's Oliver and his phone number is—" I heard as I left the room.

"Kennedy, Dr. Daniels said we needed to trade patients," I said without preamble.

"Why?" she asked.

I shrugged. "She didn't say and I didn't ask."

She removed her gloves and washed her hands. "She's pretty much stabilized. She thinks she hit her head on the driver's side window and may have lost consciousness for a few seconds. I've given her something for her headache. No other complaints. Vitals are good and she should be going for a head CT any minute now."

"You're getting a compound femur fracture. He was medicated in the ambulance, but I haven't given him anything since he arrived, though I think Dr. Daniels was entering orders for more pain medication when I left. Heart rate and BP are elevated. As soon as ortho gets here, he'll be going to surgery."

After I introduced myself and made sure she didn't need anything, my patient was taken for her scan. "Code Blue, Room Two. Code Blue, Room Two."

Son of a bitch. That was Roy's room. I grabbed the crash cart and ran to the room to help. Dr. Alvarez was calling out orders while Dr. Daniels slapped the pads on Roy's chest. We all watched the monitor for a heartbeat. Nothing. We followed the steps we all knew by heart but Roy never had a shockable rhythm and time of death was called.

"Cancel the ortho consult and see if the secretary got ahold of his son," Dr. Daniels told Kennedy.

"I can do that if you want to swap patients again," I offered.

"Don't worry about it. You shouldn't have to take care of him, dead or alive," Kennedy said.

When she couldn't get in touch with his son or find another family member to contact, I did help her take him to the morgue. "Let's make this quick. This place creeps me out," I said.

"Why? It's just bodies."

"Exactly my point."

We helped the attendant slide Roy's body

from the bed to the metal stretcher. Even though I knew it was going to happen, it still scared the shit out of me. As soon as we moved Roy's body, gasses shifted causing it to sound somewhat like he gasped.

"And I'm out," I announced and quickly fled the room because fuck that. Noises and movements from dead bodies were not on the list of things I could handle.

Kennedy emerged minutes later laughing her ass off. "I wish I had a picture of your face!"

"Shut it, bitch!"

She responded with her own version of the death gasp.

CHAPTER THIRTY-TWO

JUDGE

I was in my office trying to get ahead of the jobs I had scheduled so I could take some time off during the week to spend with River on the days she wasn't scheduled to work when I got a phone call from Copper.

"Where you at, brother?" he asked,

"In my office. Why?"

"Need to talk to you. I'll be there in a few minutes," he said and disconnected the call leaving me with an uneasy feeling.

When he arrived, he got straight to the point.

"Roy Mayfield was in a car accident last night and died at the hospital as a result of his injuries."

"What?" I shouted.

"Guess that means River didn't tell you," Copper surmised.

"No, she didn't. How'd you find out?"

He smirked. "I have my ways, but that's not the point. I also found out that Oliver Burgess is Roy Mayfield's son. So, we should be able to get our hands on the little shit in the next few days."

"Why does he have a different last name?"

"Fuck if I know. Does it matter?" Copper asked.

"No, I guess not." I sat back in my chair and rubbed the back of my neck. "Prez, doesn't it seem strange to you that basically every person we've been looking for over the past few weeks has turned up dead?"

Copper shrugged. "Oliver hasn't. Besides, it's not uncommon for people to overdose on heroin."

"Yeah, I guess you're right. So, what's the plan?" I asked.

"According to the information I was given, Roy was married. He has one son from a previous relationship, Oliver, and another son from his current wife. He also has a stepdaughter, which we met the day we were looking for Oliver and found Spring. Since he has a family, I'm thinking there will be a funeral."

"You want to grab him after his father's funeral?" I asked and acted like I was shocked when I was really just trying to poke the bear.

"Yes, I fucking do. He caused problems at my bar, he might be selling drugs in my establishment, and he helped his friend break into one of my rental properties who then had the audacity to die inside," Copper fumed.

"Easy, Prez. I was just fucking with you."

"Fucker. You'll pay for that," he laughed. "What're you doing here anyway?"

"River's working tonight. I thought I'd get some work done so I can spend some time with her on her days off during the week," I told him.

"When are you asking her to be your Old Lady?"

"Who said anything about that? She's only here for a few more weeks," I quickly replied.

Copper nodded and got to his feet. "No one needed to say anything. You took her to ride the Tail of the Dragon. I'll catch ya later, brother," he smirked.

I can't say I hadn't thought about her being my Old Lady because I had, more than I cared to admit. But she didn't have a life in Devil Springs. She only had a few weeks left on her contract with the hospital and hadn't said anything about wanting to stay in Devil Springs once it was finished.

I stayed in the office for several hours after Copper's visit, but I didn't get much work done. My mind kept wandering back to River and how much I wanted her to stay.

***

Someone banging on my door woke me. I sat up and glanced around my room, surprised that River wasn't asleep beside me. Actually, I was more surprised that I hadn't woken up when she got home from work.

I got out of bed and pulled my jeans on while the banging on the front door continued. "I'm coming," I yelled and then cursed hoping I hadn't woken River. She sometimes had trouble going back to sleep after a shift if she was woken up.

I yanked the door open to find Savior standing on my porch. "Copper wants you at the clubhouse."

"Why?" I asked over my shoulder as I

walked back to my room to finish getting dressed.

"Prez just said to get you to the clubhouse."

"He could've called me."

"He did."

I looked at the nightstand and realized my phone wasn't there. "Fuck! I must've left my phone at the office."

I quickly brushed my teeth, slapped on some deodorant, and ran a damp cloth over my face. I quietly opened the door to River's room to check on her before I headed out with Savior. When my eyes landed on her empty, perfectly made up bed, I whirled around to find Savior already heading to the front door. "What the fuck is going on?" I bellowed.

"Clubhouse," was all he said before he climbed on his bike and took off.

I hauled ass to the clubhouse and damn near laid my bike down when I recognized several bikes from Croftridge in the forecourt, particularly the bikes belonging to Dash and Phoenix.

I pushed through the front door and was met with a fist to my face. Without conscious thought, I pulled my knife from its sheath and held it to the neck of the motherfucker I'd just slammed against the wall.

In the blink of an eye, my blade was knocked from my hand and I was face down on the floor with a knee in my back. "Breathe, brother," Batta heaved in my ear.

"The fuck is going on?" I roared and tried to throw him off of me.

"You said you'd take care of her! You swore you wouldn't let anything happen to her!" Dash bellowed from across the room.

"Copper, get your boy under control. Dash, shut the fuck up and don't you dare move a muscle," Phoenix ordered.

I looked up to see Carbon's arms wrapped around Dash's upper torso holding him in place. I turned my eyes to my Prez. "What happened? I'm good. Just tell me what happened to her. Is she okay?" I spewed.

Copper nodded and Batta released me, though Phoenix did not give Carbon the okay to release Dash who was still actively struggling to free himself from Carbon's vice-like grip.

"She tried to call you. We tried to call you," Copper said and audibly swallowed. "River was arrested at the hospital this morning. She's being charged with second-degree murder," Copper said.

"What?!" I shouted in utter disbelief. "Who

do they think she murdered?"

"Brett Owens," Phoenix shared.

"That's not possible!" I insisted. "We've got to get her out of there! So help me, if something happens to her, I won't stop until every person involved has suffered the consequences!"

A familiar hand landed on my bicep. "Son, we're going to do everything we can, but you need to pull your shit together so you can help her, too."

"Mom," I croaked and choked back the sob that desperately wanted to escape.

She engulfed me in a comforting hug like only a mother can. "It's going to be okay, Jonah. Officer Dunk made sure she was placed in a cell by herself and I've already spoken with Judge Hinkley. He pulled some strings and will oversee her bond hearing first thing in the morning."

"She has to spend the night in jail?"

"She does, but Officer Dunk was able to arrange for her to have a trusted guard assigned to watch over her private cell," Mom reassured.

"I want to see her."

"You can't, baby. She can't have any visitors right now."

"Bullshit! I'm going to see her and nobody is going to stop me!"

Copper stepped in front of me and kept coming until his nose was touching my nose. "I'm stopping you."

"Step back, Prez," I growled through my clenched jaw. I was barely holding it together and if Copper didn't get the fuck out of my face, I was going to do something I was sure I'd later regret.

Copper didn't back down. "We've been friends for a long time, Jonah. You've always had faith in me. I'm speaking to you as your friend, not your President. Have faith in me now."

"She's my Old Lady," I declared.

"I know," he said and clasped my shoulder. "She's got the full support of the club."

I took a step back and nodded. Carbon had since released Dash, but was still standing in front of him ready to intervene if necessary. I surveyed the room full of concerned faces and asked, "Can someone tell me how in the hell this even happened? How did they come to the conclusion that River murdered Brett?"

Phoenix and Copper exchanged a look. At Phoenix's nod, Copper started explaining. "There's a lot of circumstantial evidence that links River to Brett. She dated him in high school and was recently involved in an altercation with him at Precious Metals. He was found dead in the house she was renting. She had two run-ins with Didi, who happens to be Brett's sister. Spring was found dead in Brett's trailer."

"And how did she supposedly kill him?" I asked.

Copper sighed. "Preliminary toxicology reports revealed Brett had fentanyl in his system. They're saying River stole the medication from the hospital and injected Brett with a large enough dose to kill him."

"She would never do something like that," I shouted.

"We all know that, brother. Not a single person in this room thinks she's guilty."

I took in a deep breath and silently counted to ten. It didn't do a damn thing to calm the rage burning inside me. My chest was violently rising and falling as I heaved in breath after breath. "You have got to be fucking kidding me! This is utter bullshit and we have to do something! Right fucking now!" I roared.

Batta put his hands on my chest and forced me to take a few steps back. "We know she's innocent and we're going to do something. Now, get your shit together so we can figure out the best way to help her."

"I can't believe this shit! Do we have a lawyer for her? And where the fuck is Kennedy? She should be able to help prove this isn't true."

"Pop made some calls and has a lawyer on the way to the clubhouse as we speak," Phoenix said.

"Kennedy's in Batta's room sleeping since she worked—" Copper started but was cut off when the clubhouse doors burst open.

Savior stepped inside and glanced around the room. "Uh, Prez, I need to speak with you outside."

"It'll have to wait. We're in the middle of—"

"It can't wait, Prez," Savior interrupted. "No disrespect, but it's urgent."

Copper's brows furrowed in anger, but he nodded and followed Savior outside, as did the rest of the Devil Springs officers. Coal was leaning against Savior's truck with his arms crossed over his chest, but he reached over to open the back door when Savior got closer. Savior reached into the truck and suddenly, Oliver Burgess was writhing on the ground in front of us.

"Picked him up at the gas station. Where should I put him?" Savior asked.

"You can't do this to me!" Oliver screamed.

Savior savagely kicked him in the ribs. "I

already told you to shut your fucking mouth. If I have to say it again, I'll sew that motherfucker shut."

"Get him to the farthest shed out back and keep his ass quiet. We're expecting company," Copper ordered. "And good work, brothers."

CHAPTER THIRTY-THREE

RIVER

I couldn't stop crying. As soon as I was led to my cell—MY CELL—I curled into a ball in the far corner of the room and sobbed. I was in such a state I couldn't even fully process what was happening.

I was walking out of the hospital with Kennedy when I was suddenly surrounded by police officers telling me I was under arrest for murder. *Murder*! I went to school to learn to save lives, not take them.

I immediately went into survival mode. "Call

Batta and go to the clubhouse," I told her. When she continued to stare at me in horror, I yelled, "Now, Kennedy! He'll know what to do." She took off running to her car as they were leading me to the police cruiser.

Being booked and processed was a complete blur. The only thing I could clearly remember was being able to make a phone call. I couldn't remember any phone numbers. Like everyone else, I was reliant on my cell phone and had never bothered to memorize Jonah's or anyone else's phone number.

"I don't know the phone number," I cried. "It's in my cell phone, but you took it and I don't know the phone number."

"It's okay, honey. I've got your phone. Whose number do you need?" a kind voice asked.

I looked up through my tear-filled eyes to see Officer Dunk with a sad smile on her face. "Jonah's," I croaked.

She let me try to call him three times before she suggested I try someone else. She gave me my brother's phone number, and thankfully, he answered on the second ring.

"Reed," I cried. "I need help."

"Raindrop? What's wrong? Where's Judge?" he asked in rapid-fire.

"I tried to call him, but he didn't answer. I've been arrested for murder, and I don't know what to do," I wailed.

"What?!" he bellowed causing me to cry harder. "Okay, okay. Stay calm and do not say a fucking word to anybody. Do you hear me?"

"Y-y-yes."

"I'm on my way. I might not be able to get you out today, but I will get you out. I'll get a lawyer to you as soon as I can. Do not answer any questions or say anything to anyone until your lawyer arrives. If anybody tries to fuck with you, you tell them you're with Blackwings MC. I'll be there soon. I love you," he said vehemently.

"Thank you, Reed. I love you, too," I whispered.

Luckily, I was in a cell by myself, but hours had passed and I hadn't heard from anyone. What was I going to do? It didn't matter that I was innocent. I was going to lose my job and possibly have my nursing license put in jeopardy.

I looked up when I heard my cell door slide open. Officer Dunk stood there with handcuffs dangling from one hand and an apologetic look on her face. "River, you have a visitor. I'm sorry, sweetheart, but I have to put these on you."

I wiped my nose with the back of my hand

and nodded. She waited for me to hold my hands out and loosely closed the cuffs around my wrists. I remained silent as she led me to a small room just a few doors down from where the cells were located.

"I'll be right outside the door. Just keep in mind, these rooms are under video and audio surveillance," she said and opened the door to the visitation room.

I was not expecting to see a familiar face on the other side of the table. "Leigh," I said and choked on a sob. "What are you doing here?"

"Oh, please don't cry. I'm not allowed to hug you and it's breaking my heart," she pleaded.

I raised my cuffed hands and tried to wipe the tears away. "I'm sorry. I haven't been able to stop crying."

"It may not seem like it right now, but everything's going to be okay," she said confidently.

"How can you say that? They think I murdered someone."

"I can say it because I know it's not true," she said simply.

I also knew it wasn't true, but I certainly did not think everything was going to be okay. "Why didn't Jonah come to visit?" I asked and hated how pathetic I sounded.

"You're not allowed to have regular visitors right now. Only your lawyer and your minister can see you."

My forehead wrinkled in confusion. "Which one are you?"

Leigh laughed. "It's an interesting story I'll be happy to share with you some time, but I'm your minister."

"I tried to call Jonah," I whispered.

"He knows, honey. He left his phone at the office and was beyond upset when he heard what happened to you. Your brother and some of the Croftridge club are here, too, but I thought it would do you some good to see a friendly face."

"It has. I'm so glad you came. I don't know what to do," I confessed and started to cry again.

"You're going to dig deep and find the strength to get through the next few days. I called an old friend, who's a judge, and he's agreed to take your case. Hopefully, the lawyer can get a bond hearing scheduled in a day or two. As soon as that happens, we'll post your bail and bring you home," Leigh promised.

"I'm going to lose my job."

"When are you scheduled to work again?"

"Tonight. Then, Wednesday and Thursday."

"I'll talk to Kennedy and see what we need to do. Maybe you'll only have to miss tonight."

I was already shaking my head. "They won't let me come back to work until I'm cleared of all charges. I will also have to be cleared by the nursing board. Not only do they think I killed someone, they think I did it with drugs I stole from the hospital."

"I know it seems like the end of the world right now, but I promise you it's not. You've got a whole lot of people who love you and are doing everything in their power to make this right for you."

I nodded and sniffled. "I just can't believe this is happening to me," I blurted and then I was consumed with anger. "I knew coming back to Devil Springs was a bad idea. I knew it with every fiber of my being. But, I've always tried to do what was right, and that meant fulfilling the contract I signed with the nursing agency." I shook my head and laughed derisively. "I didn't want to risk my career by breaking the contract, so I took the high road. But, no one told me the high road ended with me in jail and my career in the toilet. I worked so hard to get out of this place and away from my mother only to end up rotting away here."

Leigh remained silent while I had my meltdown. Finally, she said, "A bit of anger's good for you. It'll help you get through the next few days. But, you will not rot away in here; that I can promise you."

"I hope you're right," I whispered.

After that, Leigh stayed with me until my lawyer arrived. "You keep your head up, honey. I'll come see you tomorrow if you're not out."

"Thank you, Leigh. I can't tell you how much your visit helped me," I said honestly.

"Anytime, honey. You're family." When I opened my mouth to correct her, she shushed me and winked. "You will be."

As soon as Leigh exited, a petite woman wearing a perfectly tailored business suit entered the room. She couldn't possibly be my lawyer; she looked like she was a few years younger than me.

She took a seat and introduced herself. "Hello, River. I'm Tina Rivera, your attorney," she said and extended her hand.

I awkwardly extended my cuffed hands and attempted to shake hers. "How old are you?" I blurted and then gasped. "I'm sorry; I didn't mean to say that out loud."

She laughed. "It's okay; I'm used to it. I'm

thirty-two and have been practicing law for six years."

I shifted uncomfortably. "Well, you certainly do not look your age."

She smiled. "Thank you. Now, let's get down to business so we can get you out of here. All video and audio recording devices for this room have been turned off, so you can speak freely. Having said that, it is extremely important for you to be completely honest with me. In other words, if you did do it, you need to tell me. Understood?"

I quickly nodded and met her eyes, "Understood. I didn't do it."

She held my gaze for several long moments, but I didn't waiver or look away. I knew it was some sort of test, and I was not going to fail. With a curt nod, she said, "Good. Right now, our priority is getting you a bail hearing and convincing the judge that you're not a flight risk. From what I've been told, you don't have any prior convictions or arrests. Is that correct?"

"That's correct. I got a speeding ticket a few years ago, but that's it."

"Okay, the only thing I see being an issue is that you don't live in Devil Springs, because your trial is going to take longer than the few weeks left on your contract with the hospital. Now, I have no intentions of this case going to trial, but the judge isn't going to take that into consideration," she explained.

I didn't care if I had to move to Devil Springs and work at any job I could get, I would do whatever it took to get me out of jail as soon as possible, and I told her just that.

"We need to convince the judge that you're not a flight risk. Meaning, we need to show you have a future planned here—a long-term rental agreement, a serious romantic relationship, family in the area."

"That won't be a problem. Copper can give you a copy of the rental agreement and Jonah will attest to the seriousness of our relationship," I said knowingly. I didn't want to lie to the court, but I would, if it got me out of jail.

"All right, here's what we're going to do."

CHAPTER THIRTY-FOUR

JUDGE

Copper led the way to the shed containing Oliver. It was all I could do to contain myself. My girl had been arrested for a crime she didn't commit, and I had a feeling the little motherfucker tied to a chair had all the answers we needed.

"You two stay out here and keep watch," Copper told Savior and Coal. They both nodded, but the disappointment on Savior's face was clear.

"Batta, remove his gag," Copper said and

moved to stand directly in front of Oliver. "Got some questions for you, boy."

"Fuck you, cunt," Oliver said cockily and then spit in Copper's face.

Copper wiped his face with his hand and shook his head. "That was not a smart move, shitstain." He reached into his pocket and turned as if he was going to walk away, but suddenly he turned back and slammed brass knuckles into the side of Oliver's face.

"Fuck, Prez," Splint griped. "He can't talk when he's unconscious."

Copper removed his brass knuckles and wiped his face again. "He can't talk if he's dead either, and if he spits in my face again, I'll fucking kill him."

I was off to the side bouncing on the balls of my feet. I needed whatever information he had and I needed it yesterday. Bronze nudged Copper and cocked his head in my direction. Copper grimaced, "Sorry, Judge. Splint, wake him up."

Splint snorted. "I'll try," he said and pulled a small packet from his cut.

I waved him off. "I got this," I said excitedly. I had a new technique I'd been wanting to try for a while and this was the perfect opportunity.

"Batta, help me get his pants off."

"Say what now?"

"Just fucking do it," I snapped.

Being the good friend that he was, he did as I asked, but quickly stepped away when we were finished.

I ignored him and everyone else in the room while I put on a pair of disposable gloves and finished setting up.

"What in the actual fuck, Judge?" Copper asked.

"You know those videos where a man gets hooked up to a labor simulator?" I asked and held up the device in my hand. Then, I tapped the screen to send a jolt of electricity to the electrode attached to Oliver's shriveled ball sack.

Oliver's head shot up and he let out a high-pitched groan.

"Welcome back," I taunted. "Do you have anything you'd like to say?"

Oliver's eyes widened and he started trying to backpedal. "I'm sorry! I'll talk! Just don't—ahhh!" he screamed when I tapped the screen and sent another jolt to the electrode stuck to his taint.

"Tell me why you fucked with the security system at our rental property."

"That wasn't me!"

The room was filled with another scream when I increased the intensity and zapped his balls. "We already know it was you. Answer the question," I ordered and poised my finger over the screen.

"I don't know!"

Zap.

"Please, stop. I really don't know. Brett told me to do it. He didn't tell me why," he cried.

Zap.

"You're lying. So help me, I will keep going until your balls are completely fried if I have to."

"Maybe he needs a little more incentive," Batta suggested. I increased the intensity and simultaneously sent currents to both electrodes attached to him.

Oliver promptly screamed, then puked all over himself. He was panting and gasping through the tears and snot running down his face. "Okay, okay," he sobbed. "My dad's girlfriend paid me to do it."

I knew what he was going to say, but I had to ask. "Who's your dad's girlfriend?"

"Spring Lawson," he cried as he shifted and scooted around in the chair like he could somehow escape the electrodes.

"Why was Brett in the house?"

Oliver swallowed audibly and hung his head. "He was supposed to hide drugs in the house."

"Why?" I barked.

"It was a shit-ton of smack. Spring didn't want it to get stolen or to get caught with it," he spewed.

"So, she paid you to tamper with the security system so Brett could enter the house undetected and stash your junk. How the hell were y'all planning on getting it back?" I asked.

"Spring knew who lived there and knew her work schedule. She said she'd tell us when it was time to go get it."

I studied him for several minutes as I thought about what to ask next. Finally, I decided one question was more important to me than any others. "Did you know who lived there?"

"N-no. I asked once, but Spring wouldn't tell us," he said.

"Are the drugs still there?" Bronze asked.

Oliver grimaced and shook his head. "No. My dad made me go get it after Brett died."

"Bullshit! I redid the alarm after the police left. There's no way you got into that house," I roared and zapped him again.

"Ahhhh! No! No! Please!" he begged and

squeezed his eyes closed as he braced for more pain. "I ran in right after the officers left. I'd been watching the house and waiting for a chance to go in."

"How'd you even know about Brett?"

"He was supposed to go get a baggie or two from the stash. When he didn't come back or answer his phone, I went over to see what was going on. I saw them bringing someone out in a body bag and knew it was Brett. He never could wait to get his fix."

Batta took my place and wrapped his hand around Oliver's throat. "You're answering the questions; I'll give you that. But you're not telling us everything. Start fucking talking or I'm gonna put that shit on full blast."

Oliver sucked in a shaky breath and visibly shuddered. "My dad was Spring's dealer, until she became his girlfriend so she could get her shit for free. A few weeks ago, my stepmother went out of town and Spring thought my dad was with her. Spring was pissed when she found out and stole some of his product. She said she didn't do it, but it couldn't have been anyone else besides her. Dad told her not to come back without the product or the cash to replace it. She replaced it and told us to hide the rest. I don't know where it came from. I swear I don't know!" he blubbered.

"Where's the product now?" I asked.

Sheer terror washed over Oliver and he started frantically shaking his head. Batta raised the device and wiggled it in front of Oliver's face. "My ass! It's in my ass!" he screamed.

Batta tossed the device to me and stepped away with his hands held up in surrender. "No fucking way, Prez. I love this club, but I am not getting that out of his asshole."

Copper covered his mouth with his hand as he tried to stifle a laugh. Bronze, however, didn't even try to mask his amusement which resulted in the entire room erupting in laughter. "Relax, Batta, no need to open the vault," Copper said and doubled over with laughter.

Any other time, I would've been laughing right along with them, but my girl was in trouble and we were clearly missing something. I rubbed the back of my neck. It seemed like most of the pieces were there, I just couldn't put them together. I paced the room, well aware of all the eyes on me.

"What are the drugs in?" Splint asked. When Oliver looked at him clearly confused, he added, "Before you, uh, put them in your body, what did you put them in?"

"A condom," Oliver said quietly.

"Thought so. Uh, Prez, we need to get him to the hospital. If that condom breaks, and we all know how easily that can happen, we'll have a body to deal with."

"Fucking hell," Copper cursed. "Someone was trying to steal your drugs. You hid them in your ass. They attacked you when they couldn't find them. You gonna stick to that story or do I need to send you to the hospital without a tongue?"

"I'll stick to that story," Oliver promised.

"If you don't, what happened here today will be like a trip to the spa compared to what I'll do to you," Copper said in a low and menacing tone.

"Have Coal and Savior drop him at the ER. If anyone sees them, they can say they found him stumbling around on the side of the road and stopped to help," Copper announced.

The brothers started to clear out while Coal and Savior started untying Oliver. They were about to help him to his feet when a thought suddenly occurred to me. I fixed my eyes on Oliver and said, "Didi Warren."

His head turned to me and it was clear he knew the name. "What about her?"

"Who is she to you?" I asked, choosing my words carefully.

"She was my cousin's best friend."

"And who's your cousin?" I asked.

His head dropped and his shoulders slumped. "Her name was Paisley, but she's dead, just like everybody else," he said sadly. For a moment, a very brief moment, I almost felt sorry for him.

"Spazz," I called out.

"Already on it," he said as his fingers pecked away at his phone. Seconds later, he had the information I wanted. "Paisley Ellison died from a drug overdose twelve weeks ago. She was twenty years old. According to another article, she died the day before she was supposed to enter a rehab facility. Apparently, her mother is on the county council and has made numerous statements criticizing 'the lack of actions being taken to address the county's rapidly growing opioid crisis,' her words, not mine."

"I didn't realize we had an opioid crisis in Devil Springs. I mean sure, there's always been some drugs floating around here, but I don't recall there ever being many overdoses in this area."

Spazz nodded in agreement but continued to study his phone. "I'm going to go see what else

I can find. Hopefully, something that will help River," he said.

"Thanks, brother," I said and clapped him on the shoulder.

Once he left, I realized I was alone for the first time that day and I didn't know what to do with myself. Every unoccupied second was filled with worry for River. Was she okay? Was she in a cell by herself? Was she hurt? Was she scared?

I felt completely helpless. She was my woman. I was supposed to protect her, take care of her, comfort her, love her, and I couldn't do any of those things. "Fuck!" I roared as I sent the empty storage rack crashing into the opposite wall.

CHAPTER THIRTY-FIVE

JUDGE

The morning of River's bail hearing we packed the courtroom. Mom and I were in the front row with Dash, Kennedy, and Batta. The rows behind us were filled with the Devil Springs Blackwings and the majority of the Croftridge Blackwings.

We sat quietly while we waited for the proceedings to begin. Tina entered the courtroom and walked to her designated seat without so much as a glance to anyone else in the room.

A middle-aged, balding man in a suit

entered shortly after Tina and took a seat at the prosecutor's table. Unlike Tina, he surveyed the room on the way to his seat and then turned around to take another look once he was seated.

A door on the far side of the room opened and River was led into the room. She looked awful. Her skin was pale and she had dark circles under her eyes. The orange jumpsuit she was wearing hung on her body like a sack. She kept her eyes on her feet as the bailiff escorted her to the chair beside Tina.

I hoped she would look up once she got closer, but she didn't. I desperately needed her to look at me, so I cleared my throat loudly. Her head shot up and she gasped when she saw the room filled with the Blackwings. Her eyes moved to her brother for a brief moment before they came to me. And my heart broke when she started to cry.

It was out before I could stop it. "Don't cry, baby; everything's going to be okay."

She nodded once and straightened her spine before she turned to face the front of the room and take her seat beside Tina.

Moments later, Judge Hinkley entered the courtroom and wasted no time calling the court into session. I fully intended to pay attention to every single word that was uttered, but I couldn't stay focused. My mind was consumed with what ifs and possible outcomes.

Mom elbowed me in the ribs and whisper-yelled, "Pay attention, son."

"Your Honor, my client has no previous criminal charges, she's not a flight risk, and she's not a danger to the community. She's cooperated every step of the way and will continue to do so. She has no intention of leaving Devil Springs as evidenced by her signed rental agreement and her employment contract. She also has family nearby and a fiancé in Devil Springs," Tina stated.

Judge Hinkley nodded and shuffled through the papers in front of him. He removed his glasses and peered at River before redirecting his gaze to the room. "I would like to remind everyone that we are not here today to prove innocence or guilt. We are here to determine if bail is appropriate. And while a lot of points are in your favor, Ms. Lawson, you are being charged with one count of second-degree murder. But, I do believe there are many various factors to be considered in this case. Are you willing to surrender your passport, wear an ankle monitor, adhere to a curfew, and refrain from working in an environment where you would have access to controlled substances until these charges have been settled?"

"My client does not have a passport, Your Honor, but agrees to the other conditions," Tina quickly answered.

Judge Hinkley nodded. "In that case, along with the previously mentioned conditions, bail is set at one million dollars. This court is adjourned," he said and banged his gavel.

River turned around with wide, tear-filled eyes. "Jonah," she croaked. "I don't have that kind of money."

"It's okay, baby. I'll get it, and we'll have you home in no time," I reassured her.

She nodded and gave me a weak smile, but I could tell she didn't believe me. As the bailiff led her away, I kept my eyes on her until I could no longer see her. Once she was out of sight, I faced my brothers. "If the club can front me the money, I'll sell my house to replace the funds."

Before Copper could respond, Phoenix stepped forward with Dash by his side. "No, you won't. I'll take care of it."

"I appreciate it, Phoenix, but I can't let you do that," I insisted.

"You can and you will. That's a direct order," Phoenix said and clapped me on the shoulder.

"Now, if you'll excuse me, I need to figure out who I need to speak with so we can get your girl home."

With that, he walked away while I stared at his back in disbelief. "Why do you look so shocked?" Copper asked. "This is exactly what the club is all about—having each other's backs."

"The club's going to lose one hundred thousand dollars, Prez. I don't feel right about it and River won't either."

Copper snorted. "The club's not losing any money. He's bailing her out, not bonding her out. She's innocent and as soon as the charges are dropped or she's found not guilty, the money will be returned. And don't forget, you haven't officially claimed her yet, so while you feel like this is on you, he's actually doing it for Dash, technically speaking."

"You kinda suck at pep talks, Prez," I grumbled.

Copper shrugged. "I tell it like it is and that won't ever change."

***

The entire process took hours. I didn't expect it to be immediate, but it felt like everything was working against us. The powers that be wouldn't even start working on the paperwork until the bail was paid. And, it's not as simple as writing a check for one million dollars. Once the money was paid, they started on the paperwork, but then stopped for lunch. After lunch, they finished the forms, but then it was one thing after another, and I was barely hanging on to the last bit of patience I had.

Finally, fucking finally, the door to the right of the reception desk opened and River stepped out. "Jonah," she cried and ran right into my waiting arms. With her arms circled around my shoulders and her legs wrapped around my waist, she buried her face in my neck and broke.

I was already on edge, and her state did not help settle me in any way. After several minutes, I had to know. "Did someone hurt you or do something to you?"

I felt her head move, and she whispered, "N-no. Nothing like that happened. I just...I might never let go of you again."

Although I was relieved by her answer, I remained tensed and ready to strike at anyone or anything that may pose a threat to her.

"Son, maybe it would help if we got her out of here," my mother softly suggested.

"Yeah," I croaked and carried my girl out of her nightmare and into the light of day.

Dash led the way to one of the club's SUVs and opened the back door for us. I didn't even attempt to put her down; I just climbed inside with her still wrapped around me.

"Do you want to go home or to the clubhouse?"

She sniffed and rubbed her nose on my shirt. "Home, then clubhouse," she whispered.

"Did you just wipe your snot on me?" I teased.

"No," she said a little louder before she did it again.

"Ewww! Gross! Stop wiping your snot on me!" I shouted and started tickling her.

She squealed and slapped at my hands. "Stop! Stop! Please!"

"Are you going to wipe your nose slime on my shirt again?"

"Nooo! I promise. Please, stop! I'm going to peeeee!" she shrieked through her laughter.

"What did I ever do to deserve this?" I asked in mock surprise.

She sat back and wiped the tears from her face. "Thank you," she said softly. "I needed that."

"I know," I said and placed a soft kiss on her lips. "But, really, are you okay?"

She sighed. "Physically, yes, I'm fine. Emotionally? Mentally? No, I'm not okay."

"Talk to me."

"I don't even know what to say, Jonah," she said and shook her head. "Even though I'm innocent, this is going to ruin my life. I'll never be able to pay back the money the club used to get me out. Especially since I won't be able to work as a nurse until the charges are cleared. Then, I'll have to go before the nursing board to get my license reinstated. On top of all that, I'll have to pay a huge fine for breaking my contract with the agency."

"You don't have to pay back any money. The club will get it back when the charges are cleared. As for your license, it might be a pain in the ass, but you'll get that straightened out, too. Have Tina look over your contract with the agency and see if there's a clause or maybe even a loophole that can be used to help you. It's going to take some time, but I will not let this bullshit ruin your life."

"You're a good man, Jonah Jackson. I don't know what I would've done if you weren't here to help me through this."

I grinned. "Lucky for you, you'll never have to find out."

Dash cleared his throat in a loud and obnoxious manner. "Are you ready to acknowledge the rest of the world, sister dearest?"

She turned in my lap and took in the other occupants of the SUV. With a loud gasp, she covered her mouth with her hands. "I'm so sorry!" Then, she turned back to me and slapped my chest. "Why didn't you tell me they were all in here?"

I reached out and cupped her jaw as I smoothed my thumb over her cheek. "Because the only thing that mattered was having you in my arms." She leaned into my hand and closed her eyes. When she opened them, I told her what I had been wanting to tell her for a while. "You know I love you," I said softly.

Her eyes closed again while her lips curved up in a soft smile. I felt some of the tension leave her body before she opened her eyes and said, "I do. And I love you, too."

Leaning forward, my hand slid from her jaw to the nape of her neck as my lips took hers. I wanted to devour every inch of her, and would have if her brother and my mother weren't there, which I was reminded of when Dash grumbled, "Will y'all save that shit for when I'm not around to witness it?"

"Sorry, brother," I replied, even though I wasn't the least bit sorry.

CHAPTER THIRTY-SIX

River

Jonah and I were dropped off at his house so I could shower and change clothes before we went to the clubhouse. As much as I wanted to take my time and enjoy the hot water washing the jail filth from my skin, I took a quick shower, pulled my wet hair into a messy bun, and pulled on my favorite jeans and the first clean shirt I found since my time was limited thanks to my court-ordered curfew. While it was inconvenient—and mildly humiliating—I wasn't going to complain because having to be home by nine o'clock at night was much better than being in jail.

Jonah was sitting on the couch looking at something on his phone when I appeared in the living room. "That was fast. I assumed you would want to take a long shower."

"I did, but I didn't want to waste time," I said and pointed to the bulky monitor encircling my ankle. "But I plan to take a long, hot bath as soon as we get back."

With that, we climbed on his bike and headed to the clubhouse. There were more bikes in the forecourt than usual and I assumed those belonged to the members from the Croftridge chapter. As we walked to the door, I studied the bikes and quickly found the one that belonged to Reed.

I startled when "Welcome back!" and various cheers were shouted as I entered the clubhouse. The common room was packed full of smiling faces—some were familiar while others were new to me.

My hand flew to my chest as I took in the room. I wasn't sure how to react. While it was a kind gesture that I wholeheartedly appreciated, being arrested and bailed out wasn't something I wanted to celebrate.

Leigh picked up on my discomfort immediately. She stepped forward and took my hand in hers. "We just wanted you to know that we believe in your innocence and will do whatever we can to help. And, you know, we all need to eat."

I breathed a sigh of relief and smiled. "Thank you. I'm just, uh, I guess I'm a little overwhelmed by everything."

"And that's perfectly understandable," she said kindly. Then, she turned around to face the group gathered in the common room. "Y'all go find something to do and give the girl some room to breathe," she ordered.

To my surprise, the crowd dispersed. "There we go. Now, let's get you something to eat. I hear jail food is horrendous."

I absently rubbed my stomach. "It looked disgusting, but I was too upset to eat much of anything."

She nodded in understanding. "I'm the same way. I carry all of my stress in my stomach. Do you feel like eating anything now? We've got plenty to choose from, but if there's something particular you'd like, I'll be happy to make it for you."

I eyed the various dishes and plates of food

set out on one of the tables. "No, no, what's here is great." I grabbed a plate and started loading it with food. I really wasn't hungry, but I didn't want to call any more attention to myself by not eating.

Jonah joined me at the table, as did my brother, Copper, and another man who looked a lot like Copper. "River, this is Phoenix," Jonah said. "He's the President of the original chapter of Blackwings. He's also the one who posted your bail."

Phoenix extended his hand to me, but I stood and moved around the table. The man had just paid one million dollars to free me from jail; he deserved much more than a handshake. I didn't hesitate to hug him. "Thank you," I said softly.

"You're welcome, River," he said and patted my back. "You better get back to your seat before your man makes a very unwise decision."

I turned to find Jonah glaring at Phoenix. "Seriously, Jonah? You need to wipe that look off your face and get your ass over here to hug him, too," I blurted causing the table to erupt in laughter.

"Yeah, I like her," Phoenix chuckled while Jonah gave me a look I could only describe as a mix between shock, pride, and desire.

Copper pulled his phone from his pocket and held it to his ear. "Yeah," he said and paused. "Let her in." He disconnected the call and said, "Tina's here."

"What? Why?" I blurted. I knew I would have to meet with her at some point, likely multiple times, but I hadn't expected it to be so soon.

"To start working on your case," Jonah said. "The sooner, the better." Well, I couldn't argue with that. I wanted this nightmare to be over more than anyone. I still couldn't believe that I had been arrested for murder. I wasn't sure that would ever fully sink in.

Tina arrived looking like the quintessential no-nonsense lawyer, which was quite comical with her standing in the middle of a biker clubhouse. "Hello, everyone," she greeted and turned her attention to Copper. "Are we doing this here or would you prefer somewhere more private?"

"Here's good. You hungry?" he asked and gestured toward the food table.

"I may get something when we're finished, but I'd like to go ahead and get started now."

"Go right ahead," he said and went back to his food.

"Basically, here's the deal. Gwendolyn Ellison

is Chairman of the Ritch County Council. Her daughter died from a drug overdose a few months ago and she has been aggressively pushing for changes in the laws and punishments related to illegal drugs. The current district attorney is up for reelection this year and Gwendolyn has enough power to influence voters, so the DA is trying to stay in her good graces by actively pursuing any and all drug related charges," Tina explained. "Or that's what he wants her to believe. He's clearly letting a junior prosecutor or one of the paralegals review the cases and give the okay to file charges, because anyone with his experience would've realized how weak the case is against you."

I wanted to believe what she was saying. I wanted to fully exhale for the first time since I'd been arrested and sag with relief. But I couldn't, or wouldn't. Not until I heard the words from the judge's mouth.

"I feel confident I can get the charges dropped, but I need to ask you a few questions and gather some other information before I make a formal request."

"What do you need to know?" I asked.

We spent the next two hours going over my whereabouts and activities since I'd arrived in

Devil Springs. Unsurprisingly, most of the time I was at work or asleep, but thanks to Jonah's home security cameras, I could be accounted for even when I was home alone during the time surrounding Brett's death.

Tina had already received the hospital's narcotic count records for the recent weeks which showed there were no instances of missing medications, particularly fentanyl. She was also working on getting documentation from the hospital to prove that fentanyl was not routinely stocked or used in the ER. Even though I worked in the hospital, it wasn't a medication I readily had access to. In fact, I couldn't recall ever giving it to a patient in any form other than a transdermal patch in all my years working as a nurse.

"How much do you know about fentanyl?" I asked.

Tina didn't hesitate to answer with the truth. "Only what I've seen on the news recently."

"I think there is a gross misunderstanding of fentanyl thanks to the media. The actual drug is not the killer it's made out to be. Sure, any medication has the potential to be deadly when misused; acetaminophen is a perfect example, but, the 'fentanyl' that's being mixed with heroin and other recreational drugs is usually a fentanyl analog that was either created in an unregulated lab by underground chemists or one that was legitimately created for a different use. Like carfentanyl. It's intended for use as an anesthetic for extremely large animals like elephants. My point is these drugs aren't found in a hospital."

Tina was steadily taking notes as I spoke. "This is exactly the kind of information I need. Tell me everything you know about these kinds of drugs."

Because of my mother's addiction and my need to understand why she was the way she was, I'd done several research papers and projects based on addiction or the effects of illegal drug use, so I had a lot of information to share.

When I was finished, Tina looked up from her notes and asked, "Would you be interested in being a consultant for me for any cases involving healthcare related topics?"

Her question completely caught me off guard. "I'm sorry, what?"

She laughed. "Would you be interested in being a consultant? I generally don't have a lot of cases where healthcare comes into play, but I would love to have someone with your knowledge base to call on if the need arose. You'd, of course, be compensated for your time."

"Um, once all of this is over, if I still have a nursing license, I'd love to," I said carefully. I didn't want to give my word and not be able to fulfill my end of the agreement.

"You'll have a license. As soon as the charges are dropped, I'll notify the nursing board and send the necessary documentation. This isn't the same process as being tried and found not guilty. You were arrested and charged for a crime without sufficient evidence. Truthfully, they should've brought you in for questioning first. If they'd done that, you never would have been arrested. Speaking of, how would you like to handle that?"

"Are you asking me if I want to sue, uh, whomever for my arrest?"

"That's exactly what I'm asking."

"Oh, no. I just want things to be exactly like they were. I want my nursing license to be in good standing, I want to be able to work at the hospital, and I want to be able to finish working out my contract with the agency without a penalty. Oh, and I want every penny of my bail to be returned."

"Are you sure?" she asked seemingly surprised by my answer.

"Yes, I'm sure. Filing a lawsuit will only take time and resources away from more pressing matters. If my life can be restored in the next few days, I'm willing to look at this as a bad vacation," I said and then a thought suddenly occurred to me. "I want the officers, particularly the detectives, to have some additional training on fentanyl, fentanyl analogs, and other associated designer drugs."

Tina beamed at me. "That's a great idea. I know it hasn't been for you, but it's truly been a pleasure meeting you, River. I'm going to head back to my office and get started on some paperwork, but I'll be in touch with you first thing in the morning," she said and extended her hand.

"Thank you for everything. I didn't see how this could possibly turn out good for me, but you showed up and took the weight of the world off my shoulders," I said and shook her hand.

She smiled shyly. "I was more than happy to help. I think everyone around here calls him Pop, but Tommy Black was a legend in the courtroom. He'd already retired by the time I was in law school, but he came to the campus for a seminar during my first year. I arrived at the auditorium hours before the first lecture to be sure I got a front row seat. During a break, I tracked him down like the crazy fangirl I was and introduced myself. I made a complete idiot of myself, but he was unbelievably kind to me. We exchanged emails and he ended up becoming somewhat of a mentor for me. When he called and asked me for a personal favor, it was a dream come true."

I didn't know exactly who she was talking about, but I nodded and smiled like I did. "Well, I'm glad there was a silver lining for both of us."

CHAPTER THIRTY-SEVEN

JUDGE

It killed me to do it, but I left River's side so she could speak with her lawyer in private. I didn't think she had anything to hide from me, but I thought it would be easier for her to speak freely without me present, and I must have been correct in my assumptions because she didn't ask me to stay.

I couldn't bring myself to go far at first, so I claimed the empty seat at the table with Batta, Bronze, Spazz, and Splint which was only two tables away from River and Tina.

"Any updates on our little friend?" I asked.

Bronze and Batta laughed while Spazz and Splint groaned in disgust. "Turns out he'd actually swallowed the condom, so he had to spend the night in the hospital until things worked out on their own," Bronze said and cleared his throat. "He was arrested for possession." He held up his hand as he tried to stifle his laughter. "But they couldn't charge him with intent to distribute!"

I arched a brow. "How long have you been waiting to say that?"

"He hasn't," Splint answered. "That's the fourth fucking time I've heard it."

We shot the shit for an hour or so, but eventually, Batta left when he received a call from Kennedy, Splint had to go to work, Spazz said he needed to get back to whatever he was doing on his computer, and Bronze disappeared after receiving a text message. So, I picked up my empty beer bottle, tossed it in the trash, and joined Copper, Phoenix, Dash, and Coal.

"Tell me again why we picked a lawyer who looks younger than me," I said without preamble.

Copper glared at me while Phoenix snorted. "Because she's who Pop recommended. And she is older than you, but she's often underestimated because of her looks," Phoenix answered.

Copper's glare didn't relent so I held my hands up in a placating manner. "No disrespect intended, Prez. I'm grateful as fuck for everything you've done for River. But I'm not gonna lie, she looks like she just graduated from high school and my woman's future, hell my future, is on the line here."

Phoenix stood from his seat and rounded the table, which, admittedly, had me worried for a moment. "And another one bites the dust," he laughed as he clapped me on the shoulder before walking over to talk to Savior.

"Your woman?" Dash asked with an arched brow.

Fucking club politics. "I'm not asking for your permission because you weren't even on speaking terms with her until two weeks ago and that was because of me." I pushed back from the table and rose to my feet, fully prepared to physically defend myself and my woman if need be.

Dash placed his beer on the table and also stood. "So, you're telling me you're claiming my sister with or without my permission? Even if that means putting your patch on the line?"

I didn't even have to think about it. "Fuck, yes, that's what I'm saying. I love her, with every breath of my being, and if this club doesn't support that, then this isn't the club I thought it was," I stated vehemently.

Suddenly, I realized I was heaving in breath after breath and the room had fallen silent, but I didn't take my eyes off of Dash, who was currently the enemy in my eyes.

River appeared in my periphery and placed her hand on my back in a futile attempt to calm me. "Are you fucking serious right now, Reed Brook Lawson?"

A look of shock washed over Dash's face for a split second before he masked it and completely ignored the fact that she blasted his middle name in front of the packed clubhouse. "Yes, my little pain in the ass sister, I'm fucking serious right now. If he didn't have the balls to stand up to me or anyone else in this club then he couldn't claim you. But he did, so congrats, brother," Dash said and extended his hand. When I extended mine, he grabbed it and pulled me in to slap me on the back.

River scoffed and placed her hands on her hips. "Did either one of you cavemen consider asking me what I thought about all this? I mean, if I'm going to be 'claimed,' shouldn't I at least be given the chance to agree or disagree?"

I wanted to laugh because I knew exactly what she was doing, but I wasn't going to give her what she thought she wanted. No, she was going to get what she needed.

I quickly turned and slid one arm around her waist while I brought the other up and wrapped my hand around her jaw. Tilting her chin up so her eyes met mine, I told her how it was. "No, you're not getting the chance to agree or disagree because it doesn't matter. You're mine and everybody fucking knows it. Now, tell me what I want to hear."

She narrowed her eyes for all of two seconds before she licked her lips and winked. "I love you, Jonah Jackson."

I hoisted her into my arms. "Yeah, you fucking do. And, I love you, too," I said before I covered her lips with mine.

"In case y'all missed it, River's my Old Lady," I announced to the room with River still in my arms.

The guys lifted their drinks into the air and cheered. Then, my mother appeared out of nowhere with the biggest smile on her face. I knew what was coming, so I placed River on her feet. "Welcome to the family, River," Mom said and pulled River in for a hug while she mouthed,

"Grandbabies," to me over River's shoulder.

I chuckled and shook my head. "I thought you'd already gone home."

Mom waved her hand dismissively. "And miss all this? You know better than that."

"Mom, I don't want you overdoing it. I'd feel better if—" I started but was cut off by an unexpected guest.

"I'm taking her home now," Dean said. "She said she had a feeling something like this was going to happen and didn't want to miss it, but she promised to let me take her home as soon as it did."

And right there before my very eyes, my mother blushed and was suddenly tongue-tied. "Yes, that's exactly what I said, so we'll just be going now. River, you be sure to call me if you need anything. And please know, I love my son with all my heart, but don't put up with any shit from him. He was raised right and I don't want all my hard work to go to waste, you hear?"

River laughed. "I hear you, Leigh, but I don't think you have anything to worry about. Your son's a good man; one of the best I've ever known."

"Thank you, sweetheart. I haven't seen him this happy in a long time. Well, you two behave and be sure to call me in the morning," she said and hugged River again before turning her attention to me. She reached up and placed her hand on my cheek, "Your father would be so proud of you. You've grown up to be the kind of man we wanted you to be. I love you, Son."

"I love you, too, Mom." I pulled her in for a hug and kissed the top of her head while I swallowed thickly several times in a weak attempt to keep my emotions under control. "I'll talk to you in the morning."

After Mom and Dean left, River spent the rest of the evening talking with Dash and Phoenix. I tried to be patient and give her the time she needed, but I was desperate to get her home. I had an uncontrollable urge to lock her in my house where she'd be safe and no one could take her from me.

Walking up to her from behind, I slid my arm around her waist and pulled her back against my chest. "It's getting late, so we should probably get going."

"Oh, yeah, I guess you're right. I didn't realize how late it'd gotten."

"Are you guys heading back to Croftridge tonight?" I asked Phoenix while River was saying goodbye to Dash.

"Yeah, gotta get back to Annabelle and the babies," he said with a proud smile. "Tina should be able to take care of everything from here on out, but don't hesitate to call if you need me. Shaker's always looking for an excuse to put that chopper in the air."

"Thanks, Prez," I said sincerely and turned back to River. "You ready?"

"Yep," she said with a smile and returned to my side.

I extended my hand to Dash. "Catch ya later, *brother*," I said causing him to laugh.

With that, we climbed on my bike and I took my girl home.

CHAPTER THIRTY-EIGHT

RIVER

I woke to an empty bed. And when I glanced at the time on my phone, I knew why I was alone; it was almost noon. Even though I'd slept for close to thirteen hours, I felt groggy and sluggish, but I forced myself to get out of bed.

I stumbled to the kitchen and clumsily made myself a cup of coffee. "I was wondering when you were going to wake up," Jonah said from behind me causing me to scream and spill what was left in my mug.

"Holy shit," I gasped.

"Sorry, I didn't mean to scare you," he said apologetically.

"Why'd you let me sleep so long?"

He shrugged. "I figured you probably didn't get much sleep the night before and needed it."

"Shit! Tina said she'd call me today," I said and moved to retrieve my phone from the bedroom, but Jonah stopped me.

"I've already talked to her this morning," he said and grimaced causing my heart to sink.

"Just tell me," I said and braced as best I could for whatever he was going to say.

"She just said there'd been a new development and things might take a little longer than she'd originally thought, but not to worry."

I scoffed. "Yeah, right." A new unknown, at least to me, development that was going to make clearing my name take longer was most certainly something that was going to make me worry.

"I know it's easier said than done, and she does, too. She said she'd call this evening with an update."

I looked at him curiously. "Why aren't you at work?"

He slid his thumbs into his belt loops and rocked back on his heels. "Because I'm the boss," he said cockily.

I sighed. "I don't want my mess to disrupt your life any more than it already has."

"I know, but I didn't want to leave you here alone all day. I can't do it every day, but I can occasionally work from home," he said and then his face lit up. "This is completely up to you, but I could use some help at the office. It's nothing much, just answering phones and helping with invoices, maybe ordering some equipment, but it'd give you something to do during the day, and I'd pay you."

I quickly mulled it over. It wouldn't be a bad idea for me to generate some income. After all was said and done, there was no guarantee that I'd be allowed to resume working at the hospital to complete my contract with the agency. "I'll do it on one condition; you'll pay me whatever you'd pay anyone else to do this job."

He held out his hand for me to shake. "Deal," he said with a small smile. "Do you want to start this afternoon or wait until tomorrow?"

I knew he was trying to keep me busy so I wouldn't have time to dwell on the new development or the whole situation in general. "Tomorrow. I need to make some phone calls, which I'm sure will result in more phone calls," I explained.

"You don't need to do anything. Tina will take care of anything you need."

"I know, but I want to call the agency and speak to my manager myself. I've worked for them for almost four years, and I think they deserve to hear from me. Plus, I need to find out exactly who to notify since I'm licensed in one state, the agency is in another state, and the arrest occurred in this state."

"Why do you need to report anything? You've only been charged with a crime, not convicted."

"Most states require a nurse to report criminal charges to the board so they can begin their own investigation."

"That doesn't seem right. How would they're investigation be any different from a criminal investigation?"

"I can't think of an example off the top of my head, but not being convicted of the crime you were charged with doesn't automatically mean you didn't violate another law or regulation pertaining to your license," I explained.

He nodded. "Well, I'll leave you to it. I'll be in the office if you need anything," he said and kissed my forehead.

I was grateful for the privacy he gave me because I had no idea what I was going to say.

I didn't want him watching me fumble over my words while I begged and pleaded for my job.

By the time I finished my last phone call, I was emotionally exhausted and felt like I didn't get anything accomplished. If I was being honest, I was a little hurt, too. When I spoke to my manager with the agency, she informed me she was already aware of the situation and was in the middle of completing my termination paperwork. She also told me she would mail everything to my attorney, including the final amount of penalties owed.

"You okay?" Jonah asked as he entered the kitchen.

I sighed and sagged in my chair. "Yeah, I'm fine, I guess. Things didn't go as well as I'd hoped."

"What happened?" he asked and took a seat beside me.

I shook my head. "The agency terminated my contract," I said and exhaled slowly. "Please don't take offense to this, but I really don't want to talk about it right now."

"Okay, we won't talk about it," he assured me before getting up and rummaging through the cabinets.

When he continued loading the countertops

with what looked like baking supplies, I asked, "What are you doing?"

He winked at me over his shoulder. "We're going to bake shit that's really bad for us while we have a movie marathon."

"Jonah," I breathed on the verge of tears. For the entirety of my adult life, no one had taken care of me except for me. I couldn't even begin to find the words to describe how much it meant to me to have someone like him by my side.

"You have five minutes to decide what we're watching. If I don't have it, order it or whatever, but your chance to pick expires in exactly five minutes," he said and glanced at his watch, "starting...now."

I bolted from the kitchen and grabbed the remote. I already knew what I was going to choose, so I made my selection and returned to the kitchen with two minutes to spare.

"You want to start with cookies or brownies?"

"Brownies, please."

Once the brownies were in the oven and the timer was set, we curled up together on the sofa and I started the movie. I thought he'd figure it out right away, but he didn't until the title was displayed and his reaction was not what I expected.

"If this is what you want to watch, baby, I won't complain, but I will spank your bare ass if you tell anybody I watched a movie about sparkly vampires with you."

I laughed. "No, this isn't what I want to watch. I mean, they are good movies, but I picked something I thought we'd both enjoy," I said and selected the movie I did want to watch.

Jonah kissed my cheek. "Good choice. I've only seen the first one and it's been a while. Wait, do you actually want to see this or do you just want to gawk at Paul Walker?"

I grinned. "I want to see it, and I want to gawk at Vin Diesel."

In between movies, we put a batch of goodies in the oven. Jonah would get up when the timer went off and return to the living room with a plate of warm goodies and a fresh glass of milk. I'm not sure if it was due to sugar overload or sheer exhaustion, but I fell asleep not long after the third movie started.

CHAPTER THIRTY-NINE

JUDGE

When I noticed River had fallen asleep, I fully intended to move her to the bedroom, but I'd fallen asleep as well and was startled awake by my phone blaring close to midnight.

"Yeah," I answered groggily.

"Need you to come to the clubhouse. Grant's coming to stay with River," Copper said.

"Fuck," I grumbled. "I'll be right there."

I normally didn't mind being woken up and called to the clubhouse in the middle of the night, but normally, I could've brought my girl with me and let her sleep in my room while we dealt with club business. Since her bail stipulations included a curfew, taking her with me wasn't an option.

"What's going on?" River asked sleepily.

I scooped her into my arms and carried her to my bedroom. "Copper needs me at the clubhouse, but he didn't say why. Grant will be outside while I'm gone, and I'll be back as soon as I can," I said and softly kissed her lips.

"Be careful. I love you," she said with a yawn.

"I love you, too," I said and kissed her one more time. "I'll see you soon."

Grant pulled into my driveway as I was backing my bike out of the garage, but I didn't stop for pleasantries. I gave him a chin lift as I passed and headed for the clubhouse wondering what kind of hell was awaiting me.

I walked into Church and went straight to my seat before looking around the room. When my eyes landed on two somewhat familiar faces, I sucked in a sharp breath. Why in the hell was Oliver's stepsister at the clubhouse with her baby in the middle of the night? And was her cheek red and swollen?

Splint, Spazz, and Tiny entered the room

moments later and took their seats without a word. Copper snorted and shook his head, but didn't call them out.

"Sorry for the late-night call. This is Mackenzie Moore and her daughter, Brinkley," Copper introduced. "She's Oliver's stepsister and Roy's stepdaughter, but more importantly, she came to the clubhouse to ask for protection for herself and her daughter."

That had us all straightening and leaning forward on our elbows. "From what?" I asked.

Copper gave Mackenzie an appraising look as he rubbed his chin. "She won't say until we've agreed to help her. Now, y'all know how I feel about helping damsels in distress, but I thought this warranted a club vote."

He said it like he despised helping women, when we all knew good and damn well it was the opposite, so he either knew something we didn't or he was trying to see if she'd cave.

She didn't cave, not exactly. She sniffed and took in a shaky breath. "It doesn't have to be both of us, but it has to be Brinkley. I can't let anything happen to her."

"Does this have anything to do with Oliver?" I asked and slapped my palm on the table causing her to flinch. The baby stirred in her arms, but thankfully, didn't wake. I held my hands up in surrender. "I'm sorry. I didn't mean to scare you."

"It's okay," she said softly. "I'm still a bit jumpy."

I glared at Copper who was leaning back in his seat with an unreadable expression on his face. He glanced around the room and asked, "Well? What's it going to be, brothers?"

"You fucking serious, Prez?" Batta blurted and made no attempt to hide his disdain.

"Hold on a minute," I said and tried to keep my voice neutral. "You never answered my question."

I watched her carefully as she shifted in her seat and glanced down at the bundle of pink in her arms. One lone tear slid down her cheek while she chewed on her bottom lip. Whatever it was, it was enough to make her fear for her child's life, as well as her own.

"She's got my vote," I announced. The vote moved around the table and unsurprisingly, every brother voted to help the girl and her baby.

"Protection granted," Copper said. "Now, who are we protecting you from?"

"I'm not sure," she whispered.

I pinched the bridge of my nose in a weak

attempt to keep my frustration to myself. Copper sighed loudly while the rest of the brothers looked on in confusion.

Bronze leaned forward and met her eyes. "Listen, sweet cheeks, we're here in the middle of the night and we're willing to help you. But, if you don't start talking, that offer will expire in about two minutes."

Her eyes narrowed and her lips pursed. "My name is Mackenzie. Not 'sweet cheeks'."

"Noted, sweet Mackenzie. Talk," Bronze returned.

She huffed and rearranged the little girl still peacefully sleeping in her arms. "I try to keep to myself and stay away from my family because most of them are into drugs and other stuff, and I want no part of that. But I've always been a sucker when it comes to my younger brother, Tristan. His dad just died, and he asked if he could stay with me for a couple of days. Him and Mom haven't always gotten along, and I figured things were probably pretty bad over there, so I let him stay. Then, my stepbrother, Oliver, was arrested. I guess Mom told him Tristan was staying with me and gave him my phone number because he called my house. I didn't know it was him at first, because Tristan answered the phone, but I thought it was strange when he kept talking because no one should've been calling my house to speak to him. So, I listened to his end of the conversation and I think I heard something I wasn't supposed to hear. Tristan knows I overheard it, but I don't know what any of it means."

"What makes you think you weren't supposed to hear it? If Oliver called from jail, that conversation would've been recorded and anyone could hear it," Copper told her.

"Because he said, 'You really should've minded your own business,' before he slapped me a few times and shoved me into Brinkley's room so hard I fell. I got up and went for the door, but he did something to it so I couldn't get out. He said he'd deal with me when he got back. When I heard him leave, I climbed out the window with Brinkley and started making my way here," she explained.

"Why'd you come to us?" Copper asked.

"Because I'm not stupid. I've lived in this town long enough to know the Blackwings aren't the bad guys. Plus, you guys were looking for Oliver, and it sounded like Tristan was involved in whatever got Oliver arrested."

"Tell us what you heard," I said trying to

sound calm.

"He was really mad about something Oliver lost. He kept saying asshole and slamming his fist on the counter. Then, something about not being able to finish the job he was paid for and that someone, I think his boss, was going to be pissed when she found out."

"I see," Copper said. "And where does Tristan work?"

She shook her head. "He doesn't. He hasn't worked in months. That's one of the things him and Mom fight about."

"All right, this is what we're going to do. You and Brinkley are going to spend the night here at the clubhouse in one of the empty bedrooms. We have one of those pop-up baby beds we'll get set up for you. Do you have everything else you need for her for tonight?"

She nodded quickly. "Y-yes, I do."

"Is there anything you need from your house?"

Her eyes widened, but she shook her head.

"You sure? Because we're going over there to get your brother and we can grab a few things for you."

"Uh, my purse and keys should be hanging by the front door. If you happen to see my cell phone laying around, it'd be nice to have it. And, um, a pair of shoes if that's not asking too much."

"Not a problem. Brothers, we're riding out in five. Mackenzie, come with me; my woman, Layla, will get you and Brinkley settled into a room for the night. Don't leave the clubhouse for any reason whatsoever until one of the men in this room has told you it's okay," Copper said and led her from the room.

I glanced around at my brothers. "What in the actual fuck do you think this is about?"

Batta shrugged and tried to hide his grin. "Don't know, but I bet we'll find out soon."

When Copper returned, we headed out to the forecourt. He pointed to one of the Suburbans Phoenix had given to the club and we all groaned. "Quit being bitches and get in. We can't roll up on seven bikes in the middle of the night and catch him by surprise."

When we pulled up to the house, there was a car parked in the driveway and a few lights were on. I walked around to the back of the house and noted that all windows were closed, meaning he'd been back to the house and was probably still in there. Using one of the stupidest tricks in the book, we lightly knocked on the front door.

The front door swung open. "Knew you'd be back, bitch."

"Damn. I was hoping to surprise you," I said as I wrapped my hand around his throat and stepped into the house.

He gasped and flailed, but we quickly had his arms and legs bound and a gag in his mouth. As soon as we gathered the few items requested by Mackenzie, Batta hoisted Tristan over his shoulder and tossed him in the backseat.

"Are we just that good or are these fuckers getting dumber?" Batta asked. "Because that shit was too easy."

I laughed and clapped him on the shoulder. "I think it's a little of both, brother."

Batta studied Tristan for a few moments. "Do you know what we did to your brother?"

Tristan's eyes widened comically and he started shouting something behind his gag. Batta laughed. "Sorry, I didn't catch that. Oh, you want to know why they call me Batta. It's simple, really. I like breaking bones with my bat." Tristan's muffled cries became louder as he thrashed on the seat. "Calm down, boy. I'm not the one you need to be worried about. See this fucker right here. We call him Judge. Want to know why?"

Tristan shook his head frantically and yelled into his gag. Batta chuckled darkly. "Because he's a good judge of character. He can tell anything about a person—if they're lying, if they've reached their limit," he paused and lowered his voice to almost a whisper, "by the sound of their screams."

"If he pisses himself, you're cleaning it up," Copper shouted from the front.

"Oh, shit! I almost forgot," Batta exclaimed and pulled something from underneath the seat. He maneuvered his big body so he could lean over Tristan. When he was finished, Tristan was wearing an adult-sized diaper over his jeans. Batta smiled proudly. "Piss away, pussy boy."

I couldn't hold in my laughter. "I can't believe you did that."

"What? It's genius. I can scare the shit, or piss, out of him and I don't have to clean it up."

"Batta! Is that why Evelyn dropped off an industrial size box of those at the house and told Layla she was happy to help?" Copper demanded.

"Well, she has a membership to that new wholesale club, and she gets a senior citizen discount," Batta explained and we all burst into laughter.

We went straight to the shed when we arrived

back at the clubhouse, and I wasted no time getting started. "Listen, I'm fucking tired and so is everyone else in this room. Are you going to tell us what we want to know, or are you going to make me work for it?"

His face scrunched and I realized what he was about to do. "You fucking spit on me and I'll burn your tongue off with a hot branding iron." He paused and swallowed carefully.

"Prez, I say we get some sleep and see if he's more receptive to conversation in the morning," I suggested.

Copper nodded. "Sounds good. Tell Grant to come back to the clubhouse when you get home. He can guard Tristan for the rest of the night."

With that, I went home to my girl.

CHAPTER FORTY

JUDGE

I returned to the clubhouse bright and early the next morning hoping Tristan's fear had enough time to fester. During my experience in the Marines, as well as the club, I'd learned one thing was almost always true—people wouldn't talk unless they were scared. And he would be scared if he had any sense because not only was he locked up in a clubhouse full of pissed off bikers, I'd spent the night thinking of various ways to make sure he told us everything he knew.

It was fairly early when I arrived, so I was surprised to find Coal in the common room with Brinkley perched on his lap. "Morning, brother," I said and eyed him curiously.

He smirked and shook his head. "Don't look at me like that. Savior's on guard duty this morning and since I was already up, I tagged along. Figured there would be a lot going on this morning."

"Anybody else here yet?" I asked.

"Copper, Layla, Bronze, and Spazz are here, but I think they're still asleep. Grant crashed in one of the empty rooms, and Savior's with our guest.

"How'd you end up with the baby?" I asked.

He opened his mouth to answer when Mackenzie came through the door that led to the kitchen carrying a tray with three or four plates of food. I immediately got to my feet and took the tray from her. "Thank you," she said softly.

"She offered to cook breakfast, so I offered to watch Brinkley while she did," Coal said.

"I need to grab the coffee. You guys go ahead and dig in," Mackenzie said and darted back to the kitchen.

I was trying to decide if I should give him some advice or let him make his own mistakes when he took the words right out of my mouth. "You don't need to say anything. Nothing other than me being a nice guy to a girl who's having a rough time is going on," he said with a smile. "And I like kids. Isn't that right, Princess Brinkley?" he cooed causing Brinkley to erupt in a fit of baby giggles.

Mackenzie returned with the coffee and a huge smile on her face. "If you keep that up, I'll be asking you to babysit all the time. She rarely laughs like that with anyone other than me."

Coal chuckled. "Biker babysitter is definitely not what I pictured when I decided to move here."

Mackenzie laughed lightly. "I would never ask that of you. Truthfully, I don't have a need for a babysitter. If I can't take her with me, I don't go."

I was curious about the baby's father, but my attention shifted when Copper and Layla entered the room. "Food!" Layla squealed in delight and reached for a plate.

"Mornin', Prez," I said.

"Morning. I thought your ass would've woken me up hours ago."

"I wanted to, but some things can't be rushed," I said cryptically and shoveled a forkful of food into my mouth.

"We'll get started as soon as everybody else gets here," Copper said.

"Great," I said and went to the kitchen to get another plate of food.

Twenty minutes later, we entered the shed to find Tristan exactly how we left him—tied to a chair wearing a gag and a diaper.

I turned my head from side to side to crack my neck followed by my knuckles and yanked the gag from his mouth. "I don't have the fucking time or patience for any of your shit. Tell me what I want to know and I won't hurt you."

He stared at me for several long beats before his face morphed into a snarl. "Fuck you! I ain't telling you shit!"

I grinned maniacally. "Have it your way." With that, I grabbed his thumb and yanked it back until I heard a satisfying snap followed by his shrill scream.

"Fuck!" he screeched. "Why'd you do that?"

I gave his other thumb the same treatment before I answered. "I did *that* because you're being a disrespectful little shit. Tell me what you and Oliver talked about."

He grimaced and pressed his lips into a thin line. "No?" I asked and sighed as placed a large bowl of ice water on the table.

"What did you and Oliver talk about last night?" I asked again, but he wouldn't answer. I held his hands in the bowl of freezing-cold water while he screamed. Batta took a few light swings at his arms and legs. But still he refused to utter a word.

As much as I hated to admit it, I knew we'd reached the point where we were pointlessly torturing him, and that's not what we were about.

I stepped beside Copper and kept my voice low. "Prez, we can do this all day long, but he's not gonna talk."

Copper looked down at his phone. "Guess it's a good thing our backup plan just arrived."

"Just give me one second," I said and walked back to the table with a plate of food. "You hungry?" I asked.

Tristan eyed the plate of scrambled eggs, grits, and bacon. "I'll just leave it right here in case you decide you want to eat," I said and placed the plate in front of him before heading for the door.

Grant was waiting outside the shed door looking tired as hell. "Check his restraints and replace his gag. We won't be long," Copper told him as he passed.

We'd made it no more than twenty feet from the shed when we heard a shrill scream followed by gagging and grunts of pain.

"What the fuck did you do, Judge?" Copper asked.

I grinned. "I seasoned his breakfast with a Carolina Reaper."

Copper whistled low and shook his head while trying not to laugh. "Oh, fuck me, that's a good one."

"Prez," Grant called out from behind us sounding worried. "Should I..? Is he...? Uh, I mean—"

"Let him be. If he chokes or stops breathing, call Splint," Copper said.

"Yes, sir," Grant nodded and closed the door to the shed.

We walked into Church to find Coal sitting with a woman who looked like she'd seen better days a long damn time ago. She was the stereotypical woman who refused to acknowledge her age and ultimately made herself look far worse by wearing animal print leggings, a tight, lowcut black shirt, gold jewelry everywhere, way too much makeup, big, poofy hair, and a horrid spray tan.

Copper extended his hand to the woman. "I'm Copper Black. And you are?"

"Mitzie Mayfield," she huffed. "Shouldn't you know that?"

Copper ignored her and directed his attention to the rest of us. "Brothers, this is Tristan's mother, Mitzie Mayfield. I invited her to the clubhouse to see if she'd be willing to chat with us regarding her family's recent activities," Copper shared.

Mitzie sat back in her chair and made a show of adjusting her breasts while she smacked and clicked her gum. "Yeah, sure, I'll tell you whatever you want to know, as soon as I'm compensated."

Copper pulled out his wallet and placed five one-hundred dollar bills on the table. "Will that be enough for your troubles?"

She quickly took the money and narrowed her eyes. "Not for what you're wanting to know."

"How about you name your price so we can get on with it instead of wasting time with this back and forth bullshit?" I snapped.

"Fifty thousand dollars."

I opened my mouth but shut it when Copper held his hand up. "Fine. Fifty thousand dollars," he agreed.

"Prez," I protested.

"Shut the fuck up, Judge. Bronze, grab a check from my office."

Bronze returned with a check and I watched in disbelief as Copper made it out to Mitzie Mayfield for the amount she requested. He placed it in the middle of the table, but kept one finger on it while he spoke. "You can have this once we've heard what you have to say."

She leaned back, crossed her legs, and continued to obnoxiously smack her gum. "Well, see, all this shit started when Roy met that whore, Spring. I mean, he always liked to have his fun on the weekends with his drugs and his whores, but I didn't give a shit because it kept him out of my hair, you know? But that bitch, she just wouldn't go away. Well, when I found out he'd been giving her shit for free, I put a fucking stop to it. He can fuck whoever he wants, but his money's mine. Well, she didn't like that, so she convinces him to start selling, so she can still get hers without paying. And she got away with it until his dumbass got arrested."

She paused and pulled an e-cig from the depths of her cleavage. "You mind if I vape?"

Copper waved his hand dismissively. "Go ahead."

She sucked on the contraption and blew out a plume of berry-smelling vapor. "So, I had to call my brother to get the money to get him out of jail, which was this huge thing because he didn't want his wife to find out. Well, Roy got arrested two more times, so she did find out and threatened to stop paying for my house. So, I told Roy he needed to get out and make it look like we were getting divorced. Told him he could shack up with his little whore until my sister-in-law calmed down. We was just staying together for the sake of the kids anyway."

It was all I could do to maintain the blank expression on my face. Was she serious? For the kids? All three kids were grown, and I knew for a fact one had moved out years ago.

"Well, the shit hit the fan when my niece died. You would've thought I killed her myself with the way my brother and his wife were carrying on. They cut us off from everything, even after I kicked Roy out. Said some shit like 'If we weren't part of the solution, we were part of the problem.' I'm an understanding person and all, so I waited for a few days after the funeral to talk to them. Told them I wanted to be part of the 'solution'." She sucked in another lungful of vapor and exhaled exaggeratedly. "You know, blew some smoke up their hoity-toity asses."

"So, they said they believed me and everything went back to normal. But then, my sister-in-law shows up at my house and tells me the only way she'll keep paying my way is if I got Roy to get her some heroin. Said she'd make sure we didn't get into any trouble with the cops and she'd even give us some extra cash for our troubles. But I didn't want Roy to know about any of it because I didn't want Spring trying to get her hands on my money, so I asked my son to do it."

"Tristan?" Copper asked.

"Yeah, but I told him I wouldn't pay him if his dad found out. So, he says he'll do it and comes back with a brick. I gave him some money and he took off with his friends. So, I call my sister-in-law and tell her I did what she asked. Well, she says she needs me to hold on to it for a few weeks. So, I put it in my panty drawer for safe keeping."

I wanted to scream at her to get to the point. I couldn't take much more of her gum-popping and vapor-sucking.

"Now, here's the part that just pisses me right the fuck off. While my sugar daddy took me away for the weekend, someone stole the smack that wasn't even mine! So, I took all the money I could find from Tristan's room. Well, he comes home and he's pissed because his money's gone. He tells me he couldn't possibly have told his dad because no one's seen him in over a week. That's when I knew it was Spring. So, I told Tristan to go find his father and get it back from her. I don't know what Tristan told Roy, or what they did, but Tristan came back with most of it."

"There better be more to this story," Copper growled.

Mitzie leaned back and smiled smugly. "There is, but that's what you get for five hundred dollars. Judge me all you want, but I'm not as stupid as I pretend to be. What fucking idiot accepts a check for a bribe? You would've canceled it the second I stepped out the door."

"I'm not giving you fifty thousand dollars," Copper stated.

"Then, I'm not telling you anything else."

"Pretty sure you told us everything we need to know," Spazz said and looked up from his laptop with a small smirk on his face.

"Tell us what you got, brother," Copper said with a grin.

"Mitzie Mayfield nee Ellison is the sister of Paul Ellison who is married to Gwendolyn Ellison, the current County Council Chairman. The same Gwendolyn Ellison who has the district attorney under her thumb, and is on a crusade to clean up the streets of every town in Ritch County by whatever means necessary," Spazz said proudly.

Copper leaned back and rubbed his chin. "Well, sounds to me like you and your sister-in-law just landed in a heaping pile of shit. Doesn't matter why she wanted the heroin, you helped her get it. And because it was laced with fentanyl, it's been linked to four deaths, including your husband's."

She grabbed the check from the table and took a flying leap for the door. Batta caught her in midair and unceremoniously dropped her into a chair. "Don't even think about trying that shit again."

She took that to mean scream for help at the top of her lungs. "Fuck this shit!" Copper roared. "Gag her and get her ass out of here."

As soon as she was out of the room, Copper leaned back in his chair and tilted his head skyward. "We need to choose our next step very carefully, brothers, and I don't have the first fucking clue what it should be."

"Call Tina," Bronze suggested. "Make sure she knows you're speaking to her as a client so the attorney-client privilege will apply."

"Any objections?" Copper asked.

When no one objected, he pulled out his phone and placed a call to Tina.

CHAPTER FORTY-ONE

RIVER

I briefly woke when Jonah returned home in the middle of the night, but was able to go back to sleep after he crawled into bed with me. However, it was a different story when he left moments after the sun had started to rise.

Once I was up and moving, I didn't know what to do with myself, and I quickly became restless. All I could think about was the possibility of spending the rest of my life in jail. For longer than I care to admit, I seriously considered gathering my resources, cutting off the ankle monitor, and going into hiding for the rest of my life. I was weighing my chances of making it to the bunker at the cabin when my phone rang.

I looked at the screen and saw my brother's name, but I didn't answer. I was rapidly spiraling into a dark place which left me with no desire to speak to anyone. As I stared at my phone, the call went to voicemail. Moments later, a text message appeared on the screen.

Reed: Hi Aunt River!

Seconds later, a picture of my little niece appeared on the screen. As I took in her dark hair, big, blue eyes, and chubby cheeks, I found myself smiling. I could see a lot of Reed's features in her.

I continued staring at her picture for a long time before I decided I needed to do something to keep my mind from traveling further down the dark and depressing path it was on. Thinking that some physical activity might help with my overall mood, I cranked up some music and started cleaning Jonah's house.

Since his house was already pretty much clean, I had everything except his office spick-and-span within two hours. I'd just started a load of laundry and dropped onto the couch trying to think of something else to do when someone knocked on the door.

I sighed in exasperation and contemplated not getting up to answer it, but quickly changed my mind when I heard Leigh's voice after another round of knocking. "It's me, sweetie. I hope you're decent because I'm coming in."

I opened the door as she was starting to put her key in the doorknob. "Leigh, what're you doing here?" I asked and motioned for her to come inside.

She smiled. "I came by to see if you would help me with something."

I was suddenly concerned. "What's wrong? Are you feeling okay?"

She waved her hand dismissively. "Oh, it's nothing like that. I'm absolutely fine," she reassured me. "When Jonah decided to have a house built, he told me how much he was dreading having to make all the decisions about the interior. So, I wanted to see if you wanted to help me do some of it for him as a surprise."

I hesitated, unsure of how to answer her and she must have read the uncertainty on my face. "Trust me; if someone doesn't do it for him, that house will be fifty shades of boring. His other house looked exactly like this one—no decorations, no paint, no color."

"Maybe he likes it that way," I suggested.

Leigh laughed. "Oh, honey, if you're worried

about stepping on his toes, don't be. He's mentioned hiring someone to do it for him several times. I asked him what he had in mind for the interior, and he said he didn't care as long as it looked nice. Well, then he added that he didn't want flowers and pink shit all over his house."

"Well, I guess it wouldn't hurt to tag along. It's not like I'm doing anything else today," I said. "Let me go change and I'll be ready to go."

I grabbed my keys and headed for the front door. "Ready."

"Do you mind if we take your car? I'm not really supposed to be driving just yet."

"Sure," I said and headed to the garage. I backed out and noticed the empty driveway. "Uh, Leigh, where's your car?"

"At home. I had a friend drop me off." Before I could comment, she asked, "Do you know how to get to his new house?"

"Not a clue."

She entered the address and I followed the robotic directions across town to Jonah's future home. To say I was surprised would have been a vast understatement.

We turned down a driveaway almost completely hidden by the surrounding trees. It led to several open acres with a massive two-story, country-style home situated near the front portion of the property. I noticed a barn in the distance as well as a small pond before my attention returned to the house.

"It's gorgeous," I breathed. It had light tan siding with black shutters, but the best part was the porch that wrapped around at least three-fourths of the house.

"Wait 'til you see the inside," Leigh said and pushed open the front door.

She was right; the inside was breathtaking and would be even more so after it was decorated and filled with furniture. I started upstairs and walked through the house taking in room after room until I made it back to the kitchen where Leigh was waiting for me.

"Don't get me wrong, because this house is amazing, but why does he need so much space?" I asked.

Leigh gave me a small, almost sad smile. "There's a couple of reasons for that. I know my boy wants to have kids someday, but I think he also wants to have plenty of room available in case someone needs it."

My brows furrowed in confusion. "I'm not sure I understand what you mean by that."

"When Jonah was fifteen, not long after we

lost his dad, my niece and nephew came to live with us after they lost their parents. Duke was eighteen, but he stayed with us for a few months. Harper was only ten years old at the time. Anyway, you've seen my house, there was plenty of room for them. Even Trey lived with us for a year or so at one point." She chuckled, "Come to think of, even Copper and Bronze had a room at my house, though they never officially lived there."

"Wow. Not many people would open their homes to others so willingly."

"Well, Duke and Harper were family. Copper's and Bronze's mom, Goldie, was one of my best friends, so her boys were like family. And my other best friend was Trey's mom, Nicole, so again, her son was my son," she said solemnly. Then, she clapped her hands and got to her feet. "Enough of that. Let's get to work."

I hadn't noticed the size of the purse she was carrying until she pulled a laptop, two notebooks, and several pens from its depths. "Which room should we start with?"

We worked for hours picking out everything from cabinet pulls and light switch covers to wall colors and window treatments. And not once did I think about my current situation. Until my phone rang.

CHAPTER FORTY-TWO

JUDGE

Tina dropped everything she was doing and came straight to the clubhouse. She walked into Church with a serious yet concerned look on her face.

"I have to say I was quite surprised by your phone call. What's going on?"

Copper placed his elbows on the table and leaned forward. "Before I say anything, I need to be sure this conversation falls under the attorney-client privilege. Will that be a problem since you're representing River?"

Tina didn't hesitate to answer. "For all intents and purposes, I'm the club's lawyer, so there's no conflict of interest."

Copper grinned. "Perfect," he said and proceeded to tell her everything.

Tina listened quietly, occasionally jotting something down on a notepad. When Copper finished, she sat back in her chair and met his eyes. "Well, this is going to cost you."

Copper threw his head back and laughed as did the rest of us in the room. "Send the final bill to the clubhouse and I'll make sure it's taken care of," Copper told her.

She looked at her notepad and started reading over her notes while biting down on the pen in her hand. I wasn't sure if that was something she normally did, but I got the feeling it was a nervous habit, which did nothing to quell my unease.

"I believe everything you've told me, but we're going to need proof to support these allegations."

"I recorded the conversation we had with Mitzie," I informed her.

Tina's reaction was not what I expected. "In this state, only one party has to consent to the recorded conversation, which I assume will be you, but we can't use it unless we can prove it's actually Mitzie on the recording."

I placed my phone on the table and played the first part of the recording for her.

"I'm Copper Black. And you are?"

"Mitzie Mayfield. Shouldn't you know that?"

"Brothers, this is Tristan's mother, Mitzie Mayfield. I invited her to the clubhouse to see if she'd be willing to chat with us regarding her family's recent activities."

Tina smiled broadly. "That'll work. I'll need you to email the recording to me."

"Not a problem," Copper said. "What next?"

Tina's smile disappeared. "Unfortunately, to make sure this is handled correctly, it's going to take some time, which means you'll have to release Mitzie Mayfield."

"She'll disappear," I blurted.

Tina arched an eyebrow. "Perhaps there's some way to make sure that doesn't happen," she said suggestively.

Copper nodded knowingly. "There is. What about Tristan?"

"We need Mackenzie to file charges against him. One of you went over to check on her this morning which led to a physical altercation started by Tristan. It will be an obvious case of domestic violence and self-defense. He'll be arrested and out of your hair," Tina said simply. "Anything else?"

"What about River?" I asked. Surely, the new information would clear her name.

"I'm going to handle River's case completely separate from this one. I have enough evidence to get her charges dropped without the new information you provided."

After Tina went back to her office, Copper called Savior into the room. "I've got a new assignment for you, brother."

"Whatever you need, Prez," Savior answered automatically, almost robotically.

"I need you to escort Mitzie Mayfield to her home, and then I need you to stay with her until I say otherwise. Do not let that woman out of your sight."

"By whatever means necessary?" Savior asked. Copper rubbed his chin while giving him a quizzical look, but Savior didn't waiver. "I was referring to restraints, Prez."

Copper nodded. "Yeah, restraints are fine."

With that, Savior left and Copper called Coal and Mackenzie into Church. "Are you willing to press charges against your brother for assaulting you?" Copper bluntly asked Mackenzie.

"Yes," she answered immediately.

"You sure?"

"Yes. He shoved me so hard I lost my balance and fell. Brinkley was in the floor playing and I almost landed on her. I've put up with a lot of shit from him, but I draw the line when it puts my child in danger."

"Will it be a problem for you to say it happened today instead of last night?"

"No, sir," Mackenzie answered firmly.

"Good," he said and turned his attention to Coal. "You and Mackenzie are friends. You knew her stepfather just died and you went over to check on her. When Tristan answered the door, you could hear Mackenzie calling for help but he refused to let you in and then physically attacked you when you started to call the police. You got the upper hand, knocked him out, and called the cops."

"Got it, Prez," Coal said with a sly grin.

"All right, let's get this shit done," Copper said and got to his feet.

***

I pulled into my garage surprised to see River's car gone. She hadn't mentioned going anywhere, though I hadn't exactly been around for her to tell me.

I called her while I was walking into the house. "Hey, baby. Where are you?" I asked when she answered.

"Uh, I'm with your mom," she said sounding uncomfortable.

"Oh. What're y'all doing?" I asked curiously.

"Um, she needed to do some shopping and asked me if I could drive her."

"Okay. You going to be much longer?"

"I don't think so. Why?" she asked.

"A lot happened today and I want to tell you about it."

"Okay. Your mom's checking out now, so I shouldn't be much longer. Do you want us to come there first?"

"No, just come home when you're finished. I need to get a shower and find something to eat first anyway. I'll see you when you get here," I told her and disconnected the call.

I got the feeling her and my mother were up to something, but I couldn't for the life of me figure out what it could possibly be.

CHAPTER FORTY-THREE

RIVER

L eigh was already packing up her stuff before I got off the phone with Jonah. "Thank you so much for helping me today. I can't believe how much we were able to accomplish," she said excitedly as I drove her to her house.

"Thanks for asking me. I really needed something to do to keep my mind off of things and this was perfect."

She smiled knowingly. "I'm glad I could help. If you need anything, all you have to do is ask."

I found Jonah on the sofa in a pair of drawstring pants, no shirt, and sound asleep. I was slightly jealous at how effortlessly sexy he was. My eyes were making their third or fourth pass over his body when his eyes popped open and his lips curved up in a sleepy smile.

"Were you watching me sleep?" he asked.

"No, I was eye-fucking you while you slept," I confessed causing him to burst into laughter.

He sat up and reached for me, pulling me onto his lap. "Sorry for ditching you today, but some stuff came up with the club that I had to deal with and it took much longer than expected."

I sighed. "Jonah, I don't expect you to spend every waking second with me, and quite frankly, I don't want you to, but a quick text or phone call would be nice."

"Sorry, baby," he said and nuzzled my neck.

Despite how much I wanted him to continue his ministrations, since I had a good idea of where they were headed, my curiosity won out. "What did you want to tell me?"

He grinned against my skin. "You really want to know now?"

"Yes," I said. "Is it about my case?"

He lifted me from his lap and placed me on the sofa beside him. "Yes and no," he said and proceeded to tell me about his day and the night before.

When he finished, I sat quietly for several minutes trying to process everything he'd said. "So, basically, my mother stole tainted drugs from her boyfriend's wife and distributed them, ultimately killing at least four people, including herself."

"I'm sure there's more to the story, but that's the gist of it," he said.

"And nothing's changed for me?"

"Not yet, but Tina assured me that it would only be a few days at most."

I flopped back on the sofa. "Yeah, I hope so."

We sat in silence for a few minutes before he asked, "What are you going to do when all this is over?"

I sat up and faced him. "What do you mean?"

"I mean, once you're cleared and can resume working, are you going to stay here or go on another traveling assignment?"

"I haven't given it much thought," I said carefully. I really wanted to stay in Devil Springs with him, but I also didn't want to be one of those women who based their decisions on a man. And, he hadn't asked me to stay.

He reached for my wrists and pulled me onto

his lap with a knowing grin. Holding me tightly against him, he took my lips in a passionate kiss. When he broke the kiss, he rested his forehead against mine. "I want you to stay here in Devil Springs with me."

"You do?" I asked. I needed him to repeat it, to reassure me, to destroy the last piece of the wall protecting my heart.

"Yes, woman, I do. I didn't claim you as my Old Lady to help you. I did it because I meant it. I want you to be my wife and have my babies. And I don't give a fuck about how fast it is. I'm not on anyone else's timeline but my own," he stated vehemently.

"Did you just ask me to marry you?" I whispered.

With his forehead still pressed to mine, he slightly shook his head. "No, I told you what I wanted. When I ask you, it'll be on one knee with a ring."

"I'll have to find a job and a place to live."

"We'll find you a job and you'll live with me," he said.

"Okay," I said softly.

"Okay," he agreed and covered my lips with his before pushing to his feet and carrying me to his bedroom.

***

Two days later, Tina called first thing in the morning and told me to come to her office. I couldn't tell by the tone of her voice if I was in for good or bad news, so I tried not to get my hopes up while Jonah and I rushed to get out the door. Regardless, I was a ball of anxiety by the time we arrived at her office.

As soon as we arrived, her secretary ushered us into her office. Tina smiled kindly, "Good morning. Please, have a seat."

"Just tell me," I blurted and slapped my hand over my mouth. "I'm so sorry. I'm really nervous."

Tina laughed at my outburst. "Don't worry about it. I can't imagine how you've been feeling through this mess, so I'll get straight to the point. The charges against you have been dropped. I have some paperwork for you to sign after we go over it, but first, let's go have your ankle monitor removed."

I stood in stunned silence and blinked at her for several moments until Jonah nudged me with his elbow. "Are you shitting me?"

"Nope. Not at all," Tina said with a wide

smile.

"I can't believe it," I breathed and covered my mouth and nose with my hands while I tried to hold back the tears of relief brimming in my eyes.

"Believe it, baby," Jonah said softly.

"Thank you," I told Tina as the first tear fell down my cheek. "Thank you so much."

"It was my pleasure," Tina replied.

With that, she drove us to the same place I received my digital shackle. Only this time, I was more than happy to be there. They were quick about removing the device and sending us on our way.

Just when I thought things couldn't get any better, Tina hit me with another surprise. "I've already spoken with the Board of Nursing regarding your license. You'll need to wait until you have the official copy to resume working, but here's a copy of the letter declaring your license reinstated in good standing."

I jumped from my seat and engulfed Tina in a hug while I cried all over her expensive suit. "Thank you. Thank you. Thank you," I wailed.

Jonah carefully pulled me away from Tina and into his arms. "Thank you, Tina. Any updates on the other case?"

I pulled back from Jonah and saw Tina grin. "None that I can share," she said cryptically.

"I see. Well, we appreciate everything you've done for us," Jonah said and extended his hand.

After hugging her an embarrassing number of times, Jonah and I left her office and climbed on his bike. "Let's go share the good news!" he announced.

We went straight to the clubhouse to share the news with Copper and whoever else happened to be there. After a lot of cheering and shouting, Copper let me use his office to call my brother and Phoenix. I couldn't stop worrying about Phoenix's money, even after Reed repeatedly assured me it wasn't a problem, which left me wondering about how much money these guys actually had.

***

I was heading out to meet Jonah for lunch and opened the front door to find a well-dressed woman standing on the porch poised to knock. "Can I help you?"

"Hello, River. My name is Gwendolyn Ellison. I'm sorry to come by unannounced, but I need to speak with you. I only need a few minutes of your time," she said.

I stepped out onto the porch and closed the door behind me. I gestured to the wicker chairs, "As long as you don't mind speaking with me outside."

"Of course," she said and took a seat. She exhaled heavily. "I just wanted to apologize to you directly for any part I may have indirectly played in your arrest. When I started pushing to actively pursue those responsible for bringing drugs into our community, it was never my intention for innocent parties to be prosecuted. Yes, I was looking for someone to blame for my daughter's death, but I wasn't looking for just anyone to blame. I truly wanted to hold the right people accountable and put them behind bars where they belong so they couldn't destroy any more lives," she said and wiped a tear from her cheek.

"I was blinded by my grief and rage. Losing a child is a pain I wouldn't wish on anyone, even those who took mine from me. I channeled my anger and despair into a quest to save other families from the pain and heartache I was going through. I was so hell-bent on what I was doing; I didn't realize others were taking advantage of me."

She inhaled deeply and shook her head. "I'm sorry, I'm getting off track. I just wanted you to know how truly sorry I am that your life was affected by my quest for justice."

"Well, thank you, but I don't believe any of it was your fault," I said honestly.

"We'll have to agree to disagree on that one, dear," she said and pulled an envelope from her purse as she got to her feet.

"Thank you for your time." She handed me the envelope before she got into her car and drove away.

I immediately opened the envelope and unfolded the papers inside. I read over them twice before I shoved them into my purse and went to meet Jonah for lunch.

He smiled when he saw me, but his smile quickly disappeared. "What's wrong?"

"Nothing," I rasped and cleared my throat. "I just, uh, here," I said and shoved the papers into his hands.

He glanced between me and the papers before sitting at his desk and reading them. "When did you get these?"

"About fifteen minutes ago. Gwendolyn Ellison came by the house and gave them to me after she apologized for her part in everything that happened to me," I said.

"She what?" he asked.

I shrugged. "I know. The whole thing was really weird. She apologized, handed me that, and left. She obviously feels guilty if she went to all that trouble."

The envelope she'd given me contained two sets of papers. The first set was from the nursing agency I used to work for. All penalties I'd been fined for breaking my contract were gone and I was listed as no longer under contract but in good standing and hirable for future contracts. The second set of papers was a job offer for a full-time position in the ER at the hospital.

"Well, what're you going to do?" Jonah asked.

I looked at him incredulously. "Are you serious? I'm going to take the job at the hospital."

He grinned. "Just checking."

CHAPTER FORTY-FOUR

JUDGE

When I returned from lunch, Officer Dunk was waiting for me in my office. "Lana, I'm surprised to see you here. Is everything okay?"

"It's nothing like that," she waved dismissively. "Just have some information to share. Would you mind closing the door?"

"Sure," I said and felt my insides start to twist as I waited to hear what she had to say.

"What I'm about to tell you cannot be repeated to anyone, not even Copper. I shouldn't even be telling you, but I feel like you have a right to know."

"You know I can't promise to keep it from the club. If it in any way effects—"

"It doesn't," she assured.

At my nod of agreement, she began, "As you already know, we found the drugs in Mitzie Mayfield's house and arrested her as well as her son. Tests have confirmed the heroin in her house matches the heroin found in her stepson. Mitzie claims her sister-in-law, Gwendolyn Ellison, asked her to buy the drugs for her. According to Mitzie, Gwendolyn's plan was to plant it on the people who played a part in her daughter's death and have them arrested. But, Mitzie's son, Tristan, tells a different story. He says Gwendolyn asked him to take the heroin and replace it with some that was laced with something that would kill anyone who used it. He did it and she paid him handsomely for his troubles. He also said she asked him to make sure his brother and father knew about the tainted drugs."

"Are you saying Gwendolyn actually was behind this whole thing?" I asked.

She shrugged. "I'm saying it came down to her word against theirs. She's Chairman of the

County Council with a stellar reputation. She's supported Mitzie and her family for years and just recently refused to continue supporting them because of their ongoing drug use. It looks like they made these accusations against her because they were pissed that she cut them off."

"Why was she supporting them?" I asked.

"She's married to Mitzie's brother, Paul. After Roy and Mitzie married, Roy worked for Paul's company and was hurt on the job. When his workers' comp payout ran out, they threatened to sue claiming he was permanently disabled. Gwendolyn comes from a very wealthy family and they chose to handle the matter out of court."

I sat back in my chair and crossed my arms over my chest. "I see. So, you think they're trying to get more money out of her?"

She shook her head, "Off the record, I think they're telling the truth, particularly Tristan."

I sat forward and leaned on my elbows completely shocked. "You think Gwendolyn purchased tainted heroin and intended to what? Kill people with it?"

She nodded. "That's exactly what I think. Tristan said she pointedly told him to make sure his brother and father knew about the drugs. I don't believe she did that because she was trying to protect them. I think she knew one of them would steal it."

"Why would she do that?"

"According to Tristan, Gwendolyn's daughter was introduced to heroin by Brett Owens, Oliver Burgess, Tristan Mayfield, and Roy Mayfield one night when she was spending the night at her best friend's house. Her best friend was Brett's sister, Didi Warren. Now, do you honestly believe it's a coincidence that every single person involved is now dead or in jail?"

"Fuck," I breathed. "What are you going to do?"

She shook her head. "Nothing. There's no proof."

"Gwendolyn showed up at my house a few hours ago to talk to River. She said she wanted to apologize for any part she played in River's arrest. She also went to great lengths to restore River's good name with her previous employer as well as provide her with a job offer at the hospital," I shared.

"That was probably her last stop on her way out of town."

"What?"

"She resigned from her position as chairman and her husband turned his company over to his second-in-command. You didn't know?"

"I had no idea. Wait, what kind of company does her husband have?"

"He owns GP Construction and Contracting," she said and nodded. "Yeah, the city inspector used to work for him. See what I mean? It's all circumstantial and speculative, but it's all there. Everyone's greatest fear should be a mother's wrath."

"I don't disagree with you. Thank you for sharing that with me. And, I won't say a word, not even to River," I promised. Telling River about the conversation I'd had with Lana wouldn't change anything. And not knowing what was actually true would drive River crazy.

EPILOGUE

RIVER

I was on the back of Jonah's bike and we were headed to Croftridge with most of the Devil Springs chapter. I'd only ever ridden with Jonah, so it was my first time riding in a formation. I was amazed at how fluidly they moved as a unit, seeming to anticipate one another's movements.

I fully expected to be a nervous wreck during the ride, but that wasn't the case. I was definitely excited to meet my baby niece and my brother's wife, but being plastered to Jonah's back as the wind whipped around us brought me a special kind of peace I knew I'd never find anywhere else.

When we arrived at the Croftridge Clubhouse, I was surprised when we didn't pull into the forecourt with everyone else. "Where are you going?" I asked.

"To Phoenix's house. I thought you'd want to see the baby and meet your brother's wife without an audience."

He pulled up to a massive plantation style home that was on the same property as the clubhouse. Before we made it up the stairs, the front door opened and my brother engulfed me in a bear hug. "Jailbird! You made it," he crowed.

"Of course, I did Reed BROOK Lawson!" I shouted as loud as I could. "How are you, Brookie boy?" I asked and arched an eyebrow. I knew how much he hated his middle name and it gave me great pleasure to use it when he was being an insensitive asshole.

He held his hands up in surrender. "Too soon. Got it."

"Shut up and show me the baby," I said jovially.

After he shook hands and back-slapped with Jonah, we followed him to a packed living room with far more people than I expected. My steps faltered, but Jonah reached out to steady me.

"Everyone, this is my sister, River," Reed announced. "River, you know Phoenix, Copper, Layla, and Coal." Somehow, Copper, Layla, and Coal had gotten there before us. "This is Phoenix's wife, Annabelle, and their babies, Flint and Blaze. This is Annabelle's son, Nathan," he said and moved to a beautiful blonde woman who looked just like Annabelle and Layla. She placed the baby she was holding in his arms and stood. "This is my wife, Ember, and this our Raven," he said proudly and placed the bundle in my arms.

I gazed at her for long moments and gently ran my finger down her cheek. "She's beautiful," I said and tried to choke back my emotions. "Lucky girl doesn't have your nose."

Ember laughed so hard she doubled over and clutched her stomach. "Hey," Reed said sounding offended. "There's nothing wrong with my nose."

"There's nothing wrong with your nose now. But your nose has been that size for as long as I can remember. Most boys have to grow into their bodies. Not you. No, you had to grow into your nose," I laughed.

"Come sit down and please tell me more,"

Ember giggled.

"Fucking hell," Reed grumbled.

"Language," multiple women snapped.

Reed threw his hands into the air in exasperation. "They can't even talk yet!"

Ember completely ignored his outburst. "What else can you tell me? Did he sleep with a stuffed animal? Dress up as a princess and play tea party with you?"

I smiled down at my brother's pride and joy. "He was a good brother. He let me sleep in his bed when I had a bad dream or was scared. He made sure I had clean clothes to wear and I know there were times he went hungry so I could eat. He made sure I was taken care of even when he didn't' have to."

I looked up when I heard Ember sniffle. Reed was already there wrapping her in his arms. She wiped a few tears from her face and smiled. "Damn pregnancy hormones."

"Way to bring the house down, Raindrop."

"Fuck off, Brook," I retorted.

"Hey! Why doesn't she get a 'language'?"

"I didn't hear anything. Did you?" Annabelle asked Layla.

"Sure didn't," Layla laughed.

"Are you ladies ready to move this to the

clubhouse?" Phoenix asked.

With that, everyone got up and started gathering the unbelievable amount of stuff required to move three babies from one location to another.

I managed to catch Phoenix's eye and he came over to where I was standing. "Everything okay, River?"

"Oh, yes, everything's fine. Um, well, Jonah told me not to worry about it and Reed did, too, but I just wanted to make sure you got your money back from when you bailed me out," I said nervously.

His lips twisted and his eyebrows narrowed for a brief second before his face relaxed and he graced me with a warm and friendly smile. "Every penny was returned to me the day after your charges were dropped."

I breathed a sigh of relief and felt my body visibly sag. "Oh, good. I've been so worried about that," I confessed.

"All's good, darlin'," he said and went back to help Annabelle with the babies. Or that's what I assumed he was doing until he extended his arms and smacked Jonah and Reed in the back of the head at the same time.

Phoenix grumbled something I couldn't hear

causing both Jonah and Reed to turn to me. "Sorry," they both said at the same time.

I blinked in shock and glanced between the two of them. Jonah reached for me and pulled me against his chest. "I didn't realize you were still concerned about the money. When I told you not to worry about it, I meant don't worry about it because it was in the process of being returned."

"Well, you should've said it like that."

"You're right," he admitted.

"Okay, then," I said, a little taken aback by how easily he owned up to being wrong.

He smiled like he knew what I was thinking, but didn't comment further. Instead, he led me to his bike and we rode the short distance to the clubhouse.

"Brother Judge," Harper shouted and made a beeline for Jonah as soon as we walked through the door.

"Sister cousin," he returned as he picked her up and swung her around.

He placed her on her feet and she immediately reached out to hug me. "River! It's good to see you again."

When I felt something cold and wet press against my hand, I looked down and yelped at the big beast actively licking me.

"It's okay," Harper assured. "He just wants some attention, too."

"Aren't you afraid he'll get hungry and eat you one day?" I asked as I tried to calm my racing heart.

She laughed. "No way. He's a big ole baby. Aren't you, Titan? You just want some loving, too, don't you?"

"Don't talk to him like he's a baby, Harper. Treat him like the badass he is," Carbon said and patted Titan's head. Carbon extended his hand to me. "Welcome to Croftridge, River."

"Thanks," I said and shifted uncomfortably. I was beginning to feel overwhelmed with all the attention on me. I turned to grab Jonah's hand, but he was no longer standing behind me.

I started to search for him when a loud whistle cut through the noise. The room fell silent and the crowd parted revealing Jonah in the center of the room. He met my eyes and crooked his finger.

I walked toward him wondering what he was doing. When I was two steps from him, he reached for my hands and dropped to one knee.

"Jonah," I gasped.

"I knew I wanted you from the moment you

held my hand in the ER while my hand was being sewn up. I knew I wanted to know you from the night you came to Precious Metals. I knew I wanted to protect you after the fire. I knew I would do anything for you after you stepped in and took care of my mother. I knew I wanted to ride with you forever after you rode the dragon with me. I knew I would rain hell down on anyone who tried to take you from me after you were arrested. I will go to my grave loving you. Nothing will ever change that, but you'd make me the happiest man in the world if you'd agree to be my wife for the rest of our days."

He flipped open a box I didn't even know he had in his hand and presented me with a ring I didn't so much as glance at. "Yes!" I screamed and tackled him to the floor. "Yes! Yes! Yes!"

He kissed me while we laughed in each other's arms on the floor of the clubhouse with everyone watching.

JUDGE

We returned to Devil Springs after spending the night celebrating our engagement in Croftridge. Instead of going to the rental house, I decided it was time to show River the house I was having built.

I expected her to question where we were going and was surprised when she didn't.

I turned onto the long driveway that lead to my secluded house. When I came to a stop and turned off the bike, I tapped River's leg so she would know I wanted her to get off. She handed me her helmet, but still didn't ask where we were. I took her hand and led her to the front door. I pushed it open and was greeted with twin shouts of, "Surprise!"

I whirled around to see my mother and River grinning at me. Confused, I turned back to the house and walked inside.

My brand new, custom built house was fully furnished and decorated from what I could see.

"You two did this?" They both nodded. "When?"

"Two days after I was released from jail."

"You said you were helping Mom with some shopping."

She grinned. "I was. I was helping her shop for stuff for your house."

"Quit standing here asking questions and go look at the rest of the house," Mom ordered.

I took my time going through the house and taking in each room. I was amazed how much thought and time they'd put into the house. When I returned to them, I was at a loss for words.

"Well? Do you like?" River asked excitedly.

"It's perfect. Better than perfect," I said and pulled them both in for a hug. "Thank you."

Mom patted me on the back and stepped back. "You're welcome, sweetheart."

"Oh, Mom?"

"Yes, dear?"

"Well played."

She pressed her hand to her chest and gasped. "Whatever do you mean?"

"Getting River to help unknowingly decorate her future home. Nice move."

River's mouth dropped open in surprise.

Mom shrugged and headed for the front door. "I want grandbabies. I'll head out now so y'all can get started. Love you, mean it," she said and closed the door behind her.

BONUS SCENE

LAYLA

MONTHS LATER

We were getting ready for the biggest event in the history of the Blackwings. Not one, not two, but three club officers were getting married, all in one ceremony. Duke and Reese, Carbon and Harper, and Judge and River. After a bit of discussion, they all agreed to have the ceremony in Leigh's backyard, followed by the reception at the Devil Springs clubhouse.

I'm not sure how it happened, but somehow

or another, Leigh and I became the unofficial coordinators for everything involved with the wedding and reception. We'd spent weeks planning, organizing, and coordinating, and we were finally in the homestretch with two weeks left before the big day.

We did almost all of the shopping online. Anything we needed for the reception was sent to the clubhouse, while all wedding supplies were shipped to Leigh's house. She'd made a remarkable recovery from her heart attack, but I still didn't want her trying to do too much, particularly lifting any of the packages delivered. So, I made sure to be at her house when a large delivery was expected.

On the day the custom arches, aisle runners, decorating fabrics, garland, and several other miscellaneous items were scheduled to be delivered, I was waiting by the front door. The text alert came through, and right on time, the driver pulled up to the house, and proceeded to unload box after box after box until I was standing beside fifteen boxes.

"I didn't realize this much was scheduled to be delivered today. Did you?" Leigh asked and studied the boxes.

I shrugged. "No, but maybe some stuff came

early."

With that, I started moving the boxes to the room we now referred to as the wedding room while Leigh huffed and picked up a box anyway.

I opened my mouth to protest, but she cut me off. "Don't start. It weighs two pounds, literally."

Must be the tulle for the chairs, I thought. After clearing the porch in record time, we set about opening the boxes and checking over the materials to make sure nothing was wrong with our order. And something was wrong. Very, very wrong.

I sliced open the eighth box and screamed bloody murder while simultaneously punching the thing that jumped out at me. Unexpectedly, the thing bounced back and hit me in the face causing me to begin slapping and pushing at... whatever the fuck it was.

"Layla!" Leigh shouted as she ran into the room. "What the—? Are you fighting with a sex doll?"

I shoved the thing away from me and tried to get my breathing under control. My eyes landed on the naked top half of an inflatable doll sticking out of the box. I held up a shaky finger and pointed, "She started it."

We looked at each other and doubled over

laughing. I laughed so much my side started to cramp while Leigh ran to the bathroom so she wouldn't pee on herself.

When we finally got ourselves under control, I asked the obvious question, "Where did this thing come from?" I knew neither one of us had ordered it.

She gave me a knowing look. "I'm going to take a wild guess and say some of the boys ordered it for the bachelor party not knowing we changed the delivery address on the club's account."

I looked at the other boxes ominously. "We're going to have to open the rest to figure out what's what."

Leigh made a grand gesture with her outstretched arm. "Be my guest."

Those shitheads ordered three damn sex dolls. The other two sprang from the box and began to auto-inflate just like the first one.

"Those things are not staying in my house," Leigh stated.

"I'll take them to the clubhouse when we're finished here. Can you help me put them back in their boxes?" I asked.

We searched and searched but couldn't find the release valve. There were only two places left it could be and neither one of us would stick our hand in there to find out. "Fuck it!" I said and threw my hands in the air. "I'll take them to the club like this."

"I'll help you carry them out to the car," Leigh said through her laughter.

So, there we were, carrying boxes with naked, inflatable women sticking halfway out to my car. Now, Leigh's road was never busy. Never. But not that day. Oh no. Her neighbors across the street were having a family gathering. Okay, it was a kid's birthday party, but I was pretending not to know that little tidbit.

"Hey, Leigh," her neighbor shouted and started to wave.

"Hey there!" she returned and then shoved her naked doll box at me. "Fucking hell. Get rid of this!"

"What's that you got there?" the nosy bitch asked.

"Oh, just some mannequins for Layla. She, uh, she wants to put them in her windows so it'll look like someone's home all the time," Leigh lied, poorly.

"Your son runs that security company. Why not have him install an alarm?" she pushed.

"Well, Janice, not that it's any of your

business, but Jonah has installed a security system. Layla was kidnapped and watched a madman shoot her Old Man in the chest. She's got some PTSD, understandably, but we support her in whatever makes her feel comfortable," Leigh snapped. "Now, if you'll excuse us."

I was going to kill her. "You made me sound like a crazy person," I whisper-yelled.

"And telling her you were loading inflatable sex dolls into your car would have been better how?"

She was right, but I wasn't going to admit it.

"Cover me while I get the last one," I said.

"Be sure to carry it with the tits facing you!" She was so helpful.

When I shoved the third one into my backseat, I discovered Leigh had buckled the other two in. I shook my head and for whatever reason, buckled the third one in as well.

"Too-da-loo," Leigh finger-waved as I pulled out of her driveway.

I wasn't sure who was to blame, but I was going to let every single person with a penis at the clubhouse have it when I got there.

And then, the worst possible thing happened. Blue lights flashed in my rearview mirror. "Fuck me," I cursed and carefully pulled my car over.

"Good evening, ma'am. Do you know why I stopped you?"

I groaned. "I'm guessing it has something to do with the bad porno in the backseat."

"Care to tell me why you're carting naked dolls around town?"

I slapped my hand over my face. "Because someone thought it would be funny to order these for a bachelor party but they delivered them to the wrong address. I'm taking them to the correct address," I explained.

"Well, see, here's the problem. Because their top halves are exposed, it's public indecency. You're going to have to cover them up."

"With what?" I shrieked.

"Don't know and don't care, but I'm going to have to issue a citation if you don't figure something out in the next few minutes."

I should've just popped them and been done with it, but I wanted the boys to feel my wrath after the embarrassment they'd caused.

"I'll be right back," I said to the officer and darted across the street before he could stop me. There was a drug store right there. Five minutes later, I dressed naked dolls in one-size-fits-all stretchy drug store tube tops on the side of the road and the officer let me go with a warning.

I was so mad by the time I reached the clubhouse that I almost drove my car through the front door. I came to a screeching halt, jumped out, and yanked, Betty, Barbie, and Bambi—yes, I named them—from their boxes and carried them inside while their legs were still auto-inflating.

The room fell silent as I stomped to the pool table and dropped the naked dolls on top. "Who in the fuck ordered these?" I shouted.

"Layla!" Copper scolded. "What the hell is wrong with you?"

"What's wrong with me? I was attacked by a damn sex doll, made to look like a crazy woman, pulled over by the police, forced to buy clothes to dress the air sluts, and then I was given a warning for public indecency. That is what is wrong with me, Copper Black. And it's someone with a dick's fault. Now, nut up and own it!"

He'd cracked a smile when I started explaining and was full-on belly laughing by the end of my tirade. He was even wiping tears away from his eyes. "Oh, shit. This is—"

"It's not fucking funny is what it is!" I screeched. "Who was it? Which one of you perverts ordered these?"

"Um, Layla," Grant said as he entered the

common room with a box in his hand.

"You!" I seethed.

"No, ma'am," he said and pointed to one of the boxes. "I saw it when I moved your car. I think there's been a mistake. Look at the address."

I looked at the address and realized he was right. Not only that, but the boxes were meant to be delivered to the house across the street from Leigh—Janice's house.

"All right, boys, I need to borrow three pairs of pants. I've got a party to crash!"

Author's Note

To everyone who's read my books, thank you! Without you, this dream would be just that, a dream. I never imagined I would be publishing my EIGHTH book on the one-year anniversary of my first book. Judge's book is also special to me for a different reason. The events in the Prologue are based on a true story. And while the main story is fiction and for entertainment purposes, I also hoped to shed some light on addiction and show the effects from a different perspective.

Other Books by Teagan Brooks

Blackwings MC - Croftridge

Dash - Blackwings MC Book 1

Duke - Blackwings MC Book 2

Phoenix - Blackwings MC Book 3

Carbon - Blackwings MC Book 4

Shaker - Blackwings MC Book 5

Blackwings MC – Devil Springs

Copper - Blackwings MC - Devil Springs Book 1

Standalone Novella

Beached

Website

WWW.TEAGANBROOKS.COM

Made in the USA
Columbia, SC
20 July 2019